ICE AND BONE

THE RISING WIND SERIES
BOOK 2

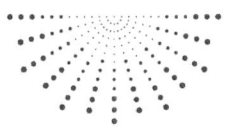

DIANE OLSEN

ISBN-10 : 1737204002

ISBN-13 : 978-1737204008

To contact the author, email to dolsen6464@gmail.com

BLACK ELK PRAYER CIRCA 1931

Grandfather, Great Mysterious One,
You have been always and before You nothing has been.
There is nothing to pray to but You.
The star nations all over the universe are Yours,
And Yours are the grasses of the earth.
Day in and day out You are the life of things.
You are older than all need, Older than all pain and prayer.
Grandfather, all over the world the faces of the living ones are alike. In
tenderness they have come up out of the ground. Look upon Your
children with children in their arms,
That they may face the winds,
And walk the good road to the day of quiet.
Teach me to walk the soft earth, A relative to all that live.
Sweeten my heart and fill me with light,
And give me the strength to understand and the eyes to see.
Help me, for without You I am nothing.

Hehaka Sapa, Black Elk December 1, 1863-August 19, 1950 Wichasha Wakan, Holy Man of the Oglala Lakota

As recorded by John G. Neihardt, trans
    lated by Ben Black Elk Used with permission from University of Nebraska Press

ACKNOWLEDGEMENTS

With Deep Gratitude to the following colleagues, friends, and family

Baha'i Publishing Trust: Baha'i Prayers, 2002

Hall, Mark A. Thunderbirds: America's Living Legends of Giant Birds 2004

Neihardt, John G. Black Elk Speaks 1932 An American poet and writer; translated to English by Ben Black Elk.

Leif Milliken: Prayers used with permission from University of Nebraska Press Rights and Contracts. I am deeply grateful University of Nebraska Press for permission to use the prayers of Hehaka Sapa AKA Black Elk in this manuscript series.

Black Elk: Prayers, and assistance - Wichasha Wakan Oglala Lakota December 1, 1863 – August 19, 1950

Nolberto Ortiz - Family Duende account - used with permission

Barbara Daniels Dena: Dear friend since high school, Writer, Beta Reader, writing instructor Copy Editor. You have encouraged me when I had no hope—which seems to happen every time.

S.G. Minae – Formatting and cover artist, good friend and great soul

Catherine Townsend-Lyon Author and Cat Lyon's Reading Den. Tireless Promoter of Lyon Media and Literary Consulting; building custom plans around an author's budget. That's a mouthful, but you have always found a way for us to move forward on this path.

J D & J Cover Design: Hats off to Dave for his excellent covers and cheerful flexibility and patience.

I would love to rave about my intrepid readers: Sandra Munoz and Valerie Inmee for being willing to read almost anything and have valid suggestions each time. My Supportive Family: Ika Toutaiolepo, Andrew Mark Olsen Pat and Fella Mulberger, Peter Mulberger, Gavin Dane Olsen, and William Munoz

I want to thank Steve William Liable an American Children's Author and Publisher at The Kodel Group For his kind wisdom, advice and interest.

Thanks also to Reader's Favorite Reviewer: Scott Cahan for his time, insight and interest.

Sagebrush Critique Group: Laura Kostad Thank you for your expertise as beta and kindness, thanks to Theresa St Hilaire for her inspiration for the character, Teresa, Norma Boswell, Esther Irwin, Pam Kindle, Lindsay Irwin, Grace Cain, Mimi Billing, and Jane Goldberg, Jeff and Patty Bailey for your assistance and encouragement.

"It is time for all of the world's healers—to heal!"
— SECORA JAMES

LIST OF CHARACTERS

Alai Santiago - A sensitive, a psychic medium

Azalea Peterson - Ex-policewoman, into forensics.

Billy Riggins - Field paleontologist specializing in mammoths and mastodons

Diego Santiago - Deceased fiancé of Secora. Spectacular healer and pure hearted Kallawaya, son of Guillermo and Alai Santiago

Dr. Donald Chastain - Chair of the Paleontology department this year.

Guillermo Santiago - Kallawaya healer

Gideon Yellow Thunder - Lakota realtor for Treasuremont Realty - Because of thunderbird visions Some call him a holy man, a Heyoka.

Iris Snowden - Secora's sister, sister-friend of Jane Roanhorse, and daughter of Dr. Sage and Dr. L.W. Dalton.

Jake Lansing - Salt of the earth caretaker of the Jamal Hasan property

Jamal Hasan - now deceased. Owner of the resort property

Jane Roanhorse - Aa teaching Assistant for Dr. Iris Snowden.

Jeannie - Most able secretary for Treasuremont Realty Devoted motherly

Jimmy Lizardeye - Half Tewa (Pueblo), Half Lakota. Wichasha Wakan (Lakota holy man), Gideon's mentor, veteran who served in Iraq.

Kamal Hasan - Jamal's son, kidnapped and murdered.

Ken and Sue Grayson - run the nearby Buckeye Dude Ranch

Kyah Roanhorse - Jane's son, Gideon's precocious nephew

Mitch - Realtor at Treasuremont Realty, Assistant and close friend of Gideon

Secora James - Teaches Paleontology at the university level, mother of Monta.

Robert (Bob) Greenwood - Biologist and tracker. A.K.A Dead Eyes.

Tarkio Cyr - Best darn graduate student around Husband of Anida and father of Frederick

William Landsing - Assistant To Mr Hasan at the resort.

1

LATE DECEMBER 1999

Wind blew out of the North as Billy Riggins, a tousled forty-year-old modern-day mammoth hunter stood over the newly unearthed cave burial between the little towns of Birch Bay and Custer in Western Washington. Something disturbed the flow of his thoughts. He'd heard a clamor that sounded like the metallic squeaking of a car bouncing down a dirt road. Looking up from the gritty work, he hopped up out of the trench and let his wary eyes scan the rock-covered hill above the cave and the dirt track that led back past other stony outcrops all the way out to the freeway. Nothing caught his eye, so he was willing to assume it was a random sound from the distant highway.

Looking back into the pit, his eyes were immediately drawn to the softened bone of the nearly perfect human skull, breathing the oxygenated atmosphere for the first time in perhaps twenty millennia. The spectacular event of its unveiling was announced by a brigade of chickadees and low flying geese in the crisp air of late December.

"Cripes! This is a miracle of Louis Leakey proportions," Billy exclaimed to his preferred companion, a small seal brown mule known as "Carrots," who kept him company on his paleontological digs.

Carrots earned his keep by hauling gear to and from Billy's pickup. In answer to Riggins' outburst, the critter twitched its tail and turned somberly toward Billy, as if he anticipated another chunk of commentary. He wasn't disappointed.

"The unthinkable has happened! The association of this burial with the skeleton of our mammoth is, well, undeniable. Worse yet, it's a credible site with reliable dates, and you know what that means..." Coincidentally, Carrots shook his large ears.

Billy reached into his duffel to grab two cameras. He leaped in and out of the trench, carefully snapping photos while expending two rolls of 35 mm film. Next, he made a pass with a brand-new video camera. "Might as well use this gadget too, Carrots. It cost us plenty."

He explored the various angles and nuances of the placement of the skeleton and the associated artifacts, in relation to the bones of the young Colombian mammoth he'd already unearthed. Next, he made a few quick sketches of the site, according to the grid system he had marked out with a plane table and alidade. Finally, he took a few wide shots of the cave and the surrounding area with the digital camera, including a shot of the mule, for no particular reason. He sighed. "Guess that'll have to do." He made some final notes then put the sketches and cameras into his blue canvas bag.

An undeniable grinding sound, like a vehicle shifting into a lower gear, caught the mule's attention and he raised his head with nostrils flaring. Another squeak generated a full-on braying event. Eee-aw, eee-aw, eee-aw.

"Quiet, Carrots," Billy barked as he strained to hear or see an explanation for the sound. After several moments, he shrugged. Maybe it was paranoia, or his imagination stimulated by the unusual find. But then why was the mule still staring at a rock outcrop a thousand yards away?

A couple of minutes later, Carrots lost interest in the rocks. With eyes half-closed, he cocked a rear ankle, transferring his balance to one hip, and then twitched a long fuzzy ear.

Seeing this, Billy's tense body relaxed, and with a sigh of relief, he sat down on a pile of freshly screened soil beside the trench he'd been working for the last week. Something was poking his side. He thrust his fingers into a pocket of his jean jacket and withdrew a sample bag that contained a glistening, semi-translucent chunk of snowflake obsidian. As he cradled it in his left hand, Billy's jaw slackened, and his focus turned to awe as he regarded the spiny branches intricately chipped into the edging of the slender projectile point. The effect was similar to the branches of a Christmas tree cut-out.

"Know something, mule?" Carrots gave no indication he did. "This rare and cherished object took an incredible amount of skill and luck to produce. Whoever made it must have struck dozens of these before he produced one that didn't shatter. Then it had to be carefully wrapped for transportation and treated with great respect when it was used for its intended purpose, whatever that was."

Billy smiled. It was probably the most beautiful piece of Solutrean style art he had ever seen–except it hadn't been found in the caves of France, but near the Washington State coast north of Bellingham.

"We'd better move all this stuff out of sight in case we aren't alone, Carrots."

The mule repeatedly stomped a forefoot, attempting to dislodge an out-of-season botfly that was trying to lay eggs on the long hairs covering the inside of his knee. Billy noticed and went over to slap the fly to the ground. "Sorry, buddy it's been so warm, you're being pestered by bugs that should have died by now.

"Weird... the bug is out of place like this piece of obsidian which should never have been found here in the United States. It miraculously survived its active life and spent thousands of years in the ever-changing ground. Even when I opened this trench, it managed to stay in one piece. No damage. Un-freaking-believable! Gotta be very careful, it would be a crying shame to break such a rare piece."

Billy regarded the burial. Not only did these bones belong to a noble and revered leader, judging from the loot, but like the obsidian point, the body was very unusual because it also remained intact, thus prohibiting any dispute about pressure distortion of the features or other nonsense.

He scratched his head through his shoulder-length brown hair. He knew all hell was bound to break loose when word of such a find streaked across the archaeological world, and Billy Riggins didn't want any part of the hullabaloo that would inevitably follow.

It was time to clean up the site. He meticulously covered the burial in a protective veil of bubble wrap. When he was satisfied, he took the shovel and backfilled his newest revelation with screened dirt from the pile beside the trench. He finished off the restoration of the natural site with the topsoil and rocks which had previously covered the grave.

He scratched the mule's hairy cheek and whispered, "Don't worry, Carrots. We've already secured samples of bone and tusk and mailed them off to the Texas lab for dating." The bored mule gave up waiting for further commentary and drifted off to nibble tufts of dried grass and weeds.

Billy grabbed his blue duffle and reached inside for a bulky, number-ten-sized can. He sighed as he looked at the Colombian coffee tin. He not only drank this brand because it reminded him of Juan Valdez and his mule, but also because his specialty was researching and locating Colombian mammoths. Earlier, he had dumped most of the precious ground coffee in order to make room for his jaw-dropping finds. He removed a bubble-wrapped pouch from his pants pocket, and after placing the delicate obsidian icon inside the pouch, he hid it in the grounds which were already concealing other bubble-wrapped samples.

Checking the remaining compartments of his Levi jacket, he eventually fished out a granite Astarte figurine from his breast pocket. He smiled at her, then reluctantly added the piece. Billy sealed the whole can in yet more bubble wrap and carefully taped the whole thing shut to keep moisture out.

Smelling the coffee grounds had made Billy thirsty. Reaching for a thermos and a sandwich from inside his backpack, he took a short break, swirling the coffee around his mouth to wash out the dust as well as brushing away another late-season fly. He tried to imagine himself on some talk show discussing the preeminence of this particular find— which would stand out against the last twenty-five years of slow, painstaking research. If it ever came to that, he'd send some other poor sucker in his place to babble niceties and snicker at pathetic little jokes.

He scanned the area before quickly scooping out a spot for the coffee tin two and a half feet down in the soft dirt behind his tent, which was staked at the base of the tumbled rocks near the cave entrance. Finishing the job, he slid a couple of heavy, loose rocks over the top as he thought, *I need to share this with someone. Who will even believe me? There's gotta be somebody I can trust.*

About twenty minutes had passed since Billy and Carrots had heard the mechanical squeak, and something else crossed his mind. If that was a squeaky truck, who might be interested in sneaking around the site? It wouldn't be a friend dropping by.

Most of the field paleontologists he knew were undeniable loners who preferred their own company and that of a few ancient bones over human frivolity. Unlike many of the others, he drank coffee rather than alcohol, and didn't count those struggling with addiction among his friends. As a result, he didn't discuss his business with anyone but the waitress at the café where he took his breakfast. She was capable, but neither friend nor peer.

Billy mulled over the short list of people he could trust to share the immense burden and joy of this dig. One by one each name was eliminated. He kicked the truck tire, and then snapped the shovel into its mounts on the stock rack of his dusty, old, Forest Service green, Dodge pickup.

Next, he swung open the stock gate at the back and lowered the tailgate, ready for the mule to hop in. Carrots must have heard it clang, because he showed up mere moments later, while Billy threw in the blue duffel and reached for the bulky cell phone on the passenger seat and stuffed it into his pocket. He rubbed the mule's neck and scratched behind his ear, then Billy returned to squat one last time beside the old grave, thoughtful, as the peaceful winter sunset began to descend.

A smile creased his sweaty features as he remembered one person who might qualify in both regards–someone knowledgeable, whom he could trust. He stood up and took the cell phone out of the jacket. I might not see Secora for years at a time, but she'll pick up the threads of friendship without a ripple. Not to mention, she's an excellent Pleistocene paleontologist and would appreciate the irony of this find. Thankfully, she doesn't buy into the lame concept held by the archaeo-logical powers-that-be, who decreed that no humans arrived on the ground of North America prior to 13,000 years ago. This guy had died 7,000 years too early by their measure!

As he began to dial the number, he stopped short, startled by the squeak of un-oiled metal, maybe a truck door opening, but not quietly enough. This time it was unmistakable. Both he and the mule had heard it. They froze, their eyes desperately searching the area for the origin of the sound. It must be close; they should be able to see something. There were several hilly outcrops, but they didn't appear big enough to hide a vehicle. Besides, it was unlikely a vehicle could have made it down the rutted road without raising dust.

Then the metal door slammed–no pretense this time. With head and ears held high, Carrots took halting steps toward the road, then wheeled and jumped unaided into the bed of the pickup for safety.

Motivated by dread, Billy knew he needed to share his secret, in case something bad was about to happen. He finished dialing the number and bolted toward the pickup cab.

2

RECONNECTING

Tears strung Secora's eyes as she and Gideon watched the last of Diego Santiago's blood seep into the earth. He had been shot through the neck by Glen Greenbriar's private militia, and there was nothing Secora or Gideon could do. In fact, they had to flee for their own lives from the mercenary's bullets. There was no choice. She and Gideon faced being on the run through three countries.

Secora awoke from the horrifying memory of the death of her fiancé last summer. It left her gasping, sweating, and needing to rise from her bed. She couldn't risk the chance of falling back into that dream. Tears overtook thought, as the sense of loss overwhelmed her. She had recently returned home to Missoula and hoped to settle in and reconnect with family and friends after spending six months healing physically and spiritually on Isla del Sol in Lake Titicaca, which straddled the countries of Peru to the West and Bolivia to the East.

Ultimately, she quit crying and hiccoughing and brushed at the tears with her one good arm; the other remained in a restrictive shoulder brace. She attempted to tie her hair back with the fingers of one hand, and then reached for a much-needed box of tissues. Her beloved fiancé had been killed six months ago, but healing from his loss would take her a lifetime–at least. He seemed to occupy every thought and action.

"I'm trying," she said, sniffing then blowing her nose. "Really trying, Diego, not to think of you all the time, but my heart feels like it's dying." She wiped her eyes again, and the gripping in her chest began to loosen. In that one relaxed moment, Monta, her adopted infant, began to cry.

"We'll be okay sweet baby." Secora cooed soothing sounds, but it was difficult to pick the little one up with one and a half arms.

She'd recently had hardware removed from her right shoulder, which had been shattered by a bullet on Massacre Mountain when she and her best friend, Gideon, along with the help of huge teratorns, broke up a wretched group of slavers and murderers who held sway over an obscure Peruvian mountain.

Though the arm was now in a brace, it hurt with a demanding ache that wouldn't ease up. Activities like driving were rough, but parenting was really tough. She looked into the baby's tiny face and prayed she could give her a good, safe life. "Monta, it's time for a morning prayer. Can you say, 'He is God! O God, my God! Bestow upon me a pure heart, like unto a pearl?'"

The baby smiled and drooled.

Awkwardly, Secora gathered the infant to her. Monta smiled as she looked deeply into her mama's eyes. Secora hugged the little one and carried her into the kitchen, remembering the day she left the hospital in Brazil and returned to the coastal town of Challa on Isla del Sol where Diego's mother, Alai Santiago, greeted her. "I see you have questions, Daughter."

Secora was surprised, mystified as to how her might-have-been Mother-in-Law, Alai, would think she had questions. About what, she had been daydreaming about her beloved Diego, but she didn't think of any questions. It was then she noticed movement under Alai's shawl.

"It's a baby girl," Alai said brightly. She had taken the infant out to show to her, and Secora had recoiled a bit. Alai stepped over to Secora's side to show her the tiny girl's face.

"Who is she?" Secora asked, then held her breath.

"We do not yet have a name. She was brought here from El Tigre Mountain, fifteen miles distant. Her mother had passed, and the infant was found with her body. She must have only been a couple of days old."

Alai's eyes looked to her left. "Oh, the mother's spirit is now here with us. She's asking me to find a loving home for her precious infant since her husband disappeared six months ago and no one is home to help. Diego is also here in spirit. He thinks this might be a chance for you to have a child of your own."

Secora said nothing. She'd never been much of a nurturer unless you asked her spoiled pets, a guinea pig named "Pete" and "Spider Woman," the corn snake.

"Please, Daughter," Alai begged, "I am too old and too pained by the loss of my own child to raise another."

Secora's eyes watered and a cry escaped her throat. She remembered this phenomenal woman had already taken in, and raised, a dozen foster children in addition to Diego, and wept openly. After what felt like an hour, she wiped her tears and resolutely stated. "I have a million questions."

Alai smiled. "I thought you might. Guillermo and I will help you."

As they sat in the Santiago family kitchen, the baby's eyes appeared to follow unseen faces, and she smiled. Secora thought it must be the mother and Diego. Maybe the infant would be a psychic medium like Alai. Soon they were all experiencing the light of love, which enfolded the little family with oneness. She smiled at the thought of Diego. It made her feel happy. Better than she'd felt in a long time. Strike that, maybe ever.

Basking in his ethereal presence, Secora shyly asked, "Did I hear your voice up on the mountain, Diego, when I tripped?"

Alai said on his behalf, "It wasn't time for you to join me here, Querida. There is more for you to do on earth."

"Thanks for tripping me so the bullet missed my head… but I'm not sure I want to carry on." She sighed as she remembered that her cherished friend, Gideon Yellow Thunder had warned her about being in love with the idea of loving a good man. Did she love Diego Santiago? Unquestionably!

After a few moments, Secora raised her eyes to Alai and Guillermo. "Since the mountain peaks mean so much to us all, what do you think about Montana, or Monta, for the baby's name?" They settled on Monta.

Secora's stay in Cha'lla with her infant daughter stretched into months while she healed and the adoption was finalized. Life with little Monta was exhausting, yet unexpectedly pleasant. Alai and Guillermo Santiago, her would-have-been in-laws, were so kind and helpful with the child. Without their help, neither Secora, nor the infant, probably would have survived. That magical time came to an end on December fifteenth. With a heavy heart, she hugged Diego's parents' goodbye, then bundled up the baby and began the journey north to start a new chapter of life in Missoula.

Secora sighed as the pleasant memories faded. Now she was home, she felt insecure and alone. There was no one to help with the baby, and no one here remembered Diego and the island, except Monta. Looking at her now, you could almost swear that the tiny girl was truly grateful to have a loving home and a mom who cared for her. Secora spent quite a bit of time losing herself in Monta's beauty.

After feeding and changing the little one, Secora held her close and wandered around, showing her the apartment. "Look, Monta, it's a table." The child looked from Secora's face to the table–then back, with an expression which seemed to say, "Mom, are you crazy? Got anything better than that?"

Secora tried again. "Oooh, see the plant?"

The doorbell buzzed, and Secora placed the baby into the carrier on the coffee table while she answered the door. Her friend, Maria, stood in the hall clutching two cages containing a tricolored guinea pig and an orange corn snake. She motioned for Maria to sit on the couch, thanked her for taking care of the pets while she was gone, and poured cups of coffee for them both. Maria caught her up with news about her family and what had happened during her time away.

When it was her turn, Secora didn't feel like talking about the things which had happened to her. So, she took the graceful red-orange, black, and russet corn snake she called Spider Woman, out of the carrier and gave her a once-over. Then she carefully leaned over to show the baby. "See the pretty snake?" Monta looked at the reptile with wide eyes, touched the shiny creature then looked back at her mom. Next, Secora held Pete, the guinea pig. He was so chubby and cute. Secora was ecstatic about seeing the "pig," and he in turn was unable to control his squeals of joy at seeing his long-time friend. Pete caught the baby's attention. Monta's eyes shone brightly, and she seemed happy to meet and touch him.

Secora stowed her pets in their usual areas and brought out her checkbook. She wrote a generous check for pet sitting and gave it to Maria, who said, "Whenever I make my tamales, that pig loves the masa. I will bring him some the next time we have tamales."

Secora knew the power of Maria's suggestions. She thanked and hugged her friend on the way out. "Don't forget to bring me two tamales while you're at it." They both laughed as Maria started off down the hall.

Monta began to sniffle until she was fed the rest of her bottle of goat's milk. Secora propped the baby up with pillows on the couch, and sat down beside her. She reviewed the feelings of her family and friends, who had mixed thoughts about Monta. As soon as she'd arrived in town, Secora had left a message for her sister, Iris Snowden.

Next, she made a call to her friend, Jane Roanhorse, who lived in South Dakota. Jane kind of understood the loss Secora was feeling and how scary it felt to be a single parent, since her own marriage had devolved into an abusive situation, and she now raised her son, Kyah, alone. He had recently turned thirteen and he said he couldn't wait to babysit Monta and teach her all kinds of "fun stuff."

Jane's brother, Gideon Yellow Thunder, had fought beside Secora in the battle on Massacre Mountain. She greatly valued his opinion, but he thought she was crazy to take on a child and wouldn't even talk supportively about the adoption. He told her, "Secora you can't take care of anyone. You're barely able to take care of yourself." Perhaps true, but not helpful.

Another close friend and Lakota holy man, Jimmy Lizardeye, paused when she told him, then thoughtfully offered prayers for the tiny one and all of her parents—dead or still in this world. At least, that had felt appropriate.

Secora's parents, Dr.'s Sage and L.W. Dalton, were eager to meet the sweet child and accept her as their own granddaughter, but as was typical since they had retired, they were out of town on a lecture tour.

Secora missed her family and friends. It had been months since she had visited them. She sighed; perhaps I should try my sister again. Maybe Iris would come over to catch her up about the preparations she and Jane were making for the trip they were about to make to Peru on behalf of the university. She carefully set Monta in a rocker swing, went to the house phone, and set the receiver on a stool while she dialed her feisty sister.

"Hey, Secora let me put you on speaker. I just arrived at Jane's place on Pine Ridge, and we're packing for the trip."

Jane's voice said, "We were talking about you, wondering what you were up to."

"You must have been home a couple of days by now, and this is the first time you're calling me?" demanded Iris.

"I left you a message, Iris, as soon as I walked in the door. Sorry I didn't try again. Girls, I'm exhausted. Things take so much longer with grief and a baby."

"I'm not sure what to think about that baby." Iris Snowden paused. "Truth be known, Secora you are totally crazy for trying to raise her alone."

"We are different, Iris."

Jane chimed in, "She's also still mad at you about the Duende thing."

Secora shook her head. "The Duendes, you mean the diminutive mountain people you found last summer?"

"Yeah, she's worried that the word will leak out. Everyone will descend on Bosque Alto to see the Little Ones and destroy their remaining stronghold."

"I certainly hope not, but why are you blaming me?"

Iris spewed, "I wish you had never told us about the Duendes. Their survival is so precarious. Because the university sent us there, we are expected to publish a monograph on their culture while struggling to protect their anonymity."

"Glad you are taking precautions. But do you really think nobody else is going to spill the beans about them and their stone cities? It's only a matter of time before the word is out."

"Because of us, there will probably be articles on them everywhere, from the Wall Street Journal to Reader's Digest. Couldn't you have left the subject alone?"

Secora scratched her head and sighed. "Could we please change the subject? I was hoping we could meet for lunch, Iris?"

"Obviously, not today, Secora. Jane and I have a lot of loose ends to tie up before we head back to Missoula to collect the ten students we're taking to Peru for the Chachapoya study."

"Chachapoya study?"

"Right, you told us about the flyer last summer. Sis, don't you remember?"

"Well, yes. I thought you rejected the idea. That's when you chose to seek out the Duendes, instead."

"At first, I didn't want to go. Then I recalled Dad telling us the legends of a holy Being called Viracocha, the Weeping God, when we were kids. The Chachapoyas may have been descendants of His followers. So, call me sentimental, Secora."

"It sounds as if you're as stuck on the thought of a 'Mystic Healer' in Bolivia and Peru as much as Mom and Dad are."

"Must run in the family."

"Iris and I have discovered that Teacher was also referred to as the 'White Mantle of Light.'" Jane enthused, "We're hoping the white robe might be a clue to His land of origin."

Secora stretched the long phone cord and sat down next to the baby. "Perhaps it wasn't so much a physical robe, as a reference to the glowing aura visible when Great Prophets reveal God's Word."

Jane ignored her friend. "Whatever. It could still be important."

"Come on, Secora," Iris pleaded. "We're hoping to bring evidence to light which demonstrates offspring of Tiahuanaco's inhabitants became the foundation stock for the paler-skinned Chachapoya people, whose survival required them to remain hidden in mountain fortresses until they were able to rebuff the punishing attacks; first by the Incas, and more recently by the Spaniards."

"I agree with you, Jane, and I am fully aware of the history of the once-grand city and empire of Tiahuanaco."

Iris sounded contrite, "Sorry Secora, of course, you are. I didn't mean to remind you of Diego's death."

Secora mumbled, "Doesn't matter, he's never far from my thoughts." She shifted gears.

"Okay, how are you going to approach this study?"

"We're inspired by your mother-in-law, Alai," enthused Iris. "She might be a living descendant of the Chachapoyas. If not, maybe she is related to the lighter-skinned Paracas or their kin. We think her people must have had tales, cultural arts, or other traditions that could support our theory."

Secora sighed, "Too bad they've all been wiped out, except for her." Taking advantage of the momentary silence, she changed the subject. "Maybe we could meet for lunch Tuesday?"

As Jane and Iris considered, Secora was distracted once again by the doorbell's tone. "Gotta go, girls, someone's at the door, and Monta probably needs a change."

She was eager to end this strangely uncomfortable conversation, and a friend at the door might be a welcome sight.

"Tuesday at the restaurant that's built over the creek?"

Iris scolded, "Okay, at 11:00. Better be on time, sis. We'll be leaving for the airport right after lunch."

"Then I'll see you girls in two days, God willing. Bye." Before they could contest her answer, Secora disconnected and hung up the receiver, feeling more embattled than assured by the call. She shook it off and hopped up to find out who actually wanted to see her.

3

GIDEON'S VISIT

Gideon Yellow Thunder was both excited and nervous as he skipped up the steps to the second-floor apartment. He straightened his camel-colored suit coat and black-checkered tie. On the landing, he picked a small mirror from his breast pocket and checked his neatly combed dark hair. It had been patchy after the lightning strike last summer, but six months later, it looked shiny, healthy, and was six inches longer than when he'd last seen Secora in July. He slid the mirror back into the pocket and took a deep breath before pushing the doorbell.

When Secora opened the door, her stare turned into a bright grin as she awkwardly gestured for him to enter with the baby in one arm, and the other bound up in an incapacitating brace.

Gideon could feel his face reciprocating her joy. Distracted, he asked, "Is that a guinea pig?"

Secora nodded. As usual, Pete had to put in his own two cents with a series of squeals.

The young realtor watched Secora's demeanor change as she added, "Hey, you're impressive, all dressed up in a suit. I'm kind of used to you in sweaty jeans, grime, and blood. But this is a nice look too." She stared at him a moment before coyly dropping her eyes.

Closing the door behind him, she indicated a seat on the couch with her chin.

Gideon felt like his presence had pleased and strengthened his friend. He dared to wonder, is she flirting with me?

"I'm so grateful you came to see us. Have a seat. If you'll excuse me, I need to change her diaper." Secora picked up one of little Monta's arms and pretended to wave it at him.

"Monta, say 'Hi' to Gideon." Monta smiled and drooled as she was carried off to the changing table in the corner of the room.

He looked at the rug. "So, today is Monday, your first day back at the university. Thought I'd take you to school."

"This is a surprise. You came all the way from South Dakota to Missoula just to walk me to school?"

"Well, I was in the neighborhood."

She rolled her eyes. "Your timing is impeccable."

"Not always," he snarked.

She laughed as she taped the old diaper together and pitched it to Gideon, who dropped it into a nearby wastebasket.

As he did, he remembered how he had hoped to save Secora in South America last summer and become the hero in her life... but when he had finally located her, it was just a few days after she'd met Diego Santiago, and things had taken a turn.

Secora tugged a sweater and cap on the baby with one hand and her teeth, and they were ready to go. "Could you please grab the diaper bag?"

He shook his head. "Uh-uh, you take the bag and give me the baby. She'll be safer in my two arms. Concentrate on walking yourself out the door and safely down those icy steps."

On the way to the university, he explained he was in town primarily to meet with lawyers who were sorting out the Treasuremont business partnership following the death of Glen Greenbriar in last summer's battle on the mountain. We have to figure out the taxes, and settle with his estate, et cetera."

"Nice cover for coming over to see me," she laughed.

Secora puffed up the stairs in the Social Sciences Building, and as they walked down the third-floor hall, Gideon watched her struggle to pull out her office key. He reached the door first and was surprised to find it was already open–even more shocking, the room was occupied by someone else, a smarmy twenty-something with oil shale and drilling posters covering the walls which once held Secora's treasures.

Gideon challenged, "Who are you?" He looked toward Secora, who was almost caught up, then back at the occupant announcing. "This office belongs to Secora James."

"Was–Ms. James office," said a smooth-talking young man, with a smirk.

Secora sidled up to the entrance and returned the stare of the smug young man.

"What changed?"

"If you're Ms. James," he hmphed, "you should ask Dr. Chastain."

Lifting an eyebrow, she corrected, "It's Dr. James." She turned and stormed down to visit the secretary. Gideon and Monta caught up with her as she entered the department office.

Directing her gaze to the new girl behind the desk she asked. "Who are you, and who is in my office?"

"Oh, I'm covering for Susan for a couple of weeks. You must be Dr. James. I was expecting you since your old office was reassigned last Friday."

"You didn't think to call me?"

"I tried once. No answer. Don't you have a cell phone?" The secretarial temp was young, maybe a grad student. She ran a hand through her hair as she glanced at Gideon. Smiling coyly, she added. "Are you her lawyer?"

Gideon returned the smile. "I'm not. Why do you ask?" Secora frowned. "Why would I need a lawyer?"

The assistant looked at the desk while twirling a chestnut curl. "Things have changed considerably since you left in June. Dr. James. Dean Franks handed the department Chair over to Dr. Donald Chastain, and some people seem to be very upset about the change. I assumed you would be one of them."

Gideon turned to his friend. "Secora, didn't you once describe him as the Grinch whose heart was at least as shriveled as his face?"

The young woman stared at him with half a smile.

Secora countered firmly, "I don't believe I ever said that."

The secretary turned from staring at Gideon, back to Secora and continued, "Dr. Chastain immediately cleaned out your office and assigned it to a new master's program graduate who specializes in oil shale fields."

Secora nailed Gideon with a frowny smile. "I never did say that."

"Bet you thought about it once or twice."

The young woman's eyes signaled approval as she went on to explain, "Although Dr. Chastain does not wield the power to fire Dr. James because of her tenured position, he did all he could to diminish her presence in the department." Her voice became a whisper, "He's hoping she might go away. Especially now she has an illegitimate baby." She wiggled her fingers out the door to emphasize the thought, then turned back to Gideon with a smile.

"Get a grip!" Secora put her good hand on the desk. "I'm still here– even if you can't see me in the shade of Mr. Yellow Thunder's glow."

The young woman frowned as she slid a drawer open and reached inside. "By the way, he had all your things packed and stored in the basement during your fall sabbatical in South America. The door is locked. You'll need a key." She handed a key which dangled from a bit of rope attached to a foot-long stick, to Gideon rather than Secora.

He accepted the key and glanced at Secora. Her eyes had turned to slits set into her reddened forehead.

"Breathe, Secora."

She inhaled and her brow relaxed. "It's unfortunate that Dr. Chastain sees me as an adversary."

After Gideon picked up the baby carrier, the pair descended four flights of stairs to retrieve her gear from the basement. He sniffed the stale air as they passed down a musty, grey concreted corridor, dimly lit at best. He brushed the dust from a number on a dreary metal door, jiggled the old key into the lock, and pushed it open.

He felt along the wall for a switch with the hand which wasn't holding the baby. The contents of Secora's office were thoughtlessly dumped in a heap, and dimly illuminated by a single naked bulb hanging from the ceiling. The air in the drab cement room was warm and stagnant. It reeked with sour stench.

As Gideon's eyes adjusted, he mused, "And I thought I had troubles at the office."

"Well, at least this guy hasn't tried to kill us like your former partner did," sighed Secora.

Gideon watched her kneel and search through her belongings, clicking her tongue against her teeth when she found a few of her fossils had been broken.

"My favorite mastodon molar paperweight is missing."

Gideon spoke to Monta as he set the baby carrier down. "Aw, don't worry, Monta. We'll find your mommy another one."

Secora craned her neck around, eyes and mouth wide open and ready to protest.

"Just kidding," he chuckled. "I'll grab the dolly over by the furnace. Why don't you look for some empty boxes in the heap by the door?"

They were able to stow the items in several cardboard boxes and stacked the first load on the old dolly. As they collected and boxed the last items, Dr. Donald Chastain himself appeared in the doorway and cleared his throat. They both did a double take at his unexpected appearance.

He removed the fingers which were pinching his nose to avoid the smell and began speaking quietly, crisply enunciating each word. "Apparently the rumor is true; you are back, Dr. James." His pasted-on smile faded as he stepped closer. "I've never liked you for a number of reasons. If you choose to stay with the department, I want you to know there will be no more keeping live pets at the office–especially guinea pigs. And visits must be brief. No more tea parties and extended communications from Iris and her teaching assistant, Jane Roanhorse. Such exchanges will be kept to a minimum. Is that clear?"

Secora once told Gideon she harbored little respect for the "Old Dads," as her favorite archaeology professor, Dr. Taylor, had called them. Nothing to do with their actual age but with a stubborn, arrogant mindset based on the ideas of an earlier time, the very inception of the modern study of human history.

She felt people in key positions had all too easily rejected or "mis-placed" crucial data which suggested the earliest inhabitants of the "New World" didn't fit the parameters they'd personally set for the appearance of humans in the Americas, and forget ever seeing the bones of "giants" which had been dutifully sent to the Smithsonian over the years. They had mysteriously vanished.

Today, Dr. Chastain was a dedicated, scholarly descendant of Franz Boas and Ales Hrdlika. He wore a navy-blue sweater and a black tie. *Must be his casual look* zipped through Gideon's mind.

"I said—is that clear?"

Gideon felt his hands ball into fists. Keep it up. I'd like to knock you on your cranky butt.

Luckily, Secora appeared to be reading his mind and stepped forward. He watched as she stood tall and squared her shoulders. A slight smile crossed Gideon's lips as she drew in a breath and held it before speaking. "Donald, I am aware you graduated in social-cultural anthropology from Columbia University in the 1950s. You also completed a full complement of courses in invertebrate paleontology, and you were picked up by our Paleontology department because there hadn't been an opening in anthropology for quite a few years. I, too, have a strong background in the archaeological and paleontological disciplines, and we do have a few things in common."

She picked up the baby seat and stood in front of the unpleasant man. "Congratulations on becoming Department Chair. As such, I will submit a bill to you for the replacement costs of materials that have been damaged or are missing altogether. I'll be keeping my eyes open to see if anyone might be using any of my missing articles in our department."

He deflected, "Of course, our budget is limited..."

"Your new Teaching Assistant will hopefully provide information about sediments which harbor coal, oil and gas deposits, or other treasures the earth might yield. That should help with the funding."

Did Gideon notice an eye twitch which showed Secora had touched a nerve?

"My interests lie in vertebrate paleontology, especially the Pleistocene megafauna which I realize is not nearly as financially pragmatic as choosing to specialize in invertebrate paleontology. I am well-aware few investors these days wish to fund gigantic skeletons that cost a great deal of money to dig and display. Yet, vertebrate paleo includes an attractive set of courses, and the rosters are always full. I am an excellent teacher and I more than earn my pay. I will continue as I have until I am ready to leave."

Dr. Chastain found nothing further to say. He abruptly turned and departed the basement. Gideon scratched his head as a sardonic smile broadened across his face.

Secora barked, "What?"

He shrugged. "Remind me not to land on your bad side."

She smirked and stared at him. "I don't have one."

His eyes lingered on her. He considered saying, my thoughts exactly but smiled and said nothing more.

She continued, "He's not a fan of my personal views and habits."

"I can see that. It sounds like he considers you to be expendable." They stopped in front of the basement elevator and Gideon pushed the call button.

"Tough. I'm not going to give or take offense. I figure I'm paid to teach not to bitch." The old mechanical doors opened. "Thank God the elevator works."

It took three trips to lug everything upstairs. Gideon returned the key to the department secretary and Secora asked her what offices were available. After grinning at Gideon for an extra-long moment, the girl grabbed another key from her drawer and made a notation in a logbook. She led them to a vacant desk in the back of another graduate student's office. Secora accepted it without complaint.

Gideon graciously assisted her in moving necessary items into the cramped new space, though he felt sick inside about the way Secora was being treated. The remaining items were left boxed beside the desk.

Her new office mate had springy blonde curls which fell past his horn-rims, and though he reminded Secora of an untrimmed Maltese. His grin was friendly and he offered his hand to each of them. "Name's Tarkio Cyr."

Gideon recognized the name was composed of designations for two tiny Western Montana towns.

"As you can probably guess by the name, I live up the canyon, almost to Idaho."

"That's a heck of a commute," said Gideon, trying to look him directly in the eyes.

"It is, but I only come to the office three days a week."

Both Gideon and Secora could see from the piles of work on his desk that he was a dedicated student, an overachiever, probably well on the path to becoming a workaholic.

"It's a pleasure, Tarkio," she said reaching out her good hand after setting Monta's carrier on the desk.

"Cute baby, oh hey, you probably noticed I have your mammoth molar. It got chipped when they were taking your stuff to the basement." He lifted it for inspection as he pointed. "I epoxied it, see?"

Secora squinted and nodded. "At least you're upfront and honest about things. Under more favorable circumstances I'd want a person with your integrity for a teaching assistant. Until then, I wonder if I could ask you to sub for me on occasion... if the need arises."

"Maybe, yeah... I mean, sure."

Gideon thought the young man looked hesitant. Wrinkles formed on his brow beneath the ringlets, like he was thinking. The sensitive Lakota glanced at Secora and offered, "Of course Dr. James will pay you part of her salary, for the missed days."

"Okay, here's a card with my number - in case. Man, it's like you read my mind. Gas isn't cheap. My wife, Anida, and I also have a new baby. Frederick is only two months old, and from what I've heard, Dr. James, it is very likely situations will 'arise'. Maybe my wife could babysit for you, occasionally?"

Monta was becoming fussy. Secora shook a teething ring and reached into the diaper bag for a bottle.

Tarkio stood, and reached for the tiny girl, hesitating until Secora's eyes gave him permission.

"Can't wait to hear about the extinct ground sloth you documented last summer, Dr. James."

Secora nodded as she let the young man take the child into his arms. "Tarkio, this is my good friend, Gideon Yellow Thunder. He's actually the one who spotted the baby hanging around the mapinguari's neck."

The young man seemed awed and offered Gideon his hand mindlessly while holding the baby to his chest with the other.

"Mr. Yellow Thunder that must have been the most amazing thing you ever saw."

"Maybe a close second." Gideon smiled and glanced at Secora. After a thought struck

him, he said, "Well, maybe the Thunderbirds topped the list." He laughed. "Let's just say, at times it was an awesome summer."

"Gideon's a master of understatement." Secora smiled sardonically as she offered Monta the bottle.

Tarkio turned to her. "Wow, I can't believe the luck of sharing an office with you."

Before retrieving the baby, Secora looked through the boxes they had stacked beside her new desk and recovered a few Clovis and Solutrean replicas she might need for one of her classes.

Gideon helped her load up the remaining items, then they bid farewell to Tarkio. He called after them, "See you in a couple of days."

Once Monta was settled in the car, she released her bottle and fell asleep. When Gideon stopped at a red light, he mulled over the shocking developments at Secora's job. "Is the kid legit, or is he a spy for the Grinch?"

Secora looked thoughtful. "Time will tell."

"Don't be so Zen, Secora, I'm still ticked off about your new accommodations, and I'm not sure I trust the kid."

Her eyes lingered on Gideon. "His actions will speak louder than mere words... so, we'll see."

While the baby was still asleep in the back seat, Gideon and Secora decided to order sandwiches and drinks at a drive-in on the way home.

Gideon regarded her as he finished chewing a bite, and she sipped her unsweetened tea. Feeling his gaze, she asked, "How's life in South Dakota?"

"It's good, but I'm here for a week or so." He stared at her. "To be honest, I was kind of lonely for my Montana friends."

She smiled and dropped her eyes. "Good to see you too, though I imagine the office takes priority over friendly visits."

4

BILLY'S ATTACK

W hen they reached the apartment building, Gideon walked down the hall with Secora. She unlocked her door, and he stepped inside with little Monta setting her on the couch. He took off his jacket and laid it on a chair, then sat beside the baby while trying to muster his courage. Secora closed and locked the door asking, "Would you like coffee?"

"Forget the coffee, please Secora look at me." He waited while she set the diaper bag down and sat across from him. "We need to have a conversation about us."

Her eyes lit up when she looked at him. "Yes, we should."

Like Secora, Gideon had spent most of the summer recovering from severe injuries. He nearly died from trauma and blood loss in Peru. There had been no time to express his feelings for her on the mountain, or even before he left the hospital. Now that Secora was back in Missoula, he couldn't wait any longer to find out if there was the slightest chance she had recovered enough from Diego's death to move on. He was nervous. It's now or never. He inhaled deeply taking strength from the inrush of air. Looking her in the eyes, he began, "I've been thinking about you... and about what happened after you left the hospital last summer."

She dropped her eyes. Gideon's heart raced. *Why did she disconnect?*

"Secora, I know you will always love Diego." She looked up. "I miss him too. He was unlike anyone I've ever met...so brave, selfless, and kind. Is there even the slightest possibility...?" His words faltered.

She softly ventured, "I'm so full of feelings. Gideon, I don't even know where to begin."

Gideon could see his smile reflected in Secora's eyes. For the first time, they were about to discuss their feelings for one another. This was the moment he'd anticipated for months.

As the Satfon began to ring, Billy looked up and his jaw dropped in shock. A large man with a shovel had stepped from behind a pile of rocks less than twenty feet away. The burly aggressor moved determinedly toward him, stopping only momentarily to glance at the mule clattering in the back of the pickup, and screeching a warning.

Billy panicked and ran to the truck. "Come on, Secora..." He groaned, as he struggled to pull his shovel from the mounting braces at the rear of the cab. Finally freeing it, Billy turned to meet the man. "Pick up, pick up!" he pleaded into the ringing phone as he clutched the handle with his one free hand.

The wall phone rang, and Secora looked at it.

"Don't." Gideon shook his head, eyes begging,

She looked worried but didn't reach for it. The ringing quit. Both sighed and began to relax again.

He took a breath as if to speak just as the phone shrilled again, demanding attention.

Thoroughly distracted now, Secora rose and picked up the receiver. "Hi, can I call you back?"

Gideon could hear the caller shout, "No, it's Billy! This-is-an-emergency! Some guy's coming at me–he's trying to kill me."

She had to hold the phone away from her for the yelling.

"I've discovered something miraculous near Birch Bay and—No. Dammit, stop! Ow…" "Wait, Billy…"

"He's hitting me, I need help. How quick can you get here?"

"**Ya Alláhu'l - Mustagháth**." Secora uttered a prayer revealed by the Bab, invoking God for protection during imminent danger.

Gideon remembered hearing the prayer during desperate times last summer. Then he heard Billy scream, "Secora, where are you?" followed by a loud clanging sound.

"That's right, buddy, I have a shovel too." Gideon could hear more banging on the other end.

"Secora, you wouldn't believe this dig." Billy puffed with exertion. "There's an entire human burial associated…7,000 years too early!"

Carrots brayed another screechy alarm. Billy yelled, "Christ! This guy's nuts! He's trying to kill me. Stop that. Shit, he just broke my arm. Please call 911 because I can't."

"Billy, I'll call 'em. Where will they find you?" Secora held the phone away from her ear, looking desperately to Gideon.

"Outside of Custer, three miles south of Birch Bay give or ta…"

Gideon thought to himself, Birch Bay, Washington is twelve to fourteen hours away with baby stops. He heard the incessant screeching of the braying mule, then silence as the connection was lost. His heart sank into his gut, not only with concern for this guy, Billy, but because of a growing realization. Secora always seemed to be unavailable, to be moving off in another direction.

She looked at him with dread in her eyes. "I have to call the police."

She was already dialing 911 but turned again to look at him. "Can we talk later, Gideon? Please?"

His eyes lowered, his composure rapidly breaking down. "I'm... not sure. What you're doing right now seems to be really important."

She put her hand over the mouthpiece. "Please?"

Their moment of vulnerability had been shattered. His eyes moved to the door. "I ought to go so you can think. I'll be in touch."

As he set the sleeping baby in the crib and covered her with a blanket, he could hear, "Nine-one-one, what's your emergency?" He grabbed his jacket and opened the door.

"Hi." Secora again covered the mouthpiece with her hand, and in a strained voice begged, "Please, Gideon."

She'd looked heartbroken and he thought he saw tears in her eyes. For him, probably for Billy he thought, as she began to talk to the dispatcher. Either way, he knew things would always be like this. He'd be lucky to come in a close second–make that third with the baby. Pain was eating away his confidence. He turned away and with a backward wave, he stepped into the hall with tear-filled eyes.

Secora's voice followed him out the door. "I'll call you–you'd better answer."

Once in the hallway, Gideon shook his head, I should have known this would never work; she'd be better off married to a dead guy. To the stucco ceiling, he said, "No offense, Diego. At least you wouldn't feel so disappointed or left out."

5

COLD TRAIL

fter 911 dispatch, Secora called the Whatcom County Sheriff's
office and reported the incident as well. She also called the
Lummi tribal police since she wasn't exactly sure who had jurisdiction.

Even though it was afternoon, she loaded up her car and immediately took off for Western Washington. During the long drive which was regularly punctuated with baby breaks for feeding, changing, and walking around with Monta, Secora recalled Billy had been in grad school with her. He was a nice guy, shy, but nice. She had been immersed in her studies until she met Rick James. He was a new biological anthropology student whose study path took him to the Amazon to study howler monkeys. She and Rick married, but within a year he died from a heart attack.

By then she'd lost touch with Billy, who had begun his long solitary search for mammoths and mastodons, a quest which had taken him around the globe. They kept in touch from time to time, sharing a common interest in Pleistocene megafauna, but Secora hadn't heard from him in years, until today.

She felt pangs of emotion when she thought about Gideon's visit.

She wasn't sure the conversation would have continued anyway; she was conflicted when she saw him. Until that moment, she had thought of no one but Diego. What was he hoping for? Was she ready to move on? She was driving through Bellingham when she realized she'd been obsessing about Gideon's feelings and her future for hours.

It had been a long thirteen-and-a-half-hour drive from Missoula to Birch Bay, about twelve minutes from the Canadian Border. Traffic had been backed up over the pass, and Secora was exhausted. The adrenaline had worn off hours ago.

Once she left the freeway, it took a while, and several dead ends, to find a promising track off the frontage road. Even as they arrived and pulled to a stop, Secora could barely discern that this was the right place.

She rolled the windows down about an inch then stepped out of the Dodge Dart, whose hot metal was making noises of contraction as the engine began to cool. Outside, the temperature felt like the mid-sixties, and there was no rain. She paused, feeling a breeze blowing perfectly into her face. It felt good to stretch as she took a quick survey of the site. There wasn't much to be seen—no bodies anyway.

Monta had slept on and off, but she was now awake and cranky. Secora released the baby from the back seat, and after adding an extra blanket, took her out of the car. Monta cooed and smiled as she was placed in the snugly.

The dig was in a shamble. Tatters of plastic, bits of string, and empty Shasta cans were tossed around the hill and a little cave. There was a ripped green tent by a pile of boulders and aging tracks made by deer, a mule, and two sets of boots. There were also two sets of tire tread marks. These were the only remnants of recent activity.

She went to the tent which had been pitched about twenty feet from the trench in the lee of a rocky outcrop. Here, she found a few shreds of rip-stop nylon. One large scrap was still staked to the ground. Pondering the situation, she watched the lightweight material flap in the lackadaisical winter breeze, as did her shoulder-length tawny hair and the fringe on her elk skin jacket.

"Billy, I hope you aren't resting beneath a pile of these rocks."

Secora thought it was odd that both vehicles would be missing after Billy's attack. It's also weird that there's no crime scene tape. *The Sheriff's department hasn't responded yet?* Guess that's not unusual since I was trying to describe a place I'd never seen from a vague reference screamed into a phone.

Secora changed the baby's diaper and strapped Monta back into the snugly on her chest before she returned to scan the rest of the area.

"Wish I had time to find a babysitter so you wouldn't have to travel so far, little one." Secora scanned the site looking for the miracle Billy had mentioned, as well as further evidence of the attack. She saw disturbed dirt and the broken grid strings as evidence of a struggle. The dig site slash grave was open and untidy. She widened her circle hoping to find evidence of photos, notes, a tape recorder, or any kind of clue about what happened to Billy. Nothing seemed to remain of his personal gear, but she noted a few sample bags, more soda cans, and a variety of candy bar wrappers along with a mishmash of fading mule tracks. Secora appropriated the sample bags, jamming them into the pocket of her jacket.

"Billy, where are you? I know you'd never leave a mess like this!" She called out to him and Carrots several times, but there was no answer.

Inside the small cave, her eyes adjusted and easily made out the perimeter of the L-shaped trench. Bending closer, she found shards of something sharp and black. Surely, it's not obsidian? *No, plastic.* This must be what's left of Billy's smashed satellite phone. She shuddered, hoping Billy wasn't also smashed to pieces.

"Now what?" She dragged over a dried cottonwood branch to prod the disturbed soil of the trench. First, she poked gingerly through the long side. The earth gave as if something soft might be under it, but she didn't feel a fresh corpse had been added to the grave. The branch did bounce off an object in the leg of the "L," but she found nothing else. The skeleton seemed to be gone—and so was Billy.

Secora cocked her head a moment, frozen in mid-step because she heard a screeching sound. "Is Mommy imagining the distant bray of a mule, Monta?" She strained to listen while the little girl stared at her, but she could hear nothing now. "Naw, you're right, Baby, probably squeaky brakes from the interstate."

She yawned and shook her head as she sauntered back to the car where she grabbed her camera and dropped it into a jacket pocket. She also picked up a little metal ruler and a trowel from under the front seat. The baby tried to turn her head to see what her mom was doing. Secora grinned and kissed her, then inspected the trowel's honed edges. It had been sharpened so often that it was half its original size. Her gaze passed beyond the trowel to the two sets of truck tire tracks again.

Not likely the police were here, no yellow tape, no extra car tracks. What is going on? Twenty hours ago, Billy and Carrots were fine. Then a man attacked Billy with a shovel. He only mentioned one guy... the second tire track could have been from the assailant's pick-up, I suppose. She uncapped the lens of the camera and knelt to take close-up photos of both sets of tire tracks with the little ruler in the frame to gauge the width.

Because it was difficult to bend over with the child in front of her, she'd brought out the carrier and nestled the baby in it, placing her beside the dig. Giving Monta another kiss, she offered a Binky, then took a spade from the trunk and returned to the trench.

"I don't want to disturb evidence, but I need to find out why you called me. Why was it so imperative that you reach me? If I find the reason, will I also find out why you were attacked?"

Secora carefully removed the fill dirt and used her trowel to take back the wall beside the object the branch had struck. With measured strokes, she cautiously proceeded to move down the side wall shaving an eighth of an inch at a time until the dried, caked outer soil was replaced with moist inner soil. This emphasized the natural strata and exposed a little more of a protruding rib tip of a juvenile mammoth, which she examined, then photographed.

"I hope this mammoth site is worth forfeiting a substantial conversation with Gideon." She squatted down to take a better look at the wall. Putting her hand into the back dirt for support, she felt something sharp cut into her palm. Secora recoiled when she saw the cut was bleeding freely, so she wrapped her hand in a blue bandana withdrawn from her pants pocket.

She was much less careful when she stood and kicked at the back-dirt pile to expose a razor-sharp metal point.

"No way, Billy. It's your trowel! Now, I am worried. No self-respecting bone-diggerologist would leave this prize behind." She smiled briefly, as she remembered that was how Billy referred to himself after he heard it on a Magnum episode.

She snapped photos of the rib, the trowel, her handprint, and the blood while trying to brush the worry from her mind. She carefully replaced the soil she'd removed then stood to scan the area making certain nobody was watching or interested in taking *her* head off with a shovel.

Secora took shots of the whole site including the tent which she scrutinized for clues. It was then she noticed a disturbance in the dirt behind what was left of the shelter. I'm onto you now, Billy boy. Removing some suspiciously placed rocks, she dug cautiously until she gently wiggled a bubble-wrapped coffee can and a worn blue backpack free of the soil. Smiling, she briefly inspected them, and then replaced the dirt and the rocks. She headed nonchalantly toward the car with the loot.

"No!" She stopped abruptly and turned back. I need a piece of that bone. She returned to the juvenile rib and cut a small segment from the distal end with an obsidian flake she kept wrapped in a little case in her pocket. She'd always preferred a flake to a metal knife. Satisfied, she dropped the sample into a bag from her jacket pocket, scribbled a few notations in indelible ink, before returning the package and marker to the temporary safety of her shirt pocket. "We'll get that right off to the dating lab, Monta."

She replaced the loose soil, then carrying the spade in her stiff hand she picked up Monta's car seat with the other. Reconnoitering one last time she shouted, "Riggins, I swear I'm going to find out what happened to you."

When she turned toward the car, she did a double take. Was that dust rising over the access road to the frontage? That's got to be a dust devil... or maybe a deputy? Probably not the deputy since they haven't been here yet. *Oh, God.*

Beads of sweat began to form on her brow as she rapidly stowed Billy's gear in the trunk of the car, buckled the baby's car seat while quickly kissing her, and hopped into the driver's seat.

If someone is coming down the road it's too late to make a run for the interstate. She drove warily behind the set of boulders to the left of the remains of the tent and waited to see what developed. Nothing happened.

After eight minutes, her breathing had returned to normal, and she chided herself for being paranoid. Secora eased the Dodge back onto the roadbed, but around the first corner, she slammed the brake pedal. To her dismay, a red and silver Ford Ranger was parked in the middle of the road. A man lumbered out of the bushes with a set of binoculars in one hand. He stopped for a moment to look at her, and then ran for his vehicle.

Secora focused on his long dark hair, the Fu Manchu mustache, and —was he limping? She hit the gas. It's only a half-mile to the on-ramp. Secora's tires dug into the sandy soil, and her car sprinted past the truck, headed for the highway. She tried to tell herself the shovel she saw in the back of the Ranger as she passed was coincidental.

Allowing herself a look at the rearview, she confirmed the truck was glued to her, but her old slant six Dodge was one of those cars powerful enough to respond to the will of its driver. Rubber screeched onto the pavement, causing her to think of the mule again. She turned up the freeway ramp wishing she could use both hands as she flew past Ferndale, heading for Bellingham. Luck was with her, and she managed to put several car lengths between herself and the pickup as she entered the city limits.

Secora was sweating as she drove the last three blocks and pulled into an angled slot. The truck slid in two spaces down. The driver came out at a limping lope, trying to cut her off as she raced with Monta toward the entrance.

The baby started to cry and Secora panicked. She bashed the wooden doors open and ran behind the desks yelling, "Stop him! I think he killed my friend!"

The eyes of the employees were opened wide, and their wordless mouths hung slack—too stunned to help.

"This is ridiculous!" The tension in Secora's hazel eyes eased into calm. She thrust Monta into the arms of the nearest clerk then sized the man up as he charged toward her. At the last moment he hesitated, but it was already too late. Her hiking boot came up with enough force to knock his chin backward and drop him to the floor. The effort pushed her body back against the wall, where she tried to regain her balance with her unbraced arm.

It was a move she'd once used on a dangerous Barbados ram which she had captured in the mountains above Clinton. Since then, she'd used it on other attacking animals, enough times to feel confident in her ability.

Deputy "Blakely Greene," according to a little sign on the wall, sauntered out from his cubbyhole in time to catch the action.

"Okay, Judy. What the hell just happened?" He pointed to Secora. "Lady, don't move!"

The clerk recounted what she'd seen, and what Secora had said about the man killing her friend. She finished by adding that the man had come rushing right up to the mother with an intense look in his eyes and spit dripping from his mustache.

Deputy Greene responded by asking, "Judy, would you be kind enough to get the gentleman on the floor some medical attention? Make sure—"

"Make sure he doesn't leave the building." Judy interrupted and then handed Monta back to her mom.

"Right." He cocked his head and indicated his small office to Secora, "Let's have a chat over at my desk."

When they were seated, he said, "You know, your awkward entrance reminds me of a dog I once had. Nearly every time I took her camping, she'd high tail it back to the fire with a bear or something awful right behind her. The worst episode involved an angry cow elk who tore right through camp as we were eating; thought we'd all die that day, for sure."

Secora rolled her eyes. "So, did you get rid of the dog?"

"No. Just quit camping." He smiled and began to put her information on a form. The belligerent assailant was being seated at the desk of another deputy. "You know that fellow might press assault charges against you."

"He was the aggressor. I was defending my baby and myself."

Greene looked up from his form and raised his eyebrows. "I guess we'll see."

"Sir, that guy was trying to stop me from reaching help. I didn't want my daughter caught in the middle of a fight. Is there *really* a possibility I might be charged?" She was exhausted and the muscles in her legs and arms began to twitch.

The good news was, in the end, it didn't look like she would be charged. The man who had chased her was detained instead because a bloody shovel was found in the back of his truck. Despite his denial that he'd never used it as a weapon to kill Billy or anyone else; he insisted the shovel was only used to remove roadkill from the highway.

Deputy Greene didn't feel the perp's story adequately explained why the blood was primarily on the bottom side of the implement.

"Hell, I'm not even sure it's legal to pick up roadkill without a permit. Judy, can you find the latest information on dead animals from Highway Patrol?" She nodded and began to tap the computer keys.

To explain the blood on the underside of the shovel, the man conveniently remembered he'd used it to smash an opossum "...that wasn't quite dead. I was just putting the poor creature out of its misery."

Needless to say, the Deputy was eager to see the DNA results for the dried "opossum" blood. In the meantime, the assailant was temporarily held on the suspicion that he had something to do with the disappearance of Billy Riggins. His face sagged, and he had nothing else to say except, "I need to make a call."

Secora shook her head as she and Monta returned to their car. She was thinking that among the problems the prosecuting attorney was going to have to deal with was the missing body, no Billy.

After filing the missing person paperwork, it took Secora the rest of the day to convince two deputies to come to the place where Billy disappeared. A unit followed Secora out to Birch Bay, where, not surprisingly, they found no trace of him.

Almost nothing was left when they arrived. Even the aluminum Shasta cans and candy bar wrappers she'd seen and photographed earlier were gone by the time they arrived to cordon off the area. She was glad she had taken samples of the rubbish as well as Polaroid photos, which she shared with them. They did find drops of blood near Billy's abandoned trowel, which Secora explained.

The wind picked up, and Secora took off a glove to test the baby's cheeks for a chill, then pulled Monta's hat down further over her little face while she waited for them to finish a sweep of Billy's dig site.

They told her she could leave; they'd take it from there. She hesitated for a moment, and then stated, "There were at least two people involved. The man in the truck, for sure; then, someone else must have cleaned the scene after the assailant was detained at your station."

"Possibly, miss, or maybe the mule just ate the stuff," smirked one of the deputies.

"Could the landowner be involved?" she asked, wondering if Gideon's real estate connections could check into who the property owner might be.

"Or an unhappy tribal member was maybe thinking Mr. Riggins had disturbed a distant relative."

The other man said, "Thanks, Ms. James, we've got this."

She turned to leave then turned back. "I'll claim the mule and take responsibility for his care until you find Billy. You have my number, right?"

"Sure, miss. If we find the animal we'll let you know."

As she climbed into her car, she noticed both men were chuckling, as if they thought it was a joke.

6

PRESUMED DEAD

Secora had done her homework. Yet, try as she might, she could not find any trace of Billy or Carrots. Now, she was physically and emotionally drained from his frantic call, the long drive to Birch Bay, and the arguably peculiar investigation into her friend's disappearance.

She grabbed a burger and fries in Ferndale, but felt so exhausted she couldn't even think about eating, and took most of the meal with her to a motel outside of Bellingham. After crawling up the stairs with Monta's car seat, she stiffly returned to the car for their luggage.

When she finished washing and changing the baby, she uncapped a jar of goat's milk from the little fridge. She found the odor a bit strong for her taste, but then Monta had had to make do from the start since neither she nor Alai was lactating when the baby was orphaned.

Afterward, Secora sprawled on the bedspread with the little girl, surrounding her with pillows. They enjoyed sharing evening prayers, finishing with, "O God, guide me, protect me, make of me a shining lamp and a brilliant star."

As she played with the baby's toes, Secora let her thoughts wander to Billy's abrupt disappearance. Was he really dead? Why had a profound discovery cost Riggins so much? The man had always been meticulous about his work, but clearly, he'd taken extra care to hide this breakthrough. What caused him to seek her confirmation of his "miraculous discovery?" Why did Billy risk a call to her–rather than the sheriff? She shrugged, and rolling over, finally gave in to a serious need for sleep.

In the middle of the night, her eyes flew open, and she sat up with a jerk. Oh m' gosh... the can! She had totally spaced it, and hadn't even told the deputies about Billy's stash. Now that she thought about it, this could be a problem. She sprang up, dressed haphazardly, flew down the stairs in the dark to her trusty Dodge, and opened the trunk.

The hairs on the back of her neck prickled at the sound of the faintest noise. Is someone watching? What if someone tries to stop me from returning to my sleeping child? She slid the can into a white garbage bag, which she snapped free from a box that remained in the trunk along with her other travel gear. A quick scan to see if other eyes had noticed left Secora satisfied that there was no one around other than a slinking black cat. She slammed the trunk and rushed back to the room to appease her curiosity.

She decided to sit in the room's single chair rather than take a chance on waking Monta. Once the bubble wrap was removed, she inhaled the smell of coffee. It made her realize she hadn't eaten since yesterday morning, and her stomach growled a warning. After a quick peek at the contents of the can, she would eat the cold fast food that languished in the mini fridge. In the meantime, she took a break to soak some of the coffee in hot water so she would be able to wash the greasy burger down.

Now back to the treasure. Whoa, what's this? She put on gloves, and then gently pried out the longer cylindrical packet. "Whoa-Ho, this is no Clovis point!" That was too loud. Secora closed her eyes, winced, relaxed, and exhaled as Monta stirred. After fussing a moment, the child resumed her slumber.

Secora admired every facet of the lovely flint point, interspersed with chewy bites of cold sandwich and mouthfuls of lukewarm coffee.

For decades there had been a debate about Clovis lance points and other artifacts in America being derived from the advanced Solutrean flint tools found in Spain, Portugal, and France which dated between 22,000 and 17,000 years ago, during the Upper Paleolithic Stone Age.

The American Clovis pieces weren't quite as refined, but they were arguably similar. There had been suggestions that certain tools from sites like "Cactus Hill" and the "Meadow croft Rockshelter" represented a transitional phase between the two technologies. The premise being that the stone craft may have been brought to America by boat-hopping travelers, who crossed the ice and snowpack along the Northern Atlantic coastline during the earliest human migrations to this continent. Not everybody agreed.

"Billy, I wonder if your dead guy found this point and kept it for a lucky charm? Perhaps, but it still had to travel to the Washington coast, somehow. Question is—did he or his friends bring it here themselves, and if so, When? Hmmm." Guess that's for me to figure out now.

It was all Billy hadn't said before he was silenced which ignited Secora's curiosity. Shifting again to a whisper, "What else did you know about the individual in the burial? Where did he come from? Was he a European traveler, or had his ancestors been Bellinghamsters for thousands of years?" And darn it, where was his skeleton?

The idea forming in her mind was impossible. Could it be true that Billy discovered a legitimate burial associated with a twenty-thousand-year-old mammoth? Her training kicked in—no, certainly not! Maybe the rib sample would give her a different date. Could there be a random association between this artifact and the mammoth bones - even less likely.

"Okay, what else is in this can?" She fished out the Astarte figurine and smiled. Oh ho, ho. You're kidding! Astarte was a female fertility goddess also known as Ashtoreth or Ishtar, who had been generally worshipped in the Middle East and parts of Europe.

"That tears it." This explosive information would not be welcomed by the general American archaeology community. Billy wouldn't want any part of this. She looked around suspiciously and checked the lock on the door. "Pretty sure I don't either."

When she sat again, she thoughtfully fingered the figurine, and then uncovered the other fragments taking care not to touch the surfaces of the objects with anything but a fresh Kleenex. Secora laid the tissue-cradled artifacts on the bedspread, photographed them, then took the time to rewrap each item and place them securely in a plastic box that she kept in a special part of her leather backpack.

She finished the last film roll, took it out of the camera, and placed it among Monta's clean diapers. Briefly, she dug through the clothes and gear in Billy's nylon backpack looking for notes or a tape recorder. They were noticeably missing. He must have had another bag. *Did I miss a stash containing the crucial information? Did your attacker see you hide it, and take your findings with him?*

Perhaps, but even with the evidence she had, one thing was looking pretty clear. The dates were way off the norm. No way would Donald Chastain, or, for that matter, anyone at the university who cared about such things, accept this burial as legit. Iris had bored Secora on several occasions, with horror stories of evidence that had been rejected and or destroyed because the dates didn't fit the limitations of current thinking. Iris would say, "Over thirteen thousand years? No way!" With a sneer she borrowed from 'the powers that be' she added, "How many times has that lame song been sung?"

"Gotcha now, Riggins! This site is taboo!" *It couldn't exist according to Ales Hrdlika and the other 'Old Dads.' Too bad we don't have any proof. No human skeleton, just a mammoth rib fragment, and some artifacts I can't connect to anything. Oh well...*

Before dawn the next morning, Monta roused Secora with her fussing, and they shared prayers. She smiled at her daughter who was again having a bottle of goat's milk.

"If this burial was Solutrean, Baby Girl, we may be talking somewhere around twenty-thousand years ago." Monta turned her head at the reference to herself, dropped the bottle, and wiggled her arms. Secora picked her up and walked around, covering her in kisses before putting her tiny arms through little jacket sleeves.

Secora shoved her brush and shampoo into the travel bag and prepared to head out. She hadn't heard anything about the mule, and the sheriff had discouraged any further activity at the site which would presumably be re-dug by an archaeologist from Western Washington University.

She would give them the artifacts later, but she wasn't going to let any grass grow under her feet waiting for their findings. There was nothing more to do in Washington State, so she closed the car door and started the engine. With the baby, she expected the trip might take twelve hours. She wouldn't be home until six o'clock—give or take.

While driving through Seattle, Secora recalled that it was Wednesday. Her first megafauna lab was this morning—from ten to noon. She woke Tarkio up to see if he could fill in for the day. He was reluctant since it would be his first venture in that arena. Since it was an introductory meeting, she explained there wouldn't be much pressure. He could grab her notebook and handouts from the desk, along with the printout of the class members, and be just fine.

She would easily be ready for tomorrow's classes, which needed very little prep time. Still, she couldn't wait to be back to check out the class rosters, organize her notes, and pull out the necessary fossils. It would be good to do something she loved, something which had a certain degree of predictability.

A few miles further down the road, Secora's smile faded and she felt her stomach flip as she remembered something else. She'd planned to take Iris and Jane out for lunch before they left—yesterday.

"Darn it, I missed saying goodbye." The girls were on their way to Peru to start the Chachapoya project. *I definitely need to contact them before they disown me.* She'd had to put everything else out of her mind when she'd received that compelling call from Billy, and Gideon's momentous visit was only the tip of an iceberg. Tomorrow morning she'd check in with the Anthropology office and they'd be able to tell her how to get in touch with the university's team. She took some comfort in the thought that they almost certainly had been assigned a satellite telephone.

A few miles further down the road, she also realized that it was January third, 2000. *Huh, wonder if all the technology blew up. Maybe there aren't any computers or cell phones because of the dreaded Y2K rollover.* She shrugged her shoulders and continued driving. "At least the car works."

The rest of the trip vacillated between boredom and thoughts of Gideon. Even though all Secora could think of was her bed when she neared Missoula, she pulled into the dark university parking lot at six o'clock. Grabbing the carrier, she climbed to her new office. It was quiet and nobody else appeared to be in the department. She flipped on the lights and checked her phone messages. It was disappointing to find nothing from Gideon. *He'd been so tangible two days ago.*

Wistfully, she tried Gideon's cellular number, but it went straight to voice mail. Next, she tried to reach Iris on her cell phone, a tool Secora personally chose not to use. She listened to the recording and left a lame message to call her back. *How could she adequately apologize over a phone anyway, a cell phone, no less?*

I guess everything electronic still seems to work, not that it's very helpful. Little Monta was cooing and wiggling energetically. Secora picked her up, checked the diaper, and held her close for a moment before offering more of her bottle.

A cell phone, Billy had used a cell phone. Did someone tap into his calls? Where are your notes and photos, Billy? She brought up the university computer to check her emails in case he had sent something to her. There she found a copy of the class rosters for her lab and her other courses, but nothing from either Billy or Gideon.

Secora gently patted Monta's back. The baby burped, and Secora gently snuggled her into the carrier before laying out the notes and fossils she would need for tomorrow. When she was finished, Secora left Tarkio a thank-you note, grabbed the keys, and closed her office door.

On the way through the darkened corridor, she became aware someone was sitting at the department office desk. She peeked in and was rather startled to see Donald Chastain. The disgruntled professor leaned back into the swivel chair, wagging his head and the pencil he was holding, at Secora.

"You missed the very first day of class, Ms. James. How very unprofessional."

"It's Dr. James. There was an emergency," she said, hoping it didn't sound as lame to him as it did to her.

"Always is." The words hit her like a punch in the stomach. "Be that as it may, I expect better from tenured staff."

"There is no reason for you to feel threatened by my tenured presence or absence in the department, Donald."

"It's Dr. Chastain." He stood up, tossed the pencil on the desk, and crossed his arms over his chest. After he had inspected the carpet a moment, he continued, "Won't you empty your mind of all your nonsense for a moment and try to appreciate the intricacy of the foundation laid by the fathers of the social sciences? You're supposed to be well-versed in the theory of these disciplines, yet you... you fall for every slick, unsubstantiated idea that comes along."

Secora set the carrier down and rose again. Squaring her shoulders, she looked him in the eyes. "Okay, we agree anthropologists stand on the shoulders of the giants of the social sciences, but paleontology has more of a hard science, geological base. As scientists, we must strive to let the evidence speak for itself. How else can we understand our ancestors or the history of life on this planet? The story suggested by our antecedents is necessarily incomplete."

He put the fingers of his right hand on the desk as if for support. "If you persist in countering me, I'll see to it that your career founders. There won't be any chance for advancement at this university."

"Dr. Chastain," Secora began coolly. "I have no interest in vying for Chair of the Department." She turned momentarily away, and then glared back at him. "And I'm not interested in competing with you in any way. Couldn't we agree to be civil coworkers without agendas? Put away your arrows. We both have a lot to offer the department. We need structure and historical ties, and maybe we'll learn something new in the process."

The fading silence was broken by Monta's tired cry, which motivated Secora. She yawned and picked up the carrier. "Need sleep, early classes tomorrow. See you in the morning. Goodnight." She struggled out of the doorway fighting the emotional and physical exhaustion. With the carrier hooked over her arm, she dragged herself toward the elevator. Once inside, she turned and glanced back at the office. She could hear Dr. Chastain on the phone. She sighed. Seems like this is going to be a rough new year.

7

LEGIT!

After finishing dinner and much-needed housekeeping, Secora put in a Johnny Rivers CD and dropped onto the bed to play with her daughter. Monta was moving her arms and legs vigorously, managing to flip from her back onto her belly for the first time. She peeked over a pillow, grinning. Secora laughed and ruffled the baby's dark hair. "Won't be long, little girl, and you'll be crawling. That's gonna make teaching a major problem. Must find you a babysitter."

Secora's heart clenched as the CD player finally reached the song *Slow Dancing*,

Her thoughts immediately snapped to her beloved Diego. She remembered standing beside him on the top of Isla del Sol, staring at the lake and the shadowy mountains beyond. The world seemed to fade as they immersed themselves in each other's presence so completely, becoming the sole occupants of their own realm.

She took a deep ragged breath as tears slid down her cheeks and dripped off her chin. To look into his sparkling dark eyes had been a heavenly gift, one she'd first experienced the day they'd met. Diego had healed her from a poisoning in La Paz, and when she had awoken, there were those amazing eyes. She later became aware there were two revered Kallawayas at her side, Guillermo and his son, Diego, and there were those... big... dark... eyes - the essence of Purity of Intention.

Their time together had only been several tumultuous weeks—and though chastity was the rule in both families, they were mentally and spiritually closer than many married couples. They could read one another's thoughts.

It seemed as if she could hear his thoughts even now, or smell his scent of rosemary, at times. She knew these sensations would likely fade. Picking up the glass of water off the nightstand, she sipped and chuckled at the thought of meeting Gideon in the middle of all that.

He had, at the suggestion of Wakinyan Tonka the Great Thunderbird, left South Dakota to find this woman he'd never even heard of, and protect her so she could help him save the Thunderbirds.

At first, Gideon thought Secora must be meant for him. Over time, he grew to appreciate and respect the young Kallawaya. So much so, that the three had fought side by side to save one another. Ultimately, Diego had given himself to that end.

Secora and Diego would never be able to give Alai and Guillermo a grandchild. But when Monta needed a home, she was brought to Alai, and it seemed like the little one was a gift. Secora tickled the baby's toes in an attempt to re-channel some of her pain into joy. Monta would smile and blow bubbles, then pull her foot away.

When her tears ran out, Secora dozed off beside the sleeping child and she dreamt she was on a boat that had pulled into the cove at Cha'lla, the town where Diego and his parents lived. Her boots splashed through the water and onto the shore. She climbed the hill, picking up her pace as she neared the cottage. Someone was standing in the door-way; he looked worn and tired until his eyes caught hers. She ran to him, gently hugged him, and cried. They stood forehead to forehead, and Secora was unaware any world existed beyond his loving gaze.

Her eyelids fluttered and she mumbled, "What?" The dream was dissipating. She thought she could hear—feel his voice.

"No… no… no, mi Querida, let me be clear. It's not going to happen that way."

"What? Diego is that you? Are you here?" She popped up, fully awake now, into a seated position.

"For always, my love, but I can no longer be part of the physical realm."

"I know, but I can't help wanting to be with you."

I am sorry you are so lonely. I love you forever. But you do realize I am not the only one who loves you? Listen to your heart."

"What..." Her agony and an unexpected feeling of shame at the thought of another love caused her to falter. "But Diego…" She felt he had left, and in the vacuum, grief took her breath away.

When the last of the tears had fallen, she managed a few more hours of sleep before Monta woke with a squall, complaining she was hungry. Secora picked the baby up and kissed her little forehead, and they said morning prayers together. "Guess it's breakfast time. Then we must prepare for class."

Before she left, Secora fed and watered the guinea pig and the corn snake, then tried Gideon's phone again, still nothing. She would try the girls as soon as the anthropology secretary opened the office and gave her their number. There were lots of questions she'd like to ask Iris and Jane, assuming they were over the broken lunch date. She smirked, thinking how that would look. She wished she could talk with Jane about the strange experience she'd had with her brother. Gideon had been open and engaging one minute... in the wind, the next.

Secora stared at the Satfon number the Anthropology Department secretary handed her. She'd dial the field team as soon as she returned to her office.

As she took a seat at her desk, she dialed the girls thinking Tarkio's not in today, they can yell all they want. Jane answered and scolded this wasn't an appropriate use of the satellite phone, but she could say from personal experience that Gideon was quite capable of shutting people out—especially if he thought he would be judged or hurt. Jane had experienced his total rejection at the hospital after he was struck by lightning.

"Gideon didn't believe in anything supernatural. So, he couldn't understand what was happening to him when the visions began. He was such a skeptic."

There was a hesitation before Jane began again. "He held everything inside and wouldn't talk about it to anyone, not even to me. Thank God Jimmy helped him unwind because I'd never felt so alone."

Then Jane's tone changed completely. "Except when we were waiting for you to show up for lunch before we left town... and I suppose you'll have a good excuse for that."

"And there it is." Secora chuckled. "After we spoke on the phone, Gideon stopped by briefly and drove me to the university. It turned out I had been kicked out of my office by the new Department Chair. You remember—Donald Chastain."

Jane faked a cough. "He's completely unforgettable."

"Yeah, anyway, Gideon helped me settle into some new digs with an eager grad student, named Tarkio."

"And...?"

"And we almost started a conversation—about us. But..."

"But what?"

"But... he left when an old friend called me during a crisis. The call couldn't wait. Billy was being attacked by a man with a shovel, and I had to dial 911. Long story short, Gideon disappeared, and I raced to Birch Bay to find Billy, which by the way I couldn't. On the trip back I realized it was Wednesday, and I would be in deep trouble with you and Iris."

"Yeah. I don't think Iris should come to the phone right now."

A little icy, Secora blew out a stream of air. "Guess I expected as much."

"Try back in a couple of days."

"Wait. Did you all make it into the jungle okay? How are the students doing?"

"Yes, we're at Ojo Redondo, and the kids are green but eager to make history, or at least dig it up."

Secora figured this was all the information she would elicit from Jane. "Tell Iris I love her, and she needs to practice detachment from little irritations."

Jane said, "Hear that Iris?" Secora heard chuckling.

"She was listening in, and I elbowed her in the ribs for you, Secora. We'll see how detached she'll be in a few minutes."

Secora smiled thoughtfully as she replaced the receiver. Everyone was gone or distant, except for Monta.

That evening, she tried calling her parents. The answering machine message squawked that they planned to be traveling for the entire month. She watched Monta's eyes wander and fix on an unseen object, perhaps a face. "Do we have company, Baby?" The little one smiled and cooed. Secora put her down for the night and took a shower.

Several relatively uneventful days passed before the dates on the mammoth rib came back from the testing laboratory. At the time, Secora was sitting on the couch with her lunch. She took a swig from a glass of cranberry juice which she then set on a side table and bit into the egg salad sandwich she'd unwrapped before the phone rang. The ringer was set on loud, and she nearly jumped out of her skin. The sharp noise also surprised Pete, and he went off on a squeaking spree. She cringed, hoping the ruckus didn't wake the baby, but this was one of the lucky times; Monta stirred a little bit but remained at peace.

Secora quickly turned down the ringer and answered with a sigh. She'd anticipated it would take months to receive the test results, so she was astonished to find it was the sample dating lab. The technician sounded cheerful when Secora explained she was helping Billy with some follow-up work on his mammoth site. As he began to read from the findings, Secora took a bite of the sandwich and closed her eyes, listening.

"The mammoth sample was dated to 20,100 years ago." The lab technician asked, "Did you want those other dates?"

There was a moment of silence as Secora was lost in her thoughts. She mumbled as she chewed. "The other dates?"

The technician cleared his throat, "Yeah, the ones from the human skull and tibia from the same site."

Secora's heart pounded, her hands were shaking, and she felt weak. The sandwich dangled, trembling in her hand. She swallowed prematurely, hurting her throat, and tried to sound calm as she croaked, "Sure. I'll take them if they're ready." She held her breath and began to sweat.

The technician's voice continued, "Of course. We'll send Billy the hard copies, but you can tell him the human skull and tibia samples dated the same as the mammoth tusk, 20,100 years before present, plus, or minus 300 years."

The egg salad slipped from her hand and splattered onto the linoleum floor. "Holy guacamole! Thanks for the great work. You're fantastic!" She hung up the phone in a daze. Hallelujah! Proof! Validation!

Billy had stumbled onto something as monumental as it was controversial: clear proof of unexpected early visits to this continent by people who were not likely land-bridge Paleo-Indians. Once that cat was out of the bag, people would be screaming their opinions from one end of the planet to the other.

"So, Billy, your secret was legit. Question is, did you die for it? And where is the skull, the whole skeleton for that matter? Were they stolen? If so, by whom, to what end, or for what purpose? How would anyone recognize its significance? There's no way someone could have known these dates before today.

"I guess the real question is who stood to gain from the destruction of that site?" Presumably, the only other people who knew samples had been taken were the lab crew,

and it was unlikely that one of the techs had gone berserk and profited from sharing the information with criminals.

Secora realized that the fallout from this discovery could be even worse than the squabbles over the origin of Kennewick Man who died around nine thousand years ago along the Columbia River.

This dead guy could have come from anywhere in Europe or Asia. Perhaps he was a wild-eyed Proto-Indo-European, who somehow found his way to North America in time to die and leave his consternating contribution to the archaeological lore of this continent. Until now, Paleo-Indians had been the presumed sequential ancestors of the Americans, although speculations about oceanic incursions from the Pacific Rim or the North Atlantic had occasionally been proposed. However, actual skeletal evidence was in short supply. Even the early giants, which were buried in the southern mounds and elsewhere, might have been remnants of voyaging populations from who knew where, had disappeared.

In the past, unusually early finds had been discredited, discarded, or dismissed. Like the possibility of Bigfoot, which Secora presumed was an earlier human form—like the Denisovans. They were conveniently ignored because they didn't fit the reigning expectations. Never mind the premise that specified scientific study must be neutral and unbiased.

A twenty-thousand-year-old American buried with what appeared to be Solutrean artifacts was a monumental find. She snickered and looked at Monta, "I can get away with believing whatever I choose, right, little one?" Secora was, after all, a paleontologist and didn't have to pretend to agree with every article written on human evolution and distribution based on thinking that clearly needed to be updated.

Secora now understood why Billy had to share his discovery with someone he could trust. Until the information had been correctly dated, documented, and rendered indisputable, it was vulnerable—and so was he. She was now in the same position. The significance of that realization made her skin crawl.

Was it worth it, Billy? She peeked surreptitiously out each of her windows to make sure she wasn't next. This whole case was beginning to drive her nuts. She called the lab back to see if they'd heard from anyone besides her or Billy, or if they'd noticed any unusual interest in Billy's work. Nobody but herself, they assured her.

"Thank you. Would it be too much trouble for you to CC me a hard copy of the results?" She sighed with relief as she hung up the receiver. Now she needed to rest and think about her next steps.

After a good night's sleep in her own bed, Secora was ready for work. At the office, Secora placed Monta in the arms of Tarkio's wife, Anida, for a half-hour respite, then settled into her office chair and turned on the computer. She searched the internet to find cave burials with Solutrean artifacts similar to what Billy had collected. Eurasia Stone Age tombs, like this one, belonged to venerated individuals whose culture may have dawned in the northern Russian Steppes.

The quality of artifacts indicated he was a leader of some magnitude. Such a man wouldn't have traveled to a new continent alone or buried himself. Perhaps there had been a settlement nearby. Not too exciting, when she realized it was likely resting beneath twenty feet of Northwest Washington's coastal waters by this time. She momentarily wished she could participate in the underwater archaeology that was bound to dominate the next decades of study. But only for a moment - she hated water.

8

GIDEON LEAVES TOWN

W hen he'd left Secora's apartment building, Gideon was a wreck. "We should be together." He gripped the railing with frustration. "Should have been from the start." Seems like she always has a dozen reasons why she can't sit still and pay attention to me and my needs.

He gritted his teeth. "Oh, why bother? Was I thinking the situation had changed and she would need me in her life? I'm such an idiot for hoping she'd let me in."

Tears burned in his eyes temporarily obscuring his vision causing him to slip on a patch of ice as he stepped onto the first-floor landing.

He caught himself with the rail and sucked in a breath as he looked to the sky. "You know, Diego, I could use a little help here."

Large flakes began to drift toward his face. The weather had changed for the worse, and he was grateful he'd already put on his snow tires.

"Hold onto the railing."

"What, Diego?"

"Be patient. Think of her needs."

"Did you really say that?"

"Do you hear anyone else? I try to tell her I am not the only one who loves her."

"I'm afraid she will do what she will do, no matter what either of us says."

"Keep trying."

"Well, Diego, if she doesn't listen to you, she'll never listen to me." Gideon shrugged.

Those words repeated in his mind as he made his way to his BMW.

Safely back at Treasuremont Realty, Gideon greeted his old friends, Jeannie and Mitch, who crowded around as he entered. The office situation had been legally complicated by the death of his partner, Glen Greenbriar.

Before Glen had died, he'd attempted to kill Gideon and Secora several times, before becoming the unfortunate victim of a gigantic raptor on Massacre Mountain. Prior to his demise, Glen filed a suit for the dissolution of their partnership.

Even though the transfer of ownership to the sole surviving owner was a legal matter now, Gideon's colleagues had never questioned who was in charge.

"You would not believe how much we've missed you around this place," Mitch said. His hands shook as he emphasized his statement.

"Please, please stay here for a while, Boss," pleaded Jeannie.

Gideon laughed, "I thought you two were happy working with no boss looking over your shoulder."

Mitch grinned sheepishly. "Well, it has its moments. But things are pretty dull without you, and you know... Glen."

"Sometimes, I miss him too," confided Gideon. "He was a good realtor and a decent educator. Unfortunately, he became addicted to money and power. In the end he wasn't afraid to enslave or kill people to get his way."

Gideon took a seat behind his polished monkey-wood desk and flipped through an accumulation of envelopes. "We have a lot to sort out; it looks like I'll be here for a week or two, at least."

"Great, then let's party!" Jeannie teased, "I made cookies along with your favorite cranberry and 7-Up punch."

Gideon—not much interested in parties, winced, and then raised his eyes to look at them. He considered these two friends to be immediate family. His smile turned into a laugh. "Sure, why not?"

Cookies, punch, and a snack tray appeared immediately. He remembered the good times with his loyal friends and realized he didn't need Secora in his life to be happy.

"When do the lawyers arrive?"

Jeannie grinned after a sip of punch. "Any minute now, Mr. Yellow Thunder. Don't worry; I have all the paperwork out and ready."

Mitch added, "I have several files I'd like you to see first if you have time." Gideon shot him a questioning look. Mitch continued, "There are two or three projects Glen started, but either they haven't been closed, or they have problems that need fixing."

"Sure, Mitch, I'll take a look."

Before they had a chance to begin, a man and a woman in sleek suits appeared and stood at Jeannie's desk. After brief introductions, they pulled documents from their briefcases which laid out the process of ending the partnership and settling with Greenbriar's estate.

It became clear Gideon would need to come up with serious money. The troubles of the summer had taken most of his disposable funds. Luckily, there was a constant stream of business revenue due to the diligence of the remaining team. Additionally, Jeannie and Mitch were eager to personally pitch in.

Going forward, the three office mates decided on a profit-sharing arrangement, rather than a partnership. They'd keep both locations.

Gideon would maintain the office in South Dakota until business picked up, and he could hire an assistant.

That night, he stayed in a motel, having given up his former apartment when he moved to South Dakota. He felt bored. Secora crept back into his mind. He tried her home phone since she still didn't have a cell. She didn't answer. He thought about leaving a message for her to call him but decided against it. Next, he tried to reach Jimmy, but he was also out. Gideon shook his head and said aloud, "Those two are ridiculous. I need to buy them satellite phones so we can keep in touch." He had already done this for Jeannie and Mitch. He went ahead and ordered Satfons which would arrive later in the week.

That night, he fell into a fitful sleep fraught with images of pistols, slaves, and gigantic birds. Remembering Greenbriar at the office had dredged up a few nightmares.

It took a few days for the team at the office to plow through the backlog of paperwork and phone calls. Their flawless progress hit a snag when Mr. Jamal Hasan called from Dubai. He complained he had paid for water rights on his lake-front resort property near Glacier Park. Apparently, the water had suddenly dropped to a ridiculous level, and he felt the property was now useless for his needs.

Mitch sheepishly injected, "That's one of the cases I was talking about."

Gideon offered to drive to the lovely resort located outside of West Glacier the next day to see if he could figure out what the problem was. If necessary, he would then fly to Dubai to work out a settlement with Mr. Hasan.

While they were tidying up their work, Jeannie asked Gideon if his friend, Secora, had returned home from Isla del Sol.

"Yeah, she returned almost a week ago. I went to see her and the baby she brought with her."

"Baby! Did you forget to tell us something, Sugar?" giggled Jeannie, teasing him like an auntie.

Gideon smirked, looking away shyly. "She adopted a six-month-old infant named Monta. But Secora has only one good arm, the other is still in a brace from last summer's injuries. She still teaches at the university, but I don't think things will work out very well. Anyway, it doesn't matter. We seem to be drifting further apart. Besides the child, she has a lot of other things going on in her life."

Mitch sat on the corner of Gideon's desk. "No time for you? Man that sucks."

Jeannie sounded perturbed. "Is she nuts? You two seemed pretty close last summer. How

could she let this happen?"

"To be fair, she had witnessed the murder of her fiancé, and had her shoulder blown apart by our dearly departed Mr. Greenbriar. So, yes, we became very close friends because we were being cruelly hunted, and our chances for survival were sketchy."

He noted the intense looks on his friends' faces. "Sorry." He put his head into his hands. "When Wakinyan Tonka first sent me to South America to find Secora, I thought she would be looking for me too, needing my help." He raised his head. "But Diego rescued her a few days before I found her."

"That's tough all the way around, Buddy," sympathized Mitch.

"She has tried to leave me a couple of messages, but the more I read the reality, the worse the situation looks. If I saw her now, I wouldn't know what to say." He rubbed the bridge of his nose with an index finger. "I can't see a realistic future for us, and I'm trying not to call her back."

"Didn't you tell us you just ordered Satfons for her and Jimmy?"

"The phone was wishful thinking, I guess."

The office telephone rang. Jeannie answered, and after a brief exchange, she said, "Turns out you'll have company at the resort,

Boss. Mr. Jamal Hasan's son, Kamal, is on his way down from Calgary."

"That's great. He'll know how the property should be, and I won't need to describe everything to his father in Dubai."

"I can reserve a flight to Kalispell and a room for overnight."

"Sounds good. Thanks, Jeannie." Gideon was happy when work kept him busy and he could put his personal feelings aside. It would do him good to think about something other than Secora. *So, why am I still thinking about her?* "Make the return for three days, please. I need time to relax and think."

On a hunch, he rang Secora's extension at work. Tarkio answered and said she was in a class and he was watching the baby. He could have her call in about forty-five minutes. Gideon told him not to bother, he was leaving town for a few days. "Thanks anyway."

Next, he and Mitch perused the file pictures of the resort.

"Why do I feel this isn't a good idea?" Mitch's tone sounded morose.

"Probably because you aren't coming with me," Gideon teased.

As he left for the airport, Gideon asked Jeannie to notify Secora when the phone arrived. He'd already sent Jimmy's phone on to South Dakota.

Though it was the middle of winter, it was a sunny day, and the highway was bare and clear until Gideon took the rental pickup down the turnoff ramp and into the snowy town of West Glacier. After he shifted into four-wheel drive there was no problem traversing the primitive road to the resort, even though the snow was several inches thick. After he crossed a bridge, he turned up the long driveway to the Hasan property and noticed there was a set of fresh tire tracks. *Kamal must have beaten me here.*

The road came to an end at the top of a ridge. He parked in front of the sprawling log mansion with its beautifully toned walls, and clusters of expensive windows. The encircling girdle of decks and porches was set among landscaped pines, firs, and shrubbery which Gideon imagined would offer showy lavender, pink, and white-yellow blooms in the late spring.

Not bad, Gideon observed as he opened the truck door and watched a little pug dog run up onto the porch to bark a greeting. Gideon looked toward a large mountain rising up the left side of the structure and surmised the lake must be on the opposite side of the main building. He'd know soon enough.

The fancy etched-glass front door opened, and a smiling slender man in his forties stepped out to offer his hand. "You must be Gideon Yellow Thunder, right?" Gideon nodded and reached to meet his hand.

"I'm Kamal Hasan. Why don't you grab your bags and come inside?"

Gideon happily complied and followed Kamal, who half turned toward another room, "Make yourself comfortable. I'll make us some glasses of fresh limeade."

"Thanks, that would be great," Gideon meant it. Limeade happened to be his favorite beverage. He stepped through the door and sat on an expansive couch, ogling the split pine log interior.

"Wow, I've never seen this property. It's amazing, Mr. Hasan."

"Perfect in every way—but one, and, please, call me Kamal."

"You're sure there was water in the lake when your dad bought it?"

"Yes, right up until two days ago, in fact. Or so I heard from Dad. He recently hired a caretaker, a Mr. Jake Landsing, to keep an eye on things. That's how he knew."

Gideon noticed several expensive lighting fixtures focused on paintings and sculptures. The subject matter reflected Middle Eastern antiquity. "Good idea. There's a lot worth protecting up here."

Kamal sipped his drink and handed the other to his guest. "I haven't been able to reach Mr. Landsing since I arrived this morning. Maybe his cell is turned off. But I can take you down to the dock, and we can take a look at what's going on."

Gideon nodded and finished his drink, then stopped by the restroom. The bathroom

startled him with three twelve-foot palm trees and beautifully appointed brass and glass lantern sconces locked into the creamy marble walls. *Why would anyone buy an American palace?*

When he returned, Gideon took off his suit coat and laid it over the back of the couch. Both men put on boots and zipped up their down jackets to shelter against an increasing

snowfall. Kamal smiled at his eager pug. "Better leave Cutesie behind on this trip."

Gideon put his hands in his pockets and pulled out knitted mittens, wishing he'd brought heavier gloves. Their boots crunched through the icy remnants of the last heavy snowfall, and Gideon awkwardly ducked tree branches which were springing back from Kamal's passage.

"Hey, seems awfully quiet. There aren't any bird or animal sounds," noted Gideon.

Kamal stopped briefly and turned toward him.

"Maybe they are preparing for a heavy snowfall."

They followed another set of boot tracks up a little rise which overlooked the dry boat dock.

"There it is—Lake of the Moon." Kamal puffed.

"Or not," Gideon reflected.

"The water has dropped almost thirty feet during last week's warm spell."

All that remained was a frozen pond nearly an eighth of a mile from the former shore.

Gideon took his mittened hands out of his pockets, to point out a figure in a heavy black jacket, halfway down the slope to their left. "Who's that guy?"

9

CHILLIN'

"Good question." Kamal stopped to melt snowflakes on his tongue. "Could be Mr. Landsing, I suppose, but I can hardly make anything out in this blizzard."

"Let's see what he knows about this." Gideon skirted lingering chunks of ice from the former water line.

Kamal followed shouting, "Hello!" and waving a hand high over his head.

The man below them turned toward the sound and lifted a stocking cap away from his ears as if to hear clearly. Slowly he moved in their direction, waving awkwardly back with his left hand in apparent greeting because his right arm was in a sling. He squinted at them through the brightness of the snow and the stinging of developing wind gusts.

"Are you Mr. Landsing?" shouted Kamal.

"Sure am. Call me Jake," the man yelled as he came close enough to greet them. "You must be Mr. Hasan?"

"Yes, I'm Kamal Hasan. I've been trying to reach you by phone since I arrived."

Jake took his phone from his pocket and checked it. "Hmm, no bars, this new phone is a cheap piece of junk—won't hold a charge. I'll get a better one today, my apologies."

"Might be this storm, but a new phone always sounds like a good idea." Kamal rubbed his hands together. "I can't get used to the coldness here—so different from the desert."

"So, what happened?" Gideon was focused.

"Not sure. I was hired two days ago, and the water was already gone. Thought I'd have a look around and see what I could find. There seems to be a canal that drains off down there by the access."

Gideon strained to see the rusty water gate visible at the new water line. "Is it broken or something?"

"Don't know. We should take a look." Jake coughed because the sideways snow blew into the back of his throat when he spoke.

They hiked across with difficulty, stumbling over the ice chunks and rocks. When they reached the rusty canal gate they saw water trickling out and forming a pool. Behind the gate was a little pump house with pipes leading up the mountain until they disappeared from sight into the thick shrubbery.

"Perhaps we should wait for better weather to check this out," said Kamal, through bouts of shivering. Gideon and Jake nodded. On the way back, the caretaker bent down to look at something. He picked up a good-sized bone fragment.

"What is that?" asked Kamal.

"It's part of a skeleton that's becoming visible now that the water is dropping," Jake said, and then he shuddered.

"What kind of skeleton?" Kamal drew instinctively away. "Maybe it belongs to the former owner who disappeared and was never heard from again?"

"Doesn't look like a regular human," said Gideon. Leaning in, he observed, "Bone's too big."

The bone exploded in Landsing's hand, followed by a distant report

65

of a rifle shot. They stood frozen in shock until a second bullet disturbed the wind between Kamal and Gideon's ears.

"Run!" shouted Gideon. When they stood puffing in the bushes at the old shoreline, Gideon encouraged them, "Don't stop; let's keep moving. He could be here any second."

Snow was blowing sideways, while Jake led them toward a paintless old shed that lay hidden from the view of the house. When they were safely inside, they heard Cutesie's faint barking, rrruff, rrruff.

"Maybe he's taken the house," Gideon said in a hoarse whisper.

"Who... who's taken my father's house—and why?"

They heard another gunshot, and the barking stopped. Kamal's words were loud and full of emotion, "Did he just kill my dog?"

Gideon clapped his hand over Kamal's mouth. "Look at me," he whispered. "We are being hunted by a person who's acting like a murderous idiot. This is a matter of our survival—do you understand?"

Kamal's black eyes were glaring wildly around the shack, but he solemnly nodded, and Gideon moved his hand away.

Jake suggested, "Maybe this is related to the missing water. Maybe he was waiting for something, like the pelvic bone to be exposed by the sinking water line."

"Maybe he is looking for some other kind of treasure—like from a bank heist," Kamal mumbled.

"Or, it could have been the bone," Jake humbly noted.

"A big human, maybe even a Bigfoot - Kamal's right, it's more likely he's after a specific treasure. Doesn't make sense he'd be out in a blizzard chasing us over a dried-up skeleton."

"Is he really trying to kill us?" Kamal looked uncertain.

Jake said thoughtfully, "I guess it depends on what he's after and what he's willing to risk."

Gideon asked, "What is that sulphur smell?"

Jake answered, "Not sure. Sometime when the wind blows just right, you'll get that stench."

"I don't like any of this. I'm calling 911," said Kamal. "Dang." He stared at his phone. "No bars." They all checked their cell phones.

Jake's disappointment showed. "The mountain must be blocking the cell tower,"

"I'll use the Satfon." Gideon felt for it in his pocket. "Unbelievable, I left it in the house when I changed jackets."

After a good half hour in the unheated building, Gideon could hear Kamal's teeth chatter. He checked his watch. 2:30.

Kamal was anxious. "I don't know how much more of this we can take. My Arab body is not enjoying the freezing temperatures. And, I have to pee."

Jake whispered urgently, "Go ahead and pee, man."

"What? Here in the shack?"

Jake nodded and continued, "Gideon what are the chances the guy left? We can't stay out here forever."

"We should be okay," reasoned Gideon. "We didn't see his face, and he's had plenty of time to leave."

As they headed for the exit, they heard a crunch of snow and a snuffling sound outside. Gideon motioned the others away. The door opened slowly, seemingly, on its own to reveal Cutesie's pug face.

That dog isn't opening it by itself, thought Gideon, and he rushed the opening, ramming it back with all his might. It missed Cutesie but found a target. Because of the accumulating snow around the base, the door didn't have the anticipated impact. Gideon watched a man wearing a ski mask and an army jacket staggered awkwardly backward instead of being knocked completely off his feet. As he stumbled back he managed to trip over a dead pine branch. As the intruder fell, he fired his pistol. The bullet was too low to hit Gideon, but it injured the dog's ribs, and it yelped in pain.

Furious, Kamal flew at the assailant uttering a string of what Gideon assumed were Arabic epithets. Hasan mauled him like an enraged lion, knocking him back into the snow when he tried to rise.

In a split second, Gideon squatted nearby, trying to reach in between the two men to grab the gun. While he struggled to grip the weapon, he could see Jake on the opposite side ripping off the ski mask with his good arm, then drawing back, he punched the aggressor's face.

Gideon didn't recognize the man with the lackluster green eyes and long beard. But before that thought had barely registered, the dead-eyed man kicked him away. The gun fired a second time, and Kamal flopped onto his back, flailing in the snow.

For a moment nobody moved except for Kamal. There was blood on his handsome face and neck. In horror, Gideon watched as Cutsie came to Kamal's chest and sniffed. She whimpered and lay beside him in the snow. Gideon's mind was racing, but he couldn't make sense of any of this. It looked like Kamal had been shot through the right jaw and the bullet had exited above the mandible on the left side. He was still breathing but severely injured.

Gideon roared "You son-of-a-dog!"

The two men eyed each other icily and the killer swung the pistol toward Gideon as he

pushed up from the packed snow with his other arm. As he stood, he sneered. "Anyone else?" Taking a step forward he touched the cold metal to Gideon's forehead.

Cutsie growled.

Gideon was enraged and batted the gun away from his face. "What the hell are you doing, jackass! You could have waited for us to leave before you started messing things up. Nothing could be valuable enough for you to shoot this man." He felt the energy of a Heyoka warrior rising inside himself.

The gunman must have noticed the change and stepped back, still in control of the pistol.

For the first time in his life, Gideon wanted to destroy another person, to rip the man's throat out with his teeth if he had to. His balled fist smashed into "Dead Eye's" face. The pistol dropped into the snow.

Gideon stepped on top of the gun, but the assailant was quick. He threw snow in Gideon's eyes and kicked his leg away from the gun. Gideon nearly fell from the force. Once again, Dead Eyes trained the weapon on the seething Lakota who said, "We will give you plenty of time to walk away, but help us carry him back to the house so we can call for aid."

"Nuh-uh." Dead Eyes shook his head, "Can't have him bleeding and leaving clues around the house." He kicked Kamal in the ribs. "Get up Arab; you're not dead—yet."

Kamal moaned. Then the attacker turned his attention to Gideon and Jake. "Let's take a walk up to the mine, shall we?"

"What mine? If you're going to kill us, do it here," demanded Jake.

Gideon hissed through gritted teeth. "What's the big deal about the mine anyway?"

"Well, it's a good place to hide bodies, for one. Yours won't be the first. Parts of the old lady that used to own this place are still up there."

"Gotta be more to it than that, tough guy. You're sluicing with the lake water," snarled Gideon. "It's illegal to mess with metals so close to a water source."

Jake grumbled, "Why kill us? How does that serve you?"

"Turns out you're the reason, jerk."

"What did I do? You're crazy."

"You're a loose end. You took something from my boss's property; he wants it back, and he wants you dead."

Jake shook his head in utter disbelief. "That's insane. What are you talking about? I never stole anything, well not since second grade. And anyway, I don't even know who your boss is."

"Oh, yeah? Tell it to God, I don't care."

"Whatever you're doing, can't be worth killing three men."

Gideon spat out the words, "Why are you still here? We've given you every opportunity to leave."

"Only reason you're still alive is to help that crip over there—haul

69

the Arab up the hill. Do it! Or I can finish him here, and you can drag his dead body up there." He pointed to the mountain that ran up the left side of the resort.

Gideon was drenched in sweat, and the cold air he sucked in was burning his lungs. It had been extremely difficult to haul Kamal uphill through the fresh snow because there was an intermittent layer of slick ice underneath. Kamal did not deserve to be shot, he kept saying to himself. Sorry, Brother.

Jake could only use his good arm, so Gideon did the majority of the work. He wanted to turn and rush the gunman, but the predator never came close enough to give him a fighting chance.

Gideon said, "Wait, I need to breathe." Looking skyward, he noticed that the snow had let up and there were tiny patches of blue sky visible. He hated that he couldn't figure a way out of this.

"Let's go!" Dead Eyes growled.

They slipped and fell many times in the thousand-yard climb straight up the slope before Gideon and Jake were finally able to stand in front of the locked mine gate. While he was catching his breath and waiting to see what would happen next, Gideon noticed the snow was already melting and it dripped from above the adit entrance. He also noticed a sulfuric odor—a stench. Here and there, Gideon could see piles of muddy tailings, both under the snow and partially revealed, confirming recent excavation activity and explaining the use of the missing water. A muddy road led toward the backside of the mountain, possibly used to transport the resources away.

"I hope whatever you took out of there was worth it."

"We found what we needed. For now. When the boss buys this place, we'll start again. Feel free to keep anything you find in there."

The man with the gun shot the lock and shoved Jake, Gideon, and Kamal inside. Then he fingered the broken lock. "Huh. Guess I can't lock you in now. Good thing I brought a stick of dynamite—better run."

He grinned as he took off his gloves. Letting them fall to the ground, he removed the stick of TNT from his coat.

Gideon and Jake lifted Kamal by the arms and scrambled as far as possible into the cave's darkness before the inevitable blast. The noise was deafening and Gideon dropped Kamal to cover his damaged ears. When he opened his eyes, he saw Jake was doing the same. He looked back toward the entrance. It was massively blocked, yet there were small spaces where light bled through at the top of the slide. Maybe he could try to dislodge some of the rocks after he caught his breath.

The cave floor was wet and muddy, and the smell of black powder smoke was nasty. Jake tried to speak, but Gideon shook his head and pointed to his ears. Then he pointed about seven yards ahead to a dry slide area where they could lay Kamal in a better position and stay dry themselves.

Kamal's breathing was ragged now. Gideon imagined his blood loss was becoming critical. He took off his coat and sweater and then used the woolen garment to cushion and wrap Kamal's head. It doubled as a bandage for the shot through his cheek. After zipping his jacket again, he sat down to rest.

Jake stumbled over to the rocks and tried to climb high enough to pick scree away from the little air spaces. He only succeeded in causing gravel to slide under his feet, but that didn't stop him. He persevered and began to pull a few pieces aside. Gideon didn't think he would make any real headway, but perhaps there would be better airflow. He soon realized his legs were too fatigued after the fight and the uphill climb to stand and help. He wished they had water.

Eventually, Jake gave up and sat down on the blockage, mouthing the words, "Guess this is goodbye, Buddy." He waved at Gideon, who waved back.

Sunset came early on the mountainside, both literally and figuratively. Gideon could tell the outside light was fading as any trace of ambient light receded, and the trio was gradually plunged into icy darkness. He repeated several times out loud the invocation he'd heard Secora use when there was imminent danger of death, "Yá Alláhu'l-Mustagháth!" The words sounded strange in his deafened ears, and he could hardly keep his eyes open. He yawned, and sleep came easily.

10

JIMMY'S CALL

Secora felt surprisingly happy dominating the third floor classroom. She was at the top of her game, and Tarkio's wife, Anida, was watching Monta back at the apartment until noon. It was the first official break she'd had since she'd left the island.

As she welcomed the students, her eyes followed the entrance of an unexpected attendee. It was Tarkio—her first thought was, is everything all right with Monta? She caught his eye, and as if he'd read her mind, he nodded and gave her a thumbs up. When the last of the students was seated, Secora looked over the roster and made eye contact with each of the fifty-odd individuals.

After checking the rolls, she removed a sheaf of transparencies from her russet leather backpack, laid one of them across an overhead projector, and turned it on.

"I'm Dr. Secora James. Most of you know me from the 'Herbivores of the Pleistocene Megafauna' classes. Let's take a moment to briefly review those herbivore categories before we jump into the predatory sequence." She swept a strand of tawny hair out of her face and back over her shoulder. "Many prey animals on the American continents came from two categories of ungulates, or hooved animals." She used a pen to point to the different hoof structures on the overhead.

"Perissodactyls were members of the odd-toed hoofed animals, who like the modern horse put their full weight on a single toe, or three toed creatures like the Litopterna, who ranged in appearance from the large camel-like macarauchenia to small deer and horse-like animals. Or, the extinct order of hippo-sized Toxodons, three-toed gnawing animals which looked a little like gigantic guinea pigs from the Late Miocene to the Middle Holocene epochs.

"And finally, there was Brontotheres, with three pairs of horn bumps, and its smaller cousin, the rhino-like Uintatherium, with two pairs of facial horns. Similar to today's Tapirs, they differed from other ungulates, because they had four toes in front and three on their hind feet." She flipped the transparency.

"As for Artiodactyls, or split-hooved animals with two toes, think of deer like the megaloceros, which is sometimes referred to as the Irish elk, and the giant Bison latifrons. Pigs have four toes, with only two usually touching the ground."

Secora put away that set of transparencies and replaced it with another. "Remember folks, these herbivores put huge smiles on the faces of the large cats and other predators."

"Like Smilodon?" asked one student.

"Yes, but we had other felines in the Americas besides the sabre-tooth cats."

A know-it-all proudly stated, "There were terror cats, vampire cats, a great American lion, and the American cheetah—along with a number of smaller varieties."

Secora stared at the student while putting up a transparency of several types of predators.

"You're right, but there were more than just cats. Check the syllabus. There were several canines, giant bears, huge snakes, and humongous birds known as teratorns. We'll spend some time on these winged creatures, which were large ice age relatives of our modern raptors. Most had wingspans of twelve to sixteen feet, and they ate just about anything they wanted. But, get this, some paleontologists speculate that larger teratorns, like the gigantic Argentavis magnificens, reached twenty to thirty-two-foot wingspans. These supersized teratorns could easily be mistaken today for small aircraft. The adults might have weighed as much as *two hundred and fifty pounds*, pretty hefty, considering birds have hollow bones and feathers. By comparison, today's largest harpy eagles weigh eleven pounds at most." Secora stopped to take a bottle of water out of her backpack, opened it, and took a long drink.

"Argentavis was reported by early Americans to be capable of grabbing large fish, humans, moose, and even sea mammals including orcas. We'll be looking at the part these creatures played, both in legend and in the ecosystem, in greater depth this quarter because it's quite possible they're not quite extinct." She turned off the overhead.

"Please take the next half hour to go over the notes I gave you and look through your text. Save your big questions for the end of class. Thank you."

Thinking about teratorns led Secora's attention back to the Andes and Wakinyan Tonka, the giant thunderbird. From there it wasn't much of a stretch to think of her beloved, Diego—and then Gideon. She remembered how sick Gideon became when he was assailed by Wakinyan Tonka's visions. The seizures were much worse toward the end. There was one time on the island when everyone ran to catch him as he collapsed, so he wouldn't hurt his head on the rocks.

Guillermo and Diego, who were sacred medicine men known as Kallawayas, prepared a remedy to help him combat the effects. With the new medication, the painful visions gave way to an even more painful reality shortly after Diego's death.

"Someone told me you thought you saw one of these."

Secora shook herself back to the present and noticed a student at the desk was pointing to a picture of a giant ground sloth known as megatherium.

She stared at the image, remembering she and Gideon had spotted the mother and baby before they began to ascend Massacre Mountain. It had indeed been a magical moment, a gift which interrupted Secora's and Gideon's worries about whether or not they had any chance of surviving the day.

Her voice sounded wispy and distant, "Yeah... If you'd like to know more, please see me in my office." She removed the teratorn transparency and tried to brush away the emotions implanted by the daydream.

"Do any of these gigantic creatures exist today?" the female student persisted. "I only ask because rumor has it you believe in cryptids."

A boy next to her sneered, "Seen any Bigfoots lately?"

There were a few snickers, but Secora answered, "Sadly, most of the megafauna succumbed to the Pleistocene mass extinction, leaving our present world much blander, and believe me, much safer by comparison."

A sullen-looking girl with shiny dark hair interrupted, "Good. You can keep those ugly monsters! I don't even believe they ever existed anyway. There's nothing about them in the Bible."

People stood and collected their books, causing Secora to glance at the clock on the wall.

"Oh boy, looks like today's class is officially extinct." She turned to face the surly young woman and smiled. "I hear what you're saying, and it's not too late to drop this course if the material offends you. For anyone who enjoys learning about megafauna, I'll see you next week." She grinned and mumbled as she turned, "Unless I have a better offer." Then she unplugged the overhead projector and stowed the cord. "If you have questions please see me at my office on the second floor."

Students rustled out of the room while Secora gathered the rest of the transparencies, flopped them and the now empty water bottle into her leather backpack, then tied the flap down. Next, she gently lifted her elegant corn snake from beneath the lectern. The sleepy creature squirmed lackadaisically as she admired its strong color pattern, with the red-orange, glossy black and russet brown, painted on a cream background. She scrutinized the animal, sighed, and then placed the snake into a small, flowered pillowcase. Twisting the neck of the bag a few times, she gently laid it on the desk beside her backpack.

The now defiant girl, and a spiky-haired person who might be her friend, stepped up. "Are you even allowed to have a snake in our classroom?"

Secora smiled and shrugged. "So, you *are* interested in being a part of this class?"

"Show us something we can touch. Prove to me there were weird, non-Ark animals," insisted the second young woman.

Secora smiled. "I cannot prove anything you aren't ready to see."

Tarkio blurted, "Oh, the mammoth molar!" He set his backpack on the table and reached in. With admiration, he withdrew the plastic six by eight-inch box, which encased the beautifully lacquered brown fossil.

Secora rolled her eyes, "You just happened to be carrying my prop in your backpack?"

Tarkio looked up sheepishly. "Yeah, I probably should have asked, sorry." He carefully removed the fossil from the container. "You girls are going to love this. Go on... touch it." They obediently touched the tooth, though their faces radiated only disgust.

He enthused, "That's half a molar from an Imperial Mammoth adult, which dates to 16,000 years ago. Not all animals made it to the ark, right? This creature lived during the height of the Ice Age."

"Says you, I mean it could be anything," the sullen girl challenged.

"True, but it is a molar. Feel the ridges. Careful."

Secora demonstrated by gingerly rubbing a forefinger across the convoluted grinding surface. The two malcontent women shoved the tooth back.

"It's probably just an elephant tooth," said the companion.

Tarkio stuck his hand into the backpack again. "Glad you brought that up." He pulled out another tooth, which was only slightly larger in total than the mammoth molar fragment. "Here's a modern elephant's tooth. Both animals were adults. Compare them for yourself."

The girl again rejected the samples. "Still not convinced."

Tarkio interrupted. "The large one is regular-sized for an Imperial Mammoth adult. The other is an adult modern elephant. You asked to touch something for proof. This was your chance." He carefully replaced the molars.

"Whatever," was the response.

Secora hefted her backpack before grabbing the pillowcase. "You have a strong mind, young lady. I suggest you challenge it at a good museum or better yet, a dig in the field. Let the discovery experience be spontaneous so you will value its meaning." Secora took a few steps forward, and the girls left with questions written on their faces.

Once they were safely in the hall, Secora asked, "Tarkio, remind me again why I love teaching?"

"Yeah." He laughed and said, "Maybe I should have gone snowboarding all day like I told you. But I thought it would be good to sit in on this class and see what I'm in for if you have to leave town on another of your mysterious outings. It was kinda fun, don't you think?"

"You must be as crazy as I am. I might have to ask for an official Teaching Assistantship for you."

He said, "I already checked into that."

Secora stopped and did a double take.

Tarkio turned to her and continued, "The department head would deny it; I was told they can't afford the expense."

Secora cocked her head sideways, digesting both his nerve and Chastain's response. If anything, this seemed to verify her office mate was not merely befriending her under the influence of the Department Chair.

"Might have to go over his head this time. We'll see what the Dean says."

When she returned to her desk, she put the snake in a plastic carrying cage. Tarkio asked, "Does Dr. Chastain allow you to have pets?"

Secora answered, "Strictly speaking, no. But I wanted to watch her today. She seems a bit sluggish; probably going to shed her skin. See how it's rough and grayish around her eyes?"

"Huh," Tarkio mused as he squinted in the snake's direction.

"Some of the scales are lifting up, and that's where the shed usually begins. She often gets quiet and cranky until the skin is off, so I'll take her home to her habitat and let her be." She thought, *if Tarkio tells Dr. Chastain I have a live animal at my desk... I'll know I can't trust him.*

When Secora set the cage down, she noticed a note on her desk stating, "Call Jimmy."

She dialed the number and Jimmy picked up on the second ring.

"That's awfully quick for such a laid-back holy man."

In a few words, Jimmy made it clear he was worried about Gideon. "Something's not right. I feel a darkness."

"You feel a darkness? Where?" Secora immediately felt sick as she wondered what in the world had happened. "Where is he?"

Jimmy responded, "Don't know, can't reach him by phone. I'm headed to Montana on Highway 2."

Secora responded, "Okay. Jimmy, I've gotta pick up the baby, run home, then I'll go over to the realty office to check with Mitch and Jeannie—I'll be in touch."

She hung up and said to Tarkio, "I need to find Gideon. He's in some kind of trouble. Hope you can be on standby for Monday, in case things take more than two days." She grimaced with a pleading look.

Tarkio sighed and nodded. "I'd rather that you take me along with you on these side trips."

"Maybe one day, but I need your help here."

"Sure, why not. We sure could use the cash."

"Would you mind letting Anida know I'm coming for Monta a little early?"

"No problem. Good luck with Gideon."

11

LIMBO

When she reached the second floor and entered the office of Treasuremont Realty, Jeannie and Mitch welcomed Secora with open arms.

"We are so happy to finally meet you in person," enthused Mitch. "I feel like we've known each other for years, well, months anyway."

Jeannie stretched out her arms toward the baby. "So, this is little Monta. Gideon has been bragging about her."

"Really, where is he? Jimmy and I can't seem to reach him by phone."

Mitch responded, "He went to meet a client at a property near Glacier Park."

Secora was thinking, if anyone knows where he is—it ought to be these two. "Well, if he's still in Montana, we should be able to reach him by phone, right?"

"Yes, or by email," Jeannie confirmed.

"How long ago did he leave?" asked Secora, trying to hide the worry she felt inside.

Mitch's face began to take on signs of anxiety. His brow was furrowed, and he was pinching his chin. He said, "He left for the airport yesterday morning to fly to Kalispell. I think he was going to rest overnight in a motel and then meet the owner's son this morning. Should be there by now; let me try his satellite phone." He looked up the number on his phone and dialed. "That's odd; it's not ringing."

Secora suggested, "Maybe it died, and he can't charge it wherever he is?"

Jeannie gave Monta back to Secora and sat back down in her chair. "Maybe we can track his credit card; just a moment." Gideon's purchases included the name of the motel, and she dialed it immediately. Putting her hand over the receiver while it rang, she said, "The property in question borders Glacier Park near the town of West Glacier." Then she returned her attention to the phone. "Yes? Okay. Thank you." Turning to Secora she translated, "He left the motel at 7:30 this morning in a rental vehicle."

"We always keep in touch." Mitch was pacing with his eyes on the carpet. "It's weird he hasn't checked in with us."

Secora nervously licked her lips. "Perhaps I should take a trip up north and see if I can figure out what's going on—discreetly, of course."

"Oh, speaking of keeping in touch," said Jeannie. "Mr. Yellow Thunder ordered this satellite phone for you. It was in this morning's mail, and I was about to leave you a message, at your home and at the office."

Mitch grabbed it from Jeannie. "Here, let me show you how it works. I'll enter our office numbers and Gideon's phone numbers, so you can see how to do it."

"Thanks for the tutorial." She rolled her eyes and laughed. "Not that I needed it," she added playfully.

"Right... so we've heard," Jeannie said as she tickled the baby under the chin.

Secora offered, "I'll put Jimmy's number in for practice. There. I have a feeling this is going to be very handy. Thank you, both."

Mitch grinned then concern spread across his face like a cloud. "Thank Gideon when you see him."

"I certainly will. It should only take about eight to ten hours to drive up there, check on him, and return."

"If you fly, it will only take minutes," Mitch countered.

"I think there's a flight leaving shortly," said Jeannie. "Let me book you a ticket. There... You can pick it up at the Frontier Airlines desk." Secora marveled at Jeannie's skills. She could see how Gideon and these two made such an excellent team.

"What about dear little Monta? Why not let Gramma Jeannie watch her?"

Secora looked skeptical. Jeannie continued, "I think she would appreciate staying with us rather than riding on an airplane and then rushing off into the forest. Besides, I'd have everything she needs right here in your diaper bag, wouldn't I?"

Secora began to feel gratitude welling up inside her. She hadn't realized how tense she was about traveling again into the unknown with her child. "It would be easier to make decisions without worrying about the baby, if you wouldn't mind."

"I would so love to share the day with her."

Mitch smiled and looked at the floor. "Actually, I think it would be a good idea given the track record you and Gideon have, for stumbling into... complicated situations."

"Do you have directions for the lake house, Mitch?"

"Of course, but better yet, Gideon's phone has a GPS locator even if his phone is dead. Look there. His, or should I say his phone's location comes up, see?"

"Nice, but I'll start with the old-fashioned directions and see how far that will get me. I'd better call Jimmy with this crazy new phone and let him know what's going on." She smiled at Monta and again dialed the number from the note left on her desk. The baby was wiggling and smiling in Jeannie's capable arms. Secora touched her tiny hand and felt a pang of remorse as she waited for Jimmy to answer.

"She'll be just fine," Jeannie assured. "It's a short separation, like babysitting, and if something is wrong, this would be a safer place for her."

Secora nodded solemnly and had to leave a message for Jimmy. While Monta reached for her mom's finger, tears filled Secora's eyes, and she kissed her. "I'll keep you posted when I know something." Then, she was off.

Secora checked her watch. It was 3:45—nearly four hours since she'd left Treasuremont. In the message, she'd told Jimmy to follow Highway 2 straight across and meet her outside of West Glacier. She felt both guilty and relieved to have a break from her precious daughter. *I miss you, beautiful Baby Girl.* She took a deep breath and acknowledged this was the better choice since she wasn't sure what the outcome of this excursion might be. She exhaled slowly as her concern for Gideon reclaimed center stage.

There were six or seven inches of snow along the side of the highway, and snow was still falling. She took the off-ramp to the little town of West Glacier. There, she picked up a few supplies for her trusty backpack: water, juice, jerky, and other dried snacks. *They're so creative with this camping stuff. Not like the old days when you needed meal plans, and a mule to haul your supplies, or simply ate Vienna Sausages and hard-boiled eggs, so many choices now.* She smirked as she remembered throwing hitches over canvas-covered loads on pack horses in the '70s.

The Satfon rang, shocking her. She was even more surprised to find it was not Gideon, but Jimmy on the other end. He was saying he was nearly to West Glacier and she should wait for him. "It's important," he cautioned.

Who was she to question the word of a visionary holy man, a Lakota wichasha wakan, who seemed to sense just about everything before it happened? She told him she'd wait for him at a friend's ranch outside of town and gave him directions.

Her rental car crawled down Camas Road and crossed McDonald Creek. Clouds parted and revealed a bright day. She reached for her sunglasses. Stopping just past the bridge, Secora stepped out to stretch and listen. She was enchanted by the little heaps of snow, which topped the rocks emerging from the creek, and listened intently to the murmur of the wild turquoise river beneath its thin coat of glistening ice. It sounded louder, where it tumbled through ice-free spaces around rocks and branches.

She looked up and noticed the sunlight twinkling from ice crystal frosting on the silent trees. Breathing in a lungful of cool air, she smiled. Ice is a beautiful adornment sometimes, resting on the earth like a diadem of jewels.

A staccato rat-a-tat knocked through the air as a pileated woodpecker searched for food. The sounds and sights faded in her mind as a gnawing urgency welled up. She needed to find Gideon. At that moment, she heard the cry of a raptor somewhere above the clouds. Could that be confirmation from Wakinyan?

As she walked, she realized her feet were wet and cold inside the leather hiking boots. Hmm... guess I needed more saddle soap. Better slide on the plastic boot covers from my leather backpack.

Sitting in the driver's seat, she kicked off the excess snow before covering the boots and bringing them into the car. Her reverie was broken as a pickup began to cross the bridge. Secora turned to look at the vehicle and check to make sure the truck had plenty of room to pass her car in the six inches of fresh snow.

The truck window rolled down as the vehicle stopped, and a friendly voice hollered, "Hau Kola."

She snapped the last of the plastic covers and stepped back outside with a smile. She welcomed Jimmy with a big hug. "So glad to see you, I haven't even made it to the guest ranch, how did you find me here?"

He waved the phone. "GPS, Gideon gave me one of these gadgets. It was a good idea. But he went to all of the trouble to keep in touch, and yet I can't find him. Maybe his phone's dead?"

Secora was confused. "I can't imagine Gideon forgetting to bring a charger."

"Where do we go from here?"

"Mitch said the place was at the end of a road that splits off to the right, just past the dude ranch run by some college buddies of mine."

"How many miles?"

"Not sure. From what I can figure, it could be three to six. My grad school friends, Ken and Sue, can tell us more about the area. They earned Master's degrees in Cultural Anthropology while I was finishing up in paleontology."

"We'd be better off parking and going in on foot. Maybe we could leave our vehicles at their place? There are only six inches of snow, but my old truck's been slipping and skidding ever since I turned off the freeway."

"I don't feel like hiking these woods in this wet snow, Jimmy. We can rent a couple of their horses."

"Okay, I'll follow you."

They parked at the guest ranch, and Jimmy walked up the front stairs with Secora. "How's the baby girl, Sloth Woman?"

Secora snickered at the reference to the "extinct" ground sloth she'd found last summer, who'd had her own baby. "She's wonderful, Jimmy —so sweet it humbles me just to look at her, but she's growing too big to lug around with one arm."

Jimmy laughed out loud. "Babies tend to do that." Then he looked around as if making a point. "You didn't bring her to meet her Uncle Jimmy?"

"No, I left her with Jeannie and Mitch."

"Probably a good idea with the way you and Gideon manage to find trouble."

"I've been hearing that a lot today."

The two were eagerly greeted at the door with big grins and hugs from Secora's old friends, Ken and Sue.

Sue said, "Glad you arrived before the bad weather started up again. It's melting now, but it's supposed to turn really cold in a few hours." A mule brayed, momentarily reminding Secora of Billy and his mule, Carrots. *Whatever happened to you two,* she wondered.

The four of them went inside and sat at a table laid with cups and a plate of snickerdoodles. Sue grabbed a pot off the stove and poured hot tea. While inhaling the aroma, Secora took in the beauty of the art and antiques hanging on the surrounding walls. There were old tin plates, spurs, coffee pots, and branding irons, placed among Remington prints.

Sue smiled. "So good to see you. Jimmy. I hear you're a Lakota holy man, a Wichasha Wakan. What an honor to meet you. I hope Ken and I have a chance to deepen our acquaintance under better conditions. Why is this friend of yours up here in the wintertime? Does he ski?"

"That's a mystery we hope to solve." Jimmy sipped the tea and looked down at the table.

Secora added, "He's a realtor and he's visiting the owner of a recently purchased property. There's a problem with the water from the lake or something."

"Ahhh, you're talking about Prissy's old place. It sat abandoned for a few years after she mysteriously disappeared," Ken reminisced.

"Maybe more like six," Sue countered. We always suspected she died in a mining accident on the mountain above her place.

"Anyway," Ken continued, "she disappeared. The place needed quite a bit of work, and so does the access road. He probably got stuck in this snow."

Sue nodded, "Come to think of it, there has been more traffic than usual headed past our place for the last few weeks. So, the road is likely to be heavily rutted. You made a good choice—asking to take horses in there."

Secora rubbed her head with an index finger. "We're eager to find Gideon, in case he's having difficulties."

"Well..." Ken hopped up, slurped the rest of his tea, and excused himself. "Time's a precious commodity, and it will be dark before we know it. I'll head out to catch and saddle those horses for you. Meet me in the corral in ten minutes, so you can go find out what that rascal is up to."

Jimmy and Secora followed Ken outside; they were far too anxious to wait. They helped him catch up three horses from the corral and curried their long bushy winter hair halos. The horses sighed, snorting clouds of steam as they exhaled during cinching. Their ears turned back to remind the humans to be gentle and not pull too tight, too fast.

Sue came out to the corral with a shovel, which she tied to the saddle on the bay. "You might need this." Secora smiled and nodded.

Once the animals were saddled and bridled, Jimmy mounted the paint and led the bay by the halter. A bridle hung from the saddle horn for Gideon, if he should need it. Secora swung onto the palomino. The horses were ready, and at long last, they could begin the search for Gideon.

Jimmy turned his horse back to stand beside Secora's. "Your friend, Ken, thought it was about three miles to the turnoff. So, I guess it'll be an easy ride to that point."

Secora squeezed her legs gently, and her horse started to move away from the ranch. "Not much traffic and it's a gorgeous day even though the clouds look like they are coming back. But all I can think about is making sure Gideon's okay."

"I should try calling him again." Jimmy started to dial. "It'd be embarrassing if he answers and we're this close." He stopped speaking to listen.

Secora pulled out her phone and said, "I'll call Jeannie, to see how she and Monta are doing. She'll appreciate an update."

Jeannie thanked her and explained Monta appeared to be having a blast at the office. One of her favorite activities was speed crawling all over the place. When she hung up, there was a grin on Secora's face. "I miss that little girl. Any luck with your call?"

"It's odd. I received a phone message this time. The signal must have been blocked before... maybe by this mountain."

"Or by the storm?" offered Secora.

Jimmy didn't answer except to mumble, "Still dark."

Secora urged her horse into a trot. "That's just creepy, Jimmy."

"It is what it is." Jimmy followed suit.

12

CAVE-IN

A half hour later they turned up the long driveway to the resort. Snow had covered several sets of vehicle tracks. They stopped a moment to let the horses blow and nuzzle the snow.

"I didn't tell you before, Secora, but I can't feel Gideon," Jimmy said, looking thoughtful.

She just stared, waiting for an explanation. "It's not just because of the phone."

Secora mounted up and urged, "Jimmy, what are you saying?"

"Only that we need to prepare ourselves for more than merely digging out a car."

Secora urged the palomino on. Here and there, deer tracks criss-crossed the road. In another fifteen minutes, they came into the parking area at the front of the lodge. Three vehicles, covered in snow, waited in the lot. The one which had been driven most recently, a Jeep Cherokee, had very little snow on it and what there was had begun to melt.

The two riders dismounted warily, and took off the horses' bridles, hanging them on the saddle horns. They tied the animals to porch pillars with lead ropes attached to the halters which had been covered by the bridles, so they could snort and rest. Then the two friends climbed the few stairs to the deck side by side.

"No signs of life," Jimmy said. He knocked. There was no response.

Secora stepped up and knocked even louder. Again, nothing. She tried the doorknob, and it was unlocked. Jimmy stepped in first and called out, "Gideon, Heyoka." Everything remained still.

Secora was feeling edgy, unnerved.

"Let's call his phone?" suggested Jimmy. From somewhere within the dwelling, they heard his ringtone and rushed to the source, a couch where they found Gideon's suit coat. Jimmy paled. "He never leaves his phone behind."

Secora felt sick, like the world had in a flash, turned evil.

They checked all the rooms to ensure the building was vacant, and then left by the back
door.

Secora said, "Here's a set of tracks that leads away from the house." They circled back to
pick up the horses. After pulling the bridles back on over the halters, they followed a set of paw prints, along with a set of large boots to an old shed.

Secora shivered with a chill as she pulled her horse up alongside Jimmy's. They heard a muffled whining. Secora dismounted to dig through the disturbed snow and found the nearly frozen, injured pug.

"This girl is bleeding along her ribs, poor puppy." Cutesie yipped when she was lifted.

"Looks like a graze from a bullet," Jimmy suggested.

Secora wrapped her in a cashmere scarf from her backpack and snuggled the animal inside her coat while Jimmy stared at the mish-mash of tracks and drag marks.

"While you are sorting all that out, I'm taking the dog back to the house. Be right back."

"Yeah, okay," mumbled Jimmy.

The wind changed, blowing directly into their faces.

Jimmy hollered, "Do you smell oil? It reminds me of the reek of oil fields in the Dakotas."

"Yeah, it's strong." For some reason, it made Secora think of the new graduate student at the university. Why wasn't his office in the Geology Department? The dog groaned, and she brushed the thoughts away. "Be back in a few."

Secora trotted up minutes later, after offering the injured animal food, water, and a warm place to curl up. "I called the sheriff to report the disappearance and asked them to also call the animal control officer about the dog."

"Good. The tracks of three men came to this shed from over there by the lake." Jimmy pointed downhill into the valley. "Someone came from the house, probably an assailant. Then all of the tracks and drag marks lead to the left, straight up that mountain."

"But what the heck happened at this spot? There's a lot of blood. Someone besides the dog must be badly injured."

Secora's heart pounded against her chest. Tears began to sting her eyes. "Could Gideon be injured?"

"Can't tell for sure, but those prints over there, the ones that are slipping so badly, look like Gideon's boots. I'm guessing he and the third man dragged someone from this place."

Jimmy looked up at Secora. Then said, "The fourth man, who met them from the back of the house wasn't a friend. No remorse for the injury, no going back to the house to get help."

They mounted the horses and guided them west toward the smelly mountain. Continuing in silence, they moved as fast as they could safely travel in the snowy dusk. Secora followed the bay and watched him skid on an ice ball that had accumulated in one of its hooves. Eventually, the ball of ice released, and it was easier for the horse to walk, at least on that foot.

"I'm so glad Ken took the time to pull the shoes off the two horses we're riding. Otherwise, we might have broken our necks on this steep trail. Should have warned him we might need a third horse, so he could have taken the shoes off the bay."

The animals' long winter coats were beginning to heat up. They became sweaty and sticky as they climbed in a zigzag pattern that deer use, for better footing and ease of climbing.

While Secora watched the puffs of steam coming from the horses' flared nostrils, she said, "I'm really worried, Jimmy."

"Me too."

They rested for a few minutes to let the animals catch their breath, and then moved as fast as the horses were able toward a dark gap that appeared to be the entrance of a cave or mine.

When they arrived, they again took off the bridles and hung them on the saddle horns and tied the horses to trees with the lead ropes.

The animals snorted, vigorously waggled their heads, and then shook their entire bodies like wet dogs. Secora noticed the palomino twitching her ears as if to catch an odd sound.

Jimmy also appeared to be listening intently. Then he said, "Hear that? Sounds like a car engine moving somewhere down below." The sound died away, and they continued to hike the last few yards to the entrance.

Everything inside the entrance was pitch black. Jimmy pulled out a pistol and a flashlight, and Secora withdrew a Maglite from her backpack and pinched her nose. They could only go inside about fifteen feet before they hit a rock wall. Secora lit up the tracks and saw that two sets appeared to lead right into the rocks, while a third milled around then turned back toward the entrance. A horrible realization grew in her mind. Jimmy hollered for Gideon as his light played over the entire wall in an attempt to find any weaknesses they might exploit. Secora also yelled, but there was no audible response.

"I'm calling the sheriff again; we're going to need emergency assistance. Next, I'll call Jeannie and Mitch, also Ken and Sue to give them updates."

Jimmy nodded. "Good idea," Then he started up the side of the collapse.

Secora went outside the cavern and requested aid cars for three victims and rescue equipment that could break through a cave-in. She could hardly feel her toes as she walked back and caught up with Jimmy at the slide pulling at the slippery, muddy stones near the top of the heap. As she pitched in to dig beside him, she became concerned when she noticed his lips were turning blue. Every once in a while she could hear the horses pawing the snow, shaking their halters, or snorting. The temperature was still dropping, and she couldn't imagine how Gideon would handle the cold if he was, somehow, still alive. She yelled his name again, hoping he could hear. Jimmy remained silent but he never quit trying to budge a rock here or there.

The sky was darkening into velvet blue when they heard the grumbling of engines and a noise that sounded like the strain of a winch. Rescuers began to arrive with the roar of chainsaws, as they cleared a path for trucks equipped with the winches, Jaws of Life, and other tackle.

Lights were set up, and trucks were sliding as they took their positions. Everything outside was a cold mess. But inside the adit, there was plenty of activity. A fireman approached Jimmy and Secora, who had taken seats under a tree for refuge. He told them, "The rock fall apparently happened recently, so it's coming apart easily." Even though he was yelling, she had to read his lips because of the racket caused by the equipment. Another man grabbed a bullhorn and tried to reach the ears of anyone who might be inside.

Sue and Ken arrived on ATVs and approached Secora and Jimmy, whose teeth were chattering. They carefully helped them to stand and guided them to one of the aid cars for treatment of hypothermia and exertion. They didn't resist.

Secora was offered a warm blanket which she gratefully wrapped around herself and Jimmy. After a few minutes, the tears began to come.

Her friends offered to give them the ATVs and take the horses back.

It was a kind thought, but Jimmy and Secora wisely refused.

"Heck of a time to learn how to use one of those machines," coughed Jimmy.

It felt as if the digging and pounding took forever, but eventually, a couple of men went inside a breach with huge lamps. About half an hour later, they brought someone out on a stretcher, which they hurried to an aid car. They brought two other bodies from the cave, and then announced, "That's it. There was no one else, except part of an old skeleton the Sheriff needs to collect."

That caught Secora's attention. Her ears strained for the rest of the conversation. A man carrying a jackhammer out of the mine asked, "Do they allow oil drilling or fracking this close to Glacier National Park?"

Another man in a fireman's coat yelled, "No sir, I don't believe they do. Let's get 'em outta here."

Jimmy hopped out of the ambulance as they prepared to load one of the victims encased in a body bag. He put his arm protectively around Secora as they approached the fireman who seemed to be in charge of the operation.

The man said, "Bad news, guys. They aren't conscious, and we're pretty sure that two are clinically dead." He tried to look optimistic as he continued, "But it wasn't freezing in there, maybe mid-forties. So, one might have made it. You did the right thing."

Secora bit her lip. "Could we please see our friend?"

"Sure." The fireman took them to the aid cars. They didn't recognize the first man as the body bag was unzipped. He had a bullet wound in his face.

Secora whispered, *Ya' Baha'u'l-Abha!* a short prayer for his transition. The second one seemed like an icy stone, somehow familiar, but

Secora couldn't place him. They were barely able to recognize Gideon as the third man. His eyes were shut, and he looked like he was frozen solid with blood and dirt smearing his face. The doors closed, and the vehicles headed down toward MacDonald Creek and out to Kalispell. Both Jimmy and Secora began immediately to chant prayers for the departed.

The mountain returned to pitch black as lights were packed up and engines roared to life. Shrouded in tears, Jimmy and Secora dutifully bridled the horses and used their flashlights to guide the animals as they walked them down the slippery mountain to the parking lot. Secora wished they could go into the resort lodge to rest and warm themselves, but of course, it too, was taped off as a crime scene.

Jimmy said, "Look, someone took the third vehicle. We should tell the sheriff."

Secora nodded as he stepped over to an officer and told her the hours which the third vehicle might have been parked there.

"It was a Jeep Cherokee." Jimmy told her the license number.

Secora relayed her concerns about the injured dog. The officer took the information down and turned away to call dispatch.

When he exhausted friends mounted up and rode off into the night, crunching their way down the frozen driveway, the snowfall was sporadically lit by the rising moon.

Secora updated Jeannie and Mitch about the catastrophe and suggested they meet at the Kalispell Regional Medical Center.

When Jimmy and Secora reached her friends' ranch, they unsaddled and brushed the weary horses before walking them. Ken and Sue came outside to take over the horse duties.

Ken looked like he had something to say. "Sue and I remembered. At about 4:15 we heard a distant explosion, like a sonic boom - but it might have been dynamite. We thought that might help with pinpointing a start time for the cave-in. It's now 7:20."

"That could mean they were on their own from 4:15 to 5:30 when we got up there, and it was nearly another hour and a half before they were taken away from the mine. That's about three hours, plus they were undoubtedly cold, hungry, and wet to begin with."

Jimmy said, "Not good," He returned to his pickup.

Secora told Ken and Sue she was grateful, and she gave them an envelope for the rental of the animals. The payment was brushed away. Instead, they invited her to come back and spend spring break with them so they could catch up on all that had happened in the last twenty years. She said she might take them up on that, but now she needed to dash to the hospital. She wearily hugged and said goodbye to her friends, then began to brush off the snow that had accumulated on her vehicle.

Jimmy had already climbed into his pickup and left, and it wasn't long before her rental crept through the dark after him.

Ice crystals began to pelt the car. She shivered and thanked God that they got the men out before this started. The freeway was a mess with several inches of rutted slush. Secora didn't even see a snowplow until she was almost in Kalispell.

Her breath was coming in frosty puffs as she hurried into the emergency room, where she was relieved to find Jeannie and Mitch already waiting. She ran up to them, hugged them both, and grabbed her baby from the carrier. Monta's little angel face stared back at her.

"Thank you so much for keeping her warm and safe."

Jeannie's eyes were red from crying. "Thank you for finding Gideon."

"And for getting him out of that tomb," Mitch added.

Secora couldn't find words to answer. Tears were streaming down her cheeks. She looked around. "Did Jimmy make it here okay?"

"Yes, they're letting him sit with Gideon as spiritual council," said Mitch.

Her face was twisted in a picture of anguish. "Is he...?"

Jeannie answered, "Yes, he's alive, but in critical condition. They say its touch and go."

Mitch sighed. "When the ambulances arrived, they wouldn't tell us much, but we overheard a tech talking about three men who'd arrived. One was dead from exsanguination and the other two were severely hypothermic. One—we don't know which one, died of a heart attack en route. But we might have overheard someone say he responded to the EMTs' efforts to start his heart. Not much to go on."

Jeannie explained, "Apparently, they've been able to revive the patient, and he's still fighting in one of the trauma bays."

Mitch added, "It looks bleak. They've called two cardiac arrests since the ambulances arrived." He hesitated, and Secora noticed his lip began to tremble. "Neither of the men has regained consciousness, and..." he paused. "They aren't expected to."

"To live?" Secora moaned.

At that point, Jeannie fully broke down. Mitch placed his arm around her and said, "Gideon is strong, Jeannie. He has a chance."

Secora began to shake, and she tried to control the reaction by hugging Monta close to her.

Mitch continued, "The coroner arrived a few minutes ago to pick up the man who was DOA."

Secora nodded, remembering the man whose face was shot.

Two police officers found the huddled friends, asked questions about who the three men were, and about the vehicles at the resort.

Secora mumbled, "I remember the distinct smell of oil, but we didn't see any rigs."

Everyone was fatigued from crying, but Mitch told them the only one they knew personally was Gideon Yellow Thunder. One of the others must have been Mr. Kamal Hasan, son of the property owner, Jamal Hasan, who lived in Kuwait. Mitch worried out loud, that his death might cause an international incident.

The guy who seemed to be in charge said, "Great. Better call the FBI." Then he left the corridor.

Mitch told the officer who remained about the water problem at the resort property outside of West Glacier. He made it clear he would not be able to identify the third man, who he supposed was either a guest or client. Secora was only half listening because she was emotionally drained and content to hold her little one.

13

CRITICAL CARE

S ecora was just finishing the potent Long Healing Prayer, and looked up in time to see the ER doc step over to Jeannie and Mitch. With a long sigh, he rubbed his eyes beneath his glasses. When he was ready, he said, "I'm sorry to say that the only good news I can give you is that his heart is still beating. He's still unconscious, but he's stronger than the other man. We just have to wait." The doctor went on to explain Gideon had been chilled for so long there was no guarantee he would be the person they remembered if he did live.

That hit Secora between the eyes. In many ways, Gideon had been her strong companion. Their relationship was not the same as the infinite love she and Diego shared, but there was an undeniable closeness. There had been a trust between them which allowed them to stand together against hellish odds.

Mitch and Jeannie were openly weeping for their beloved family member. Even Jimmy, who had been chanting prayers for hours, broke down and sobbed. Secora stepped close to him and rubbed his shoulder. There wasn't a dry eye in the bunch, though Monta's tears were likely due to hunger rather than gut-wrenching sorrow, fear, or guilt.

The doc suggested they take rooms at a nearby motel and return in the morning. Jeannie mentioned she had already arranged rooms for the five of them. Bless her heart. Secora needed to take care of Monta and try to rest. Heck, they all desperately needed rest, and Gideon's condition wasn't likely to change before morning. The doctor's next words broke through the wall of her thoughts.

"We'll call you if Mr. Yellow Thunder's condition changes— significantly." They thanked him and left. All the way to the hotel, Secora was repeating, "Is there any Remover of difficulties save God? Say: Praised be God! He is God! All are His servants, and all abide by His bidding."

After checking in at the desk, they move to the rooms. Once they were settled in for the night, poor little Monta fell asleep with her bottle, and Secora wasn't far behind. She slipped into a fitful dream, in which she saw Billy Riggins' smiling face. He was thanking her, profusely, for finding him. She sat up, fully awake and gasping for breath. There were beads of sweat on her brow. She said aloud to no one, "What do you mean I found you? How? Where are you?"

When Secora and the others checked in at the critical care desk the next morning, they were briefly allowed to visit Gideon. Secora couldn't believe what she was seeing. He was still asleep *and on a ventilator*. He is so still. It doesn't seem possible. What lunacy could have possibly led to this tragedy?

A nurse entered the room and said Gideon's temperature was normal, but since he hadn't regained consciousness, they would be running an EEG to see what was happening inside his brain. He then asked Secora and the others, "Have you contacted all of Mr. Yellow Thunder's next of kin?"

Jimmy said he'd spoken with Gideon's mother and grandmother, and they should be arriving from South Dakota, tomorrow at the latest.

Secora mentioned she would contact his sister Jane, who was currently in Peru, as soon as the time shift allowed.

The nurse nodded and left, pulling the door shut behind him. Secora looked at the floor thinking, this call is not the way I envisioned making amends with Jane.

Jeannie and Mitch approached the bed and reached for Gideon's hands. Jeannie said, "I hope you didn't push your guardian angel too far this time, Mr. Yellow Thunder." She bent down and did her best to hug him. "Please, God, help him." Her face twisted in agony, and she couldn't speak anymore.

Mitch said, "Hey buddy…" Then he slowly shook his head back and forth with his eyes closed, also unable to speak.

Jimmy slowly drew out the sacred pipe from its intricately beaded elk skin bag, revealing the polished red stone bowl and two owl feathers hanging from a beaded suede strip that encircled the stem. Jimmy chanted.

"I offer the 'Between Worlds' prayer
for my dearest friend.
Hey-a-ho.
First, I offer this pipe to Wakan Tanka,
the Great Spirit who is One."

He raised the pipe with both hands toward the sky.

"Behold this sacred pipe.
Behold us on this sacred earth.
O Wakan Tanka, you are our Father and Grandfather.
You are everything.
You have always been."

Jimmy took a braid of sweetgrass from a pouch but did not light it. Instead he waved its perfume to grace the room.

"Grandfather, this is your herb, its fragrance belongs to you.
Behold this good young man before you.
He suffers between worlds now.
I beg of you to cause him to move toward you, as is your will.
Be merciful. Help him."

He offered the pipe to the Earth.

"Our Grandmother and Mother, you are sacred.
Every step upon you should be taken as a prayer.
It is from you that our bodies come.
Help this brave man.
He wishes to be one with all things.
He serves the good of all your peoples, the four-leggeds,
the two- leggeds, the wings of the air.
Help him."

Jimmy turned his feet to the West.

"I now beseech the four directions to help this man.
First to you, O winged Power from where the sun goes down.
Send your servants, ancient and sacred.
The Thunder Beings who come to us in the terrifying storm.
Send us your two sacred red and blue days. Help him."
He then turned to the South, the East, and the North,
beseeching aid for Gideon. Finally, Jimmy announced,
"Hetchetu aloh. It is finished."

It seemed to Secora that Gideon tried to move his arm. They all waited. Nothing further appeared to happen.

Secora's voice softly began the powerful Long Healing Prayer brought to earth by Baha'u'llah.

"He is the Healer, the Sufficer, the Helper, the All-Forgiving, the All-Merciful. I call on Thee O Exalted One, O Faithful One, O Glorious One! Thou the Sufficing, Thou the Healing, Thou the Abiding, O Thou Abiding One! ..."

Secora had to stop several times to stifle sobs. When she finished several minutes later, everyone was still sniffling, as the pain of detachment from the outcome of Gideon's condition began to twist and tear at their hearts. When she finished, she asked God to unite their wills with His in this matter, then she put her hand on Gideon's arm and closed her eyes noticing the sniffles around her had diminished.

She heard a sound like shuffling feet and turned to see a group of men squeeze into the room. One of them showed a badge and said, "We are from the Kuwaiti Embassy, here with Mr. Jamal Hasan regarding the demise of his son. We wish to speak with Mrs. James and Mr. Lizardeye regarding this matter."

Jimmy wasn't willing to leave Gideon's side. Secora nodded and stood. "I would be happy to tell you what I know, which, unfortunately, is almost nothing. The only people who know—can't speak, yet. And of course, the person who did this to them is not available."

At their request, she left the room to speak privately. Secora relayed everything, beginning with Jimmy's worry about Gideon going dark, their arrival on the property, and what they didn't find at the residence. She told them of finding the injured dog at the shed and what she did with her. The deputy said the animal would be taken to an emergency vet and could be picked up on Monday.

Mr. Hasan nodded and spoke with his companions in what Secora assumed was Arabic based on the few words she could pick up. Then his gaze returned to her. "The dog is Cutesie, Kamal's long-time pet. I cannot take her with me, but I will cover her expenses with the vet. What else did you find?"

"Jimmy said he could make out three sets of tracks in the snow and drag marks leading from the shed, where there had been an obvious scuffle. The men probably tried to overpower the gunman, and that is how your son was shot, but he didn't die there. The other two men tried to help him up the mountain to the mine entrance. Their footprints led inside the mine, with drag marks apparently made by your son. It looked like their tracks slipped as they tried to run. One person turned away from the mine and left."

"Mr. Lizardeye is a tracker?"

Secora nodded, adding, "And a holy man among other things. The blast hadn't happened too long before we arrived. My friends Ken and Sue Grayson who rented us the horses heard a noise around 4:15. We were outside the entrance hollering and digging with our hands somewhere around 5:00, maybe 5:30. The emergency assistance was there around 6:30 and had them out within the hour. Sadly, it was too late to help your son."

Secora stopped respectfully, because it seemed the men were praying. When there was a pause, she mentioned, "Jimmy and I heard a vehicle drive off while we were still on the mountain, and we noticed the Jeep Cherokee was missing when we returned to your parking lot later that evening. Apparently, the killer had been lurking around, avoiding contact until he could leave unobserved."

Mr. Hasan thanked her for caring for Kamal's dog. One of the men took her contact information and said they would now speak with her friends.

"One more thing, Mr. Hasan, the EMT said that the two men had made a pillow for your son's head out of Gideon's sweater. So maybe he knew he was with people who cared about him." Secora smiled, and offered, "A Salam Alahem, and Allah'u-Akbar" as they left. She remained outside the room with Monta, wondering if her life would ever be normal again. Then, she realized it hadn't been "normal" before. Not for a long time.

The three other companions joined her on chairs in the waiting room, as each finished with their interrogation. Eventually, Jeannie reached into her purse and grabbed some rubber bands and a brush and she moved her chair behind Secora's.

"I would like to put braids in that lovely hair—you don't mind, do you?"

Secora answered, "Not at all. I've been wishing I was able to do that for months now. Thank you." She relaxed as she felt the strands tighten against her scalp.

"Do you think we'll ever find out what happened, or why?"

Mitch answered, "I expect we will, but I wonder how much pain we'll find along that dark path."

Secora said, "I have a strong feeling Mr. Hasan will be conducting a separate investigation, which won't end with a question."

14

OLD FRIEND

That afternoon, when visiting hours were over, Jeannie grabbed Monta from Secora and put her in the stroller.

"We're going for a walk. She helps take my mind off... you know." Her eyes flicked over to Gideon.

Secora nodded as she handed the precious child over. She watched Jeannie and Mitch saunter down the hall in the direction of the cafeteria.

A few minutes later, she felt compelled to check at the desk for the progress of the third man, who was still teetering on the edge of existence.

The nurses didn't want to say anything about him because she wasn't next of kin.

"Do you even know who he is?" they asked.

"Yes, and I seriously think I might be the only name on his visitor's list if you had it here."

They said they couldn't help her. So, Secora made a call to the sheriff's office to ask if they had a name for the third man. When they replied that they didn't, Secora explained that she might be one of the few people who knew him. Then, she asked if they could arrange for her to see him, for the purpose of identification.

"Let me talk to his nurse," came the answer.

She handed the phone over to the RN, who was still reluctant. She told the deputy that if he wanted to see the patient—he should arrive sooner rather than later.

Secora went back to the critical care waiting room. There, she found Gideon's mother and grandmother. She stepped over to greet them and told them visiting hours were over. They acknowledged they knew, but the nursing supervisor was making plans for them to be with him and Jimmy. She smiled and called Mitch to update the situation. He and Jeannie were heading back from the cafeteria to see the women.

Nearly an hour later, the sheriff's deputy appeared and Secora stood to introduce herself. "Can you arrange for me to see John Doe?" She looked down considering her next words. "I think he might be Billy Riggins, a long-time friend, and colleague of mine. I've known him since graduate school.

"A little over a week ago he was attacked by a man with a shovel near Birch Bay, Washington. I was on the phone with him when the guy started hitting him and broke his arm. He begged me to call 911 and our connection was lost. After I arrived at his last known location, I had no luck finding him and never again heard from him. I was beginning to assume the worst."

"Oh, Birch Bay, huh. Then why do you think he'd be here?"

Secora shook her head. "Honestly, I have no idea, except he came to me in a dream last night and thanked me for finding him."

The deputy shifted his weight, obviously uncomfortable with her statement.

She continued, "Billy never mentioned having a family. He's a loner, never married. Can you arrange for me to see him? I would recognize him if I saw him."

"Guess it couldn't hurt." The deputy, whose name tag declared

"Wilkins," accompanied her to the critical care desk. The doctor happened to be looking at John Doe's chart. "He's struggling. Coded again last night. If he stabilizes, we may have to remove his frostbitten digits unless we can find a spot for him in a burn recovery unit."

Deputy Wilkins nodded. "This woman might be able to make an identification. Okay if we go in?"

"Go ahead. Maybe we can notify next of kin."

The RN led them into a darkened room. Flipping on the overhead light, she commented, "We need this bed so this may be the only time you'll be able to visit him here." She

pulled back the curtain with a whoosh. "He may not be able to hear you; his eardrums are damaged."

Secora and the deputy nodded and respectfully walked up to the bed. Gauze bandages covered the patient's forehead, nose, and ears, as well as both hands. After a silent moment, Secora leaned close and scrutinized him for clues to his identity. She said, "He had shoulder-length dark hair when I worked with him, but even without the hair, I suppose those could be his features."

The nurse acknowledged his hair had been shaved in the ER, so his head injuries could be adequately treated.

"I wish he'd open his eyes. They are a turquoise blue, rather striking against that dark hair." The deputy stepped closer and lifted an eyelid. "Yep, they're blue all right. We might be able to obtain prints." He picked up a bandaged hand, then set it down. "I'll go check the name in the system. Where did he live?"

"Not sure. He traveled all over the world recording mastodon and mammoth sites. I can probably find some old pictures of us from fourteen years ago." The doctor stepped back into the room.

"Wait a minute," Secora asked the doctor if the man had a broken arm.

"He did have a nasty bruise and a cut on his arm, as well as a fractured ulna when he came into the ER. The X-Ray showed the damage was from an earlier injury and had done some healing. A couple of weeks maybe."

"This woman thinks his name is Billy Riggins. I'm going to check it out." Deputy Wilkins shook the doctor's hand, and nodding to Secora, took his leave. The doctor followed him out.

Secora asked the RN if she could spend a few minutes alone with Billy to pray. The nurse nodded and left. She moved a chair closer to the bed to again offer the Long Healing Prayer and the Tablet of Ahmad.

After a silence, she asked, "Billy, what's going on with you? Who did this?" She touched his arm but couldn't be sure which arm was broken through the bandages and wraps for the frostbite. To her relief, the man opened his eyes and blinked.

He attempted to speak in a hoarse whisper after he looked at his bandaged hands. Instead, his eyes filled with tears and he had to cough when they flooded his nose and throat. Secora felt horrible watching him struggle.

After a few minutes, he tried to speak again. It was difficult to make out the words, but Secora had the impression he wasn't interested in living without fingers and toes. She could understand his plight. If this was Billy, he would no longer be able to function in his lifelong profession. She smiled and tried to find a part of his arm that might be safe to touch since his hands were so badly injured.

She had a strong feeling this was her friend, but she couldn't be one hundred percent sure. So, because of his hearing impairment, she decided to take the tablet from her backpack and write notes.

As Secora wrote her questions, a different nurse came in, a look of surprise seizing her concern hardened her features. Secora thought maybe the shift had changed, and this woman had no idea why she was there.

"Excuse me, who are you? There are no visitor names on his chart."

Secora explained who she was and asked to have her name added to his visitor list so she could continue to come and see him, wherever he was transferred.

She was told it would not be possible without his written consent, and if she didn't have this, she needed to leave.

"And how do you expect this to happen? He can't use his hands."

"I repeat, what are you doing here in the first place?"

"I realize you have concerns, but I came in with the doctor's consent and with a deputy to identify my friend."

"Am I blind? I don't see anyone here but you."

"Deputy Wilkins felt convinced this man might be Billy Riggins, and he stepped out to check for him in the system."

"I think you should leave until there is proof."

Secora scribbled on the tablet and held it up. "Billy, do you know me? And do you want me on your visitor list?"

He nodded several times.

"That's not proof," countered the nurse. "He could be a homeless guy who thinks you're hot."

Secora sighed. "Please call the doctor and the house manager so we can work this out once and for all."

"I will. The supervisor and security will meet you in the waiting room."

Secora understood the bum's rush and felt compelled to leave. "Hold on a minute." She scratched large visible numbers on a scrap of paper she tore from the tablet. "Billy, here's my new phone number. Don't let them take this." After glancing at the nurse, she added, "Maybe you should memorize it." She tucked the note in an arm wrap.

"I'll be back in soon." She moved obediently toward the door but turned back long enough to write in big letters, "The dates were Legit." The patient's eyes became huge, filling rapidly with tears, and a sound escaped his throat. It sounded like the croak that an overjoyed person might make when presented with a precious gift.

She smiled. "You changed pre-history!" She hit the pen on the paper repeatedly, leaving several dots of ink for emphasis near the words, and added, "Put me on your visitor's list ASAP. Call me, or have a nurse call me."

He nodded.

Later, she and Monta found a table in the cafeteria. It would be a while until the house manager or supervisor could fill her request, but Secora was confident that between Billy's acknowledgment and the deputy's information, she would indeed be added to his visitors' list as a close friend, and that is exactly what happened. The House Manager notified her in the cafeteria.

When she and Monta finished eating, they returned to the critical care waiting room, and Secora made a call to Peru on the Satfon. She connected with a voice she didn't recognize, but the man said he would take the phone to Jane. It took several seconds before Secora heard her friend's gruff, "Hello, this better be good."

She had thought a lot about what she was going to say. "There has been an incident up near Glacier..."

Jane said, "Oh, my God. What happened this time?"

Secora explained her brother had severe frostbite and gave the details of the situation to Jane, who immediately wanted to fly back to be with Gideon. Secora suggested she wait another day for him to return to consciousness and then make her decision based on what Gideon would say.

Jane agreed she would call the hospital tomorrow.

Jamal Hasan and an aide approached Secora, as she sat in the waiting room watching Monta sleep in the stroller between herself and Jeannie. She hadn't noticed how tall and slim he was. His hair was salt and pepper, as would be normal for a man in his late fifties or early sixties. The man was an iron-clad presence. He walked straight to her and picked up the medallion on her necklace. He looked at it for a moment then dropped it back to her chest. "I see you are Baha'i." She nodded, wondering if he would choose to be a friend or foe.

"Baha'u'llah said God wants justice for all the people of the earth, right?"

Secora took a long breath, nodding again.

"I want you to know I also believe in justice. And I will find out who is responsible for what happened to my son and the others." He bent close and whispered, "And there will be justice."

Secora knew what he meant, but she didn't know how to respond at that moment. She nodded as the embassy fellow she'd met before, and two plainclothes men, possibly FBI, came up to stand beside him.

Words immediately came to her mind. "Justice, not vengeance, right?"

It was his turn to take that in. He nodded once.

She continued, "The trick will be finding a motive for this tragedy."

Her attention was drawn away from her visitors by two EMTs who swiped a badge and pushed an empty gurney through the doors into the CCU. Mr. Hasan followed her gaze.

"Is someone leaving?"

"I believe they are taking my old friend, to a Seattle burn unit. Would you please excuse me? I would like to say goodbye. Jeannie?"

"No worries." She smiled.

Mr. Hasan started to speak, but Secora cut him off. "I know you want to know everything etched in his brain, but he still doesn't talk, and can't yet tell you. Maybe you can meet up with him in Seattle?"

Secora buzzed to be let into the CCU and walked up to the desk. The RN looked up from a chart.

"Is there any chance I could have one minute to say goodbye?" There was hesitation. "I know time is precious, but literally one minute?" The nurse came around and led her to where he was being prepared for transport.

Billy's eyes caught hers, and he tried to sit up but was restricted by tie-down straps.

"Billy, I hope to see you at the new unit. Get better. You still have my phone number, right?"

He was trying to speak and sounded frightened, "Don't leave. They'll kill..." He was cut off by a coughing fit.

"We need to leave," said one of the transport techs. Everyone moved out of the room and down the hall. Secora was hanging on to Billy's wrist. "I know there's danger, Billy, but focus on the power of strength and healing. We have lots of work ahead of us." They were heading for the exit.

"Billy, my phone number is for a satellite phone. Do you have it?" He nodded.

"Call me as often as you can. There is so much I need to know about why this happened."

She touched the arm of the nearest EMT to attract his attention. "Keep him safe! Please." He nodded. "Of course, ma'am, that is literally our job."

She moved to face the tech's eyes. "He's not being paranoid. These injuries are the result of a second attack on his life. Be careful."

The EMT grasped her meaning and even looked momentarily alarmed.

"I'll find you, so please don't worry, Billy." Then the gurney was out the door and out of sight. Even though Secora's system was full of adrenaline, she felt lost as she wandered back to the waiting room, thinking, if he survives, how will I find time to travel over to the burn unit? Will I ever see him again?

15

KIMIMILA

When she peeked in, Secora noticed Jimmy was back in Gideon's room. In fact, everyone was crammed inside, and Gideon's eyes were open. The moment she entered, things became awkward. Everyone was too quiet.

"If I was more self-conscious, I'd think I was the topic of conversation." After greeting each person, Secora squeezed in close to Gideon and gently picked up his wrist, so as not to further damage his hand.

She stared at his eyes hoping he would listen. "What happened, brother? Why can't, or won't you speak to me?" Gideon stared straight ahead and wouldn't even look at her. Aching loneliness gripped her heart. Tears slid from her eyes past her jaw. She ignored them. Smiling gently, she released his hand.

"I feel like you are talking to everyone but me, which hurts." She looked down at the glistening floor tiles. "But I don't want you to be any more uncomfortable than you already are." She picked up Monta from Jeannie's arms and tucked her into the stroller. "We'll be in the cafeteria." There was an uncomfortable rustling as she left.

She sat forlorn for a good half hour with only a cup of tea, while

Monta fussed in a highchair. She looked up and noticed Jimmy coming toward them. He was acting a bit squirrelly when he sat beside her at the table.

"What's going on, Wichasha Wakan?"

"He called you Kimimila."

"What, 'butterfly?'"

Jimmy looked straight ahead like he hadn't heard her.

She took her teacup to the dish collection area, and then took the unhappy baby from the highchair. "I'm thinking Monta and I should head back home." She bent down to grab her purse with the fingers of her braced arm. "Would you remind him I have this satellite phone if he ever wants to talk?"

Jimmy stood in front of her and looked directly into her eyes—something Secora had rarely seen him do.

"Why did you call him 'brother'?"

She felt crushed as she absorbed his words, then she looked at the carpet, swallowing tears. She was doing her best to hold Monta with her injury, so Jimmy dabbed her eyes with a napkin.

"Don't know. Guess I think of us as family."

"Nothing more?"

Secora searched his stern face.

"Will you always fly away?"

She returned his stare in amazement, saying nothing. From the sides of her eyes, she noticed Mitch and Jeannie approaching. Jeannie reached for the fussy little girl and walked around bouncing the child and cooing whispers of comfort.

Mitch announced, "Visiting hours will be over in ten minutes."

Secora glanced intently at both men then hurried to the open elevator. "Thanks," she called back in their direction.

The light was off in his room, but there was enough light coming through the open door. She entered cautiously as if awaiting permission.

When she stood about two feet away, she noticed tears slipping from Gideon's closed eyes.

"Gideon?"

His eyes opened then brightened as he looked at her.

She smiled and sat beside him. He lifted his hand toward his ear, and she nodded. A nurse knocked on the door, distracting Secora momentarily, as she adjusted the IV, and left.

Secora half stood so she could lean over and kiss Gideon's cheek. He put his elbow around her neck and pulled her in for a kiss even though there was goop all over his damaged lips. She resisted slightly, and he dropped his arm.

"You know, I uh, prefer to keep my distance in these situations, right?"

"Chastity, I know. See how far that got you last time?"

The words felt like a punch as she remembered that she and Diego had never kissed. She seated herself and cradled Gideon's face in her left hand.

His eyes were still moist. "I think I've loved you since... well, even before I met you. When the Great Thunderbird first told me to find you, I knew we were meant to be together."

"I remember," replied Secora, her heart surging with adrenaline as she watched him wipe tears of frustration from his face.

Gideon looked nervous but steeled in his conviction. "I love you," he said firmly.

Secora nodded as she opened a little scrap of paper she had taken from her purse and held it up so he could see the words, "Me too, Heyoka." She laid the note on his chest.

For precious moments, they smiled tears of joy. Secora could feel the intensity of their smiles grow until she was grinning.

The nurse ended the link when she came to ask Secora to leave. Gideon reached out for a hug. When she was close, he said, "This time, don't fly away."

As she turned to exit, she said, "Gideon, if I do, you know I'll always fly back, even if I'm not quite ready to nest."

His face caught in a half-smile, registering a partial win.

"I definitely care. I have feelings to process, but without question, I do love you." She was grinning as she left the room, and she noticed Gideon's eyes quietly followed her.

As Secora was rousing rom a brief nap in the waiting room, Jeannie was vibrant as she greeted her. "Guess what?"

Little Monta was smiling in her arms as Mitch strode up beside them. His frantic arms betrayed his excitement as he prepared to speak.

"What is it?" Secora asked, taking the baby.

Mitch couldn't wait to spill. "They're discharging Gideon." Jeannie added, "Wahoo!"

"He's able to stand and walk, eat, and everything. But he must take extra care of the frostbitten areas. He can hear even better if you talk close to his ears. But... you already knew that, right?" He winked at Secora.

She smiled and looked down. "Where's Jimmy, and Gideon's family?" she asked. "They're gonna want to hear this."

"They're in his room," said Jeannie. "Let's go see them."

On the way, Secora asked, "Do you think he'll go back to South Dakota right away or stay in Missoula?"

Jeannie grinned as she answered, "We've rented an apartment for him and Jimmy, and we'll be able to monitor his progress from the office."

Secora and Monta swooped into the room as Gideon was fixing his belt and beginning to run a comb gingerly through his hair.

"Hey, Heyoka, great to see you dressed and upright." Secora walked directly to him and hugged him to the best of her ability, with Gideon having to help hold the little one with only his wrists and arms during the process. Secora knew his fingers must be burning with pain. Maybe not, she hoped. "Can you use your hands?"

He shook his head. "Not very well." She and the little girl sat in a chair behind him.

Gideon turned toward her and appeared to pout as he continued, "Everyone says you've been seeing Jake Landsing."

Secora was puzzled and said nothing as she thought about his words.

"How do you know him?" Gideon's words sounded too loud because of the deafness.

Secora squinted back, looking as if she'd smelled a Bigfoot. "I don't think so. Who is Jake Landsing?"

"The caretaker of the Hasan property."

"Well how in the world would I know him? She shook her head in confusion. "Don't know any Jake."

"You know the other guy who was found with me—the one with all the heart attacks."

Recognition grew in her eyes. "Ohhh, Billy. How long did he work for Mr. Hasan?"

"He said he'd been there a couple of days, but he seemed quite capable. In fact, he was the one who first noticed the lake water was gone."

"Interesting, I know him as Billy Riggins. You remember. He's been missing since he was attacked a little over a week ago while we were talking."

After that sunk in, Gideon was astonished. "You're kidding—the same guy?" Everyone else considered the information in silence. "He was wearing a sling on his right arm. I had no idea."

Secora was thoughtful. "Yeah, I might never have known it was him, but he came to me in a dream at the motel, thanking me for finding him. I assumed he'd passed away and was saying goodbye, but I guess he could have had an out-of-body experience during one of the heart attacks."

Jeannie said, "How did you put two and two together?"

Secora cocked her head to the side and said, "I asked about the third man at the unit desk; they said they didn't know his identity and had listed him as a John Doe. On a hunch, I called the sheriff, who went with me to see if I could identify him. It was hard to say with all the bandages and no hair, but when I mentioned his mammoth dig—his turquoise eyes lit up."

Secora watched as Mr. Hasan and a three-man entourage squeezed in at the door. She returned her attention to Gideon as he spoke.

"That reminds me of something that murdering bastard said on the mountain." Gideon's eyes turned black as he watched Mr. Hasan, who had stopped short at the vehemence in his voice. Gideon's whole body shook as he continued. "He said he was killing all of us because Jake took an object from the boss' property. Then Jake said he never stole anything from anyone—not since second grade." Gideon was still glaring at Mr. Hasan, demanding an answer, "What does that mean? Would you kill your own son?"

Secora felt like a deer in headlights. Shocked not only about Gideon's accusation; but trying to think about what alternative—the assailant's words might in fact describe.

Mitch turned to the tall man and asked, "What could he have possibly done that would make you so crazy with anger, Mr. Hasan?"

Jamal drew back in horror and dismay. When he found his voice, he said roughly, "Excuse me, what are you saying? You think I did this? Are you crazy?" Every eye in the room was staring at him, except Secora's. She was still thinking.

"I love my son." His voice cracked, and he broke down crying. When he could speak again, he continued, "I had no complaints about theft, except for the water. Was Landsing responsible for that? I think not." He shook his head. "Never mind. It doesn't matter. Even if he was responsible, I would not kill him."

Secora sat wordlessly a moment longer then slowly drew another possible path from the words. "The man you hired as Jake Landsing is a renowned paleontologist named Billy Riggins. Before you hired him, he was completing a mammoth dig on a site in western Washington. Certainly, he would have obtained a signed permit for that excavation with the property owner's name on it. He'd already been working there for over a month with no interruptions or complaints. Yet..."

Mitch was beginning to connect the dots. "If *that* property owner had a problem..."

Secora nodded. "Out of the blue, Billy called me. He was in trouble. I was on the phone with him when he was viciously attacked by a man who beat him with a shovel. Gideon was with me; he heard it too." She looked up into Gideon's brown eyes for confirmation. The solemn Lakota nodded.

"I went to Birch Bay immediately, but Billy had vanished after the attack. I thought he was dead, but apparently the incident left him fleeing for his life, with several injuries, including a broken arm."

Mr. Hasan confirmed, "The man I hired did mention he had a broken arm, but he sounded like it wouldn't be an issue. And, Allah be praised, it should not have been!"

Secora nodded. "Until today, I thought he'd been killed since I never heard from him again. It was completely frustrating because I never found his body, his pickup, or his mule, Carrots. I wasn't even able to find the human skeleton he was alluding to in his excitement. But such a backlash never made sense. He was very professional and very respectful with the site."

Mitch inquired, "It might have been his practice, but how would you know he was respectful at that particular site?"

"Good question, Mitch. I know because I went there myself and completely followed up on his work, trying to find answers."

"You went there alone?" Jeannie disapproved.

"Yes, Monta and I left immediately to go to western Washington..."

"Oh, even better, young lady." Now Jeannie was beside herself.

Secora continued, "I didn't know the outcome of the attack, but I figured he was either badly injured or dead. While I was there, I poked through the whole dig, looking for clues. I was hoping to help him, but I guess Billy was able to escape on his own."

Mitch stepped in, placing his right index and middle finger to his forehead, as he said, "He was rightfully feeling paranoid and thought no one would ever find him on your remote northern Montana property, Mr. Hasan. Guess I owe you a big apology."

"Yet, a murderer did find him, and my son is dead," he replied coldly.

Everyone went quiet again.

Secora took the opportunity to begin a Baha'i prayer for the departed.

"O my God! O Thou forgiver of sins, bestower of gifts, dispeller
of afflictions! Verily, I beseech thee to forgive the sins of
such as have abandoned the physical garment and have
ascended to the spiritual world.
O my Lord! Purify them from trespasses, dispel their sorrows,
and change their darkness into light. Cause them to enter
the garden of happiness, cleanse them with the most pure water,
and grant them to behold Thy splendors on the loftiest mount."

As was his way, Jimmy raised the pipe and a voice for transition assistance in Kamal's name when she was finished.

Jamal Hasan was visibly moved. With bloodshot eyes, he thanked Secora and apologized to everyone before departing with his men. There was a brief discussion in Arabic outside of the room, and then they returned. Jamal looked at his shoes.

"My colleagues wonder what else Mr. Yellow Thunder can tell them."

"That crazy man with the dead green eyes, started to shoot at the three of us down by the drained lake. We hid from him in a shed. The dog inadvertently led him to us and..." Gideon teared up and was unable to continue.

Jimmy carried on with the tale about the fight, the dog's injury, and Kamal's wound. With an occasional nod from Gideon, he told how they were forced to climb the mountain, run into the mine with Kamal, where they all suffered, and nearly perished.

Gideon added, "I hope it helps you to know that your brave and kind son took his final breath among new friends".

After several minutes of perfect quiet which united everyone in the room, Mitch began to pace and wonder out loud, "How does either of these attacks even make sense? Was there a reason?"

"Weirder still," Secora interjected, "it wasn't the burly man who attacked Billy at the dig site, he was already in jail at the time, detained because he'd chased and tried to attack me too – all the way to the police station. So, the one who hurt Kamal, Gideon, and "Jake" had to be a totally different guy."

Later on, the entire company was visiting in the waiting room while Gideon was speaking with the doctor about his being released.

"One moment, Ms. James." Hasan uncrossed his arms and stepped forward. "What could the owner of the mammoth site consider valuable enough to kill for?"

"No idea, really." Secora thought for a moment and shook her head. "Billy would have taken samples and collected artifacts as usual, but there would have been permission granted, and they would have agreed on the disposition of the collection."

Mitch pitched in, "So, Billy was well respected?"

Secora nodded. "Of course but there was one extraordinary find. I dug up some artifact samples he had cached on-site, and I followed up on Billy's lab findings. It became clear to me this was a bizarre discovery. It was a fluke. But it's highly unlikely anyone would have appreciated the results, except a digger who thinks like Billy, or me."

"How so?"

"Because... there was a human burial associated with bones from this particular young mammoth. They appeared to be purposely entombed together in a ceremony after the man's death. Dates from the lab verified the deceased was buried over seven thousand years too soon. Too soon, that is, for early humans to live in America according to the accepted archaeological standard.

"So, Billy's work was either wrong, and I asked the techs to double-check the dates for both the animal and the man, or a *very* controversial find. Either way, what would that matter to the property owner? Besides, Billy told no one until he called me in the middle of the attack —and even then, his words wouldn't have raised anyone's eyebrows."

Mitch cut in, "None of this makes sense. Who stands to gain from this? Why should anyone be attacked or killed over bones—however old?"

"Funny you should say that," announced Gideon. "We were actually shot at when Jake, I mean Billy, picked up a huge human pelvic bone from newly exposed mud at the lake site. The first bullet blasted the bone to dust."

"Seems clear Billy needs a safer occupation," Mitch commented with a fleeting grin.

Secora moved her head slowly from side to side. "I'm mystified." She became quiet as she remembered her own attack and the dread she'd been feeling since.

Hasan was staring at her very intently. "Then you are in danger, as well, young lady. Do you not worry for your own life, and that of your child?"

She turned to face the bereaved father. "It's like you're reading my mind." She shivered. "There was an attack when I was out at Birch Bay. I noticed a burly guy watching me with binoculars, and when I tried to drive past him, it became a race to the police station."

Jeannie caught her breath, and she and Mitch shouted simultaneously, "What?"

"In the end, he came after us, right *into* the police station and I knocked him onto his backside. The clerk had no idea what happened. In the end, he was jailed for assault and suspicion he had knowledge of the disappearance of Billy Riggins."

Agent Toliver, One of Mr. Hasan's plain clothed companions introduced himself and said, "Apparently, you're able to look out for yourself. But a bullet would have cut all of that short for you—or the baby."

Secora shifted to a standing position. "I need to return home. Maybe my friends here will be safer if I do."

The agent said, "Looks like all we'll have to do, is follow you and Mr. Riggins to find out what's going on."

Jeannie stated, "Mister, if you're trying to make everyone paranoid...it's working."

Secora became thoughtful again. "I know of one man, who would hate the results of the dig, but there's no way he or anyone else could have known about it - only Billy, and now me."

Agent Toliver locked eyes with her. "...And now all of us." He reached out and shook her

hand. "We'll be in touch."

Before he or anyone else could leave, a nurse came out of the unit with Gideon in a wheelchair and discharge papers, and they led the group out the hospital door. Everyone took the opportunity to share hugs and joy at his release. Jeannie and Mitch stood to give Secora great big hugs, while Jimmy stood and shook her available hand. "Hetchetu aloh, Kimimila." She hugged him for an extended moment.

"So, I'm not Sloth Woman anymore? I've descended to the station of butterfly?" Jimmy laughed. "Take it however you want."

Gideon reached up to her. "I need one of those hugs."

Mitch joked, "Oh look, two cripples and a baby hugging it out." Afterward, Secora stepped back. She and Gideon regarded each other shyly. She couldn't quite wipe the tears in her eyes, but Jeannie grabbed Monta's t-shirt and dabbed them for her.

"I really can't thank you enough, Jeannie... for everything."

"My pleasure." Now she dabbed her own eyes with Monta's shirt.

Monta smiled at the adults' funny behavior.

"Well, friends, it's late and I need to drive back to the university, not to mention Monta and I need fresh supplies," Secora laughed.

Gideon nodded and smiled, shyly. "I'll see you there."

"Maybe." She winked and started to leave, then turned back. "You know I have this satellite phone now. Hope everyone has me on speed dial."

Agent Toliver said, "We'll be at your apartment by 6 a.m."

"Way to take the fun out of goodbye." Secora laughed.

Toliver said, "Wait a minute. I can drive you since Jimmy will be taking Gideon, and you don't have a vehicle."

Before Secora could answer, Jeannie said, "That's a generous thought, Agent Toliver. Mitch and I have room in our car, and I really don't want to let that baby out of my sight."

"Thanks anyway, I'll see you bright and early." Secora waved and warily walked with Monta and the others to the parking lot to begin the lengthy trip home.

Jimmy hollered from his pickup, "Don't worry about Heyoka, Sloth Girl. I'll keep eyes on him."

"That's, Kimimila," she shouted nonchalantly without turning back.

16

PERUVIAN GUEROS

G ray mist swirled over the Peruvian mountains but cleared by noon, revealing dark patches of foliage punctuated with beautiful flowers and showy avians whose voices immediately filled the air with raucous songs. Gilgamesh Spitama flowed through the abundant vegetation. His movements were smooth, like those of a reptile. He was not alone. Several other holy healers from four local villages were on an herb gathering expedition. There had been an outbreak of a disease which caused painful rashes, vomiting, and in some cases, the victims were not expected to live.

Moments ago, rain had drenched the forest beneath the clouds, and he heard the tick, tick, tick of water spattering the leaves around them. Still, they made their way confidently through the lush forest growth, purposefully bending down to collect the roots of a small ground orchid that could help with the pain and nausea.

As they did so, Gilgamesh cocked his head. He thought he could hear unintelligible voices in the distance, and it surprised him because he was not expecting to find any people in this area of the watershed.

He signaled his companions with gestures indicating they were not alone and should be alert to possible trouble. There were eleven men and women who quietly awaited his guidance as breezes wafted their flowing off-white tunics which were bound around their waists with colorful hand-woven sashes. One of the men kicked at a snake with the toe turned up at the tip of a leather shoe, fashioned to protect one's feet and ankles from scratchy brush, snakes, and thorns.

The Guero people were strikingly tall and graceful. Their skin was pale, and they had unusual gray or hazel eyes. Several wore their ash blond or light brown hair in braids that wouldn't catch easily on the trees. Flowing reddish beards, like the handwoven cloth of their garments, undulated in the soft breezes. The gray eyes of the women adorned beautiful faces, concealing their strength and cleverness.

"I want to know who these people are and why they are in our forest before we move forward," Gilgamesh whispered. He struck out for the rocky outcrop above their heads, where he could look down the valley on the other side of the hill, to find out what was happening below.

Two men asked to accompany him. After thinking over this request and rubbing his brow with the back of his hand—his palm being soiled by the dirt of digging the roots—he asked the two men and two of the women to stay with him, "The others should return immediately to give the medicine to our ailing villagers. Please leave us three of the balsa boats at the river." Those who remained with Gilgamesh gave their medicine bags to companions leaving for home. They obeyed and silently left the area.

As Gilgamesh and the others reached the top of the rocky ridge, the chattering became clearer. He and the other medicine seekers crouched down to avoid detection. He crept as close as he deemed wise. The only thing that moved was a gray and white feather tied in his hair. From this elevated vantage, the voices were near enough to make goosebumps rise on his bangled arms. Squatting even lower, he peered down through the underbrush covering a slight cliff that fell away thirty feet below him. The others joined him in silent observation. Between the slopes of the valley, they saw a dozen young women and men. Many were speaking excitedly about a significant find at the base of the very stone wall above which Gilgamesh and his group squatted.

Even though he listened intently, Gilgamesh could understand none of the words and couldn't make sense of any of the actions. His eyes engaged each of the devout beings who chose to accompany him. "Aparu?"

One of them nodded, "Anglish," he softly answered.

On closer inspection, Gilgamesh noticed two women on their hands and knees carefully removing layers of soil and rock at the base of the short cliff. He pulled thoughtfully on his red mustache. The others seemed mesmerized as they tried to understand the activity below. They were watchful because art in this region was carved into these stones by their ancient predecessors. He answered in a whisper, "It looks as if they are taking an interest in the stonework of our people." Everyone pulled back as they considered their options. Should they talk to the strangers, try to chase them away, or continue with medicine collection?

Iris and Jane knelt at the base of a finely carved Chachapoya frieze carved into the thirty-foot cliff. Jungle undergrowth still hung over the upper end of a stone tablet. Iris was carefully scraping soil away from the base of the object. As her gentle strokes revealed more of the frieze, it became clear the stone had been buried beneath accumulated dirt and detritus for quite a while. The subsoil portion still retained a bit of color, which gave the carved impressions better definition.

"I suppose what you say is true enough, Jane. But this whole South American trip idea was originally Secora's. We should have stayed home and worked on the Heyoka project, now that we know one."

Kyah, Jane's slender thirteen-year-old son, appeared to be listening intently. He commented, "Uncle Gideon is the only actual Heyoka we know." Nobody cared to answer him.

Jane stated emphatically, "You are in a bad mood, Iris! That's usually my specialty. I think Secora would be surprised that you blamed her for this, don't you? Besides, I don't think Gideon considers himself, heyoka—at least not like the great visionary, Black Elk."

Iris returned to scraping soil. "We could have taken the ethnological stance of 'The Making of a Contrary Warrior.'"

Both women were now on their hands and knees, carefully removing tiny layers of soil and rock while students recorded depths and photographed the various discoveries around the camp.

Iris took a slightly dirty finger out of her work glove and scratched her head. "Guess I'm still anxious about the safety of the Duendes, now that they've been 'discovered'." A moment later she admitted, "Maybe you're right in thinking I should stop blaming Secora."

"Really." Jane rested an arm on her knee and looked over at her sister-friend. "Don't stress, girl, because we can't play God. Do you remember Secora telling us last summer she didn't have the power to save anyone she cared about? Not Rick, not the Arauque hunters, or even Diego, no matter how amazing he was."

"And she very nearly lost Gideon on Massacre Mountain."

"Yeah, I know. And don't forget, she almost lost her own life. We need to take what is handed to us and make the best of those circumstances."

Jane stopped talking as a trickle of dirt and moss fell around her from the clifftop. She swept dirt from the back of her neck and scrunched her face into the sun's glare, scrutinizing the jungle above.

Iris stopped working and looked toward Jane. She noticed some of the dirt had fallen on Jane's neat, dark braids and blue beaded earrings. She reached to dust it off with her fingers and said, "I'm hoping this Chachapoya study will go well enough that we can use the findings for your thesis. I can also publish an article from this material, and then we can leave the Duendes alone."

"Ah, I see, we can't hurt the Chachapoyas—because they're already extinct." Jane rubbed her nose and looked at Iris. "By the way, there's a worm dangling from one of your curls."

Gilgamesh pulled back from the rim a few yards so he and his friends could talk.

Aparu said in his graceful language, "I think I'm in love."

"Me too—the girl with the golden hair," sighed Kantun. "No, the one with dark hair," countered Aparu.

Sarai, a middle-aged grandmother, whispered, "Idiots."

"What is wrong with you?" asked Gilgamesh, shaking his head in disbelief. The two men didn't know how to respond.

Iris smiled sardonically, her lip curled in a smirk as she placed the worm back into the soil. Then, she stood, fixing Jane with a stare. "Jealous?" She chuckled and walked over to join two students who were screening and scrutinizing the back-dirt she and Jane had been sending their way.

"Finding any charcoal or anything?" she asked.

Mariah, a young woman with flossy light brown hair was busily bagging and marking the resultant samples. She tossed the newest bag in a bin for future testing or reference before sifting through a new pile of debris.

"Not really."

Iris took her eyes away from the soil screening activity. "But in the meantime, here we sit, sweltering on this rock pile while Secora is doing, what?"

"Pipe down, Iris! I realize you miss your sister, and you almost lost her..."

Iris cut in, "She pretty much raised me, you know."

"Yes, I know, but this place really isn't so bad." Jane ambled back to the stone they were uncovering at the cliff base. She knelt and continued, "I've never been on a dig that offered up anything more than the rare charcoal pit or the occasional bead up to now."

Iris rubbed her nose with a muddy finger which left another streak, causing Jane to suppress a snicker.

"Secora managed to blow off our farewell lunch, didn't she? I don't think she cares now that she has that baby."

"In her defense, she was trying to save a fellow mammoth hunter at the time."

"She's probably out chasing down another two-bit side job, or still mooning over Diego and the Thunderbird incident."

"Look, Iris, that's enough. She and Gideon nearly died in that battle." Jane leaned in toward the basalt rock and purposefully drew her fingers across the stone slab, tracing the faded lines of an image. "Hey, speaking of thunderbirds, what is this rock thing turning into? A figure maybe, what do you think?"

Iris leaned in. "Not sure." Her fingers also began searching the rock for depressions the eyes couldn't easily see. "It does feel like there may be the shape of wings, doesn't it?"

"It does. We aren't far from Condor Lake. Maybe it's a condor?"
"Yeah possibly, but Jane, wouldn't you expect the condor to be a masked deity?"

"Well, there's no mask. Just the opposite, it has a human face with the bird's wings."

Iris seemed surprised. "I'm struck by the shape. They remind me of the Egyptian Falcon's wings, or the wings of Isis, or the angels on the Ark of the Covenant. Different from anything we've seen out here this far."

"What the heck! Is this a skirt, or a tail?" Jane continued to brush the dirt and gravel away from the wall fragment in precisely controlled increments.

Iris became animated and focused. "Maybe a skirt... or maybe both, huh, and there are shoes! Not just any shoes. They have upturned toes. This reminds me of a Zoroastrian Farvahar."

"Or, Iris, maybe it's a condor wearing Dr. Denton's PJs. How can you tell?"

"Jane, have you ever seen a Farvahar—it's a representation of the essence of the great Prophet, Zoroaster?"

Jane wagged her head, as did Mariah who had stepped over.

"It's kind of a cross between a man and a falcon. The legs are encircled with a ring sometimes depicted as a serpent. Heaven and earth—like with Quetzalcoatl the 'Feathered Serpent' hence the tail-robe."

Iris stood with her hands on her hips. Could you take the dirt back a little further on your side, Jane?"

"Why of course, my liege."

"Did you know that the Prophet, who came to Bolivia and Peru, actually lived during the same vague era as Zoroaster?"

"I did not, Iris. Do you think there could be a connection?"

Iris nodded. "I do, and my father certainly did. As you know there were several great civilizations prior to the reign of the Incas. However, until recently their vestiges were swallowed by mists of time and decay. Back then, their virtuous Lord was referred to by a flurry of names. In Peru and Bolivia, he was called Viracocha, meaning 'light as the sea foam,' and also, 'Hyustus.'"

"And you actually suppose he could also be the guy who was known as Quetzalcoatl?" asked Mariah.

"Interesting question, because that name was used up further north, and at a later time. During their reign, the Inca described one they knew as Viracocha with reverence. Declaring He and His companions were fair skinned. Several had red-gold hair and beards, and blue or hazel eyes. Thor Heyerdahl said Viracocha had long ears, as did some of the flat-headed people with him. Coincidently, high-born people of the Middle East had long ears in those days due to the custom of wearing spools, as with Zoroaster and Buddha.

"Anyway, the people here dressed in tunics, and their hair was topped with a cap. At times, the head covering was depicted as having four corner points; elsewhere it was portrayed as a two-tiered hat. The accounts varied, but there were hats, and you'll see the long earlobes in the Incan depictions."

Jane smiled. "You must not be mad anymore, Iris. Your eyes are shining."

"Ya think? This find is potentially huge, Jane."

Jane thought for a moment. If Iris is this stoked... we need to document everything. Though half of the students were on lunch break, Jane started pulling students in to work on this one piece.

"Hey, Bruce!" She gestured to the photographer who was protecting his red-freckled face from the sun with a scarf. "Come over here and get some shots of this, will you?"

Then Iris spoke to everybody else. "It's time to trade places, the five of you who were on lunch, back to work. Be very careful when you take down the dirt around this section of the wall. The rest of you can take your break."

Grudgingly, half of the crew acknowledged the end of lunch and ambled over to the wall, while the other half were relieved to sit.

Jane said, "Thanh and Sarbjeet, I want you to be careful when you record this section. Dr. Dalton thinks we might have found a very special and ancient feature."

Iris added, "I'd also like to see a twenty-four-inch trench opened in front of the engraved figure. We expect an altar. Keep your eyes peeled for any changes in the soil. If you find something juicy, give Jane or me a call, okay?"

Thanh answered with his strong Vietnamese accent. "Right away, you want the dirt screened and sampled?"

Iris nodded and turned to Jane, who was suggesting to a girl with a wide smear of zinc oxide on her nose, "Amy, map the figure for us, please. You may have to feel some of the lines, it helps."

"Yes, ma'am, I'm on it."

Iris sighed with relief. Jane said, "This is what it's all about."

17

OF WORMS AND ALWOOD

It was their turn for lunch. The two women wandered over to the piece of ground that served as a kitchen. Iris yawned and Jane stretched as they flipped open the lid and dug through the ice chest which perched on a mossy boulder. "Ice chest," was a euphemism—nothing inside it was cool.

"Okay, wise guys. Who brought the beer? Better own up!" Jane held up a ring of three cans. "Anyone claim these?"

Everyone acted innocent. Iris reached past the beers and grabbed two sodas. Handing one to Jane, she popped the top on the other. Jane still had no takers, so she dropped the beer cans to the ground. "Okay, we'll have a sacrificial ritual for this grain beverage in about fifteen minutes. Everyone should wear their Sunday best."

Iris ignored Jane and bit into her snack crackers with cheese, then a sip of pop as she watched Sarbjeet and Thanh excavate the base of the wall. Jane sat on a rock to eat her sandwich and sip a Coke. The teens appeared to be joking and discussing the birdman figure, but then they became quiet. She rose and left with her sandwich to walk along the little cliff as she ate. Once she reached the rock, she felt the imperative urge to look up to the hill above the rock face, but when she looked; nothing moved or otherwise grabbed her attention. She hesitated another moment because the feeling was so overpowering. Still no sounds, nothing moved. She sighed and moved her eyes to the birdman.

"Hey, Iris, you should come here." She pointed with a twist of her chin in the direction of the wall. Iris seemed to consider the request but remained seated with her lunch.

"My muscles feel too stiff to move."

But curiosity overcame her weariness when Jane said, "Take a look at this." She was pointing at something dark near the base of the figure. She scraped the toe of her boot for emphasis.

Iris finished her bite as she joined Jane. Then the two of them knelt beside the students who were gently removing dirt with a trowel and brush.

Iris inspected the dark, flat basalt stone. "Hey, Amy, what do you think this is?"

Amy thought and answered. "I think it will turn out to be some sort of grinding stone."

Iris pointed. "Could be, yeah. What about the carbonized smears in the depression?"

Amy ventured, "Roots or charcoal?"

Bruce commented, "I think it is charcoal."

Iris focused. "Back off, everyone, let's get samples from the surface of the stone—and some photographs! Over here with the cameras please."

Iris, also, grabbed a video camera. "Keep samples of the dirt all around this thing; I think we might have an altar stone here." She panned the location.

Jane looked intently at Iris. "Could it really be an altar?"

"Naah, probably not! It would be unlikely to find such a thing still here, but it's worth a look." She called out to the others, "Hey kids, let's find out what was on the 'barby'."

Jane asked, "Sammy, can you make a notation of this stone's position in the grid?"

Among Sammy's favorite shirts was the one he wore now. It featured a trowel, with the caption, *I dig your bones.* "Your wish is my command!" The spiky-haired sophomore made his way to the plane table.

Jane called her son over. "Hey, Kyah, draw this feature in on the map, will you please?" The rest of the work stopped except for the action around the altar area.

"This could be important!" Really, really, important! Iris was getting excited, "We should

fax these pictures back with the weekly notes this afternoon. I wish Professor Dalton was here."

"You mean your father, Dr. Dalton?"

"My mother," Iris snickered. "Easy to confuse them."

Jane's attention was once again drawn to the hill above the place where she and Iris had crouched earlier. She stood tall and watched as Kyah started to walk in her direction, his eyes also scanning the hill.

"I can't see anything, Mom, but I smell a faint perfume."

"Me too." Jane closed her eyes and switched to her other senses. There was a warm pungent scent, not unlike sandalwood. "But it disappeared almost instantly."

"What's up, Mom? What is that perfume smell?"

She waited a moment longer, but there was nothing more. "I'm not sure."

Mariah came to join the two, also sniffing the air. "I've been feeling something too. Maybe it's nothing."

Jane stretched her stiffening legs. "Keep your eyes peeled, Mariah. I have a feeling; things are about to change."

. . .

Gilgamesh had seen enough. He gestured for his companions to turn around and leave. When they were partway down the back of the hillside he said, "Aside from bewitching these two men with thoughts of passion, I don't think they mean us or the stones any harm, so let's go."

They continued toward the valley in single file, but as they walked, all the forest sounds quieted, and then disappeared altogether.

Aparu said, "Wait, something's wrong."

"I hate to admit it," Sarai said, "but I agree."

Iris breathed deep as she came to stand beside Jane. "Do you smell cigarette smoke from across the meadow?"

Warily scanning the tree line, her senses on alert, Jane nodded and turned her head away from the cliff, "I guess I do." She then returned her gaze to the hill above the wall, still nothing.

She spoke sharply, "Heads up everybody! Something is going on."

Everyone in the crew ran toward the older adults.

The robed healers returned at the sound of alarm in Jane's voice, and once again, peeked out from the brush atop the cliff wall at the two women and the children. Unexpectedly, Gilgamesh noticed the woman with long dark braids turn her head and look in his direction.

His eyes snapped to the forest beyond the meadow. Guerillas burdened with rifles were creeping low in the grass, apparently intent on surprising and containing the crew. Aparu and Kantun gestured excitedly, their attentions riveted on the approaching danger. They pointed and whispered.

Several of the girls couldn't help but scream as they spied the seven camo-clad men entering the clearing and moving quickly toward them, hunched over with rifles at the ready. The leader signaled his men to encircle the students. Fanning into an arc, the predators closed in pressing their quarry against the wall.

In a dialect understood by Gilgamesh and the others, one of the aggressors, perhaps the leader, asked, "What are you doing here?"

There was no answer from the two women who appeared to be overseeing the younger ones.

The man continued, "So, maybe these are the students from Norte America, trying to prove white supremacy or something stupid." There were a few snickers from the other men.

"Should we kill them now? Or find out if their parents are rich?"

Another man answered, "Maybe both?"

This time there was laughter, and then they raised their guns as if to shoot.

The healers, though they had no weapons, raised their own startling cry of alarm, yelling, "Ur Mazd! Ur Mazd!" This caught the guerillas and students, completely off guard.

There was an immediate answer from the assault rifles as bullets shattered across the hill above the glade, flushing birds from hidden bowers.

Screams erupted from the surprised teenagers, who covered their faces or hit the dirt. The guerrillas roughly rounded up both the archaeology crew and the five robed healers who appeared as if from nowhere.

The man in charge shouted in broken Spanish, "All right everyone, I am Juan Quintos, and this is my elite force." He pointed to his soldiers. Then he continued shouting at the students, whom he referred to as "Gringos," and to the robed ones, as "Gueros."

The students stared at the robed people in awe, wondering how and why they came to be part of the group.

Jane's heart immediately went out to her son, but she made no move that would specifically identify Kyah. She sniffed the man who was now next to her and caught the scent of sandalwood. Kyah noticed and grinned slightly.

There had been little time for the archaeology research team to react, but Iris had unobtrusively kicked loose soil and moss over the controversial artifact near the rock wall. She was afraid these or other roving looters might simply rip it out and try to sell it. One of the Guero men moved beside Iris and assisted her effort. Meanwhile, the gunmen found the beer, looted the camp, and ransacked the tents and tables. They made the captives carry anything they deemed valuable and threw the rest into the fire pit. Hungry flames laughed at the notes, maps, and other offerings, as the humans departed.

18

CONTACT LOST

On the way out of the Kalispell Regional Medical Center in Jeannie's SUV, Secora was delayed at by the two agents. "One last question, please."

"I told you what I know, and you have my contact information," Secora said patiently.

"We'd like to know more about what happened between Glen Greenbriar and Gideon."

"Glen was Gideon's real estate mentor, but as he neared retirement, he turned greedy. He delved into human trafficking, slavery, and murder. He tried to kill Gideon and me—several times. And, in the end, he was eaten by a teratorn. Is that somehow relevant?"

"We're just being thorough. We'll see you in the morning. Hopefully, you will recall other details of the sad events at the Hasan Property. Oh, *what* is a teratorn?"

Secora paused, "A giant carnivorous bird. One weird thing I noticed was that there were three vehicles when we arrived at the Hasan Resort. One of them had very little snow on it, so it probably had been driven recently. Jimmy and I thoroughly searched the house and yard before moving up the trail towards the cave. When we returned there were only two vehicles. Someone, the culprit perhaps, passed us unseen and left. You might try looking for outlying tracks."

You mean, the Cherokee, SUV?"

"Perhaps Jimmy, I mean, Mr. Lizardeye might remember. I'm not sure if it came up the road – or from another place, by the mountain for instance. I'm not interested in cars and didn't notice defining details. Also, how about you call me rather than come over so early? Monta and I are pretty tired, and I imagine you are as well."

"Yes Ma'am, see you at 6 a.m. sharp."

The next evening, after fielding more questions from Agent Toliver, and a brief call to Gideon who was feeling the pains of his ordeal, Secora finished up a busy day of work. She fed the baby who fell asleep while eating; leaving her mother again wishing there was a friend with whom she could chat. The loneliness inspired her to look at her personal emails, a task she undertook at least semi-annually, and there, a surprise awaited her.

It was a file containing twenty-odd shots of Riggins' mammoth site. There were close-ups of a skeleton and a number of the startling relics in the burial; and one of Carrots, with her rear leg cocked and ears laid back. The photos, along with all the other evidence Secora had already accumulated, made an outstanding case for Billy's find.

Billy must have sent them directly from the site to my personal email, somehow. *Via his cell phone, amazing!* Then a more chilling thought crossed her mind: Could anyone else open my email and see these pictures? Then it crystalized—was a data transfer interception how someone found out about Billy's taboo site in the first place?

Anida and her son Frederick came by early the next day to watch Monta, allowing Secora to slide into her desk by 7:30 a.m. She was greeted by a typed memo which she found taped to her jumbled desk—a note about a missing archeological crew.

Secora reread the words. She was officially being notified that the university had lost contact with the research crew led by Iris Snowden and her assistant, Jane Roanhorse, while they were excavating a suspected Chachapoya site called Ojo Redondo in Las Yungas. Secora saw in her mind's eye, the warm eastern slopes of the La Paz region of the Peruvian Cordillera Real.

A faxed note was attached to the memo from the Peruvian National Antiquities Foundation, dated January 1st. It read:

To those it may concern:

We deeply regret to inform you we have lost all contact with the members of the archeological team sent to Ojo Redondo by the University of Montana. We have sent a tracking party to look for them. However, they found nothing of interest. It could be that they fell victims to a group of culture terrorists who have begun to plague some well-known archaeological sites.

It may be possible that the crew has returned early from their explorations. If so, we would appreciate an immediate notification if you have an update. And we would also like to remind you that all prehistoric artifacts are to remain in Peru.

Thank You.

Sincerely, Paulo Angelo Rodrigues De la Mar

"What?" Secora roared as Tarkio entered the office.

"Whoa there... a little loud, don't you think?"

Stunned, she handed him the memo.

"Dang, you're kidding!" he exclaimed. "Interesting timeline sequence."

"What are you talking about?"

"Well, first your paleontologist friend was beaten up and disappeared. Then your cool buddy—pun intended—Mr. Yellow Thunder was turned into a Popsicle, and his client is murdered... and now this. I'm beginning to reconsider my decision to share an office with you."

She sadly looked down. "Whatever, you're not wrong."

"Luckily, I'm a bit of a mystery buff, if you can't tell."

"That makes one of us," she groaned and pivoted to leave the office. "I need to go over to the Anthro Department and find out what's going on."

Secora trotted across campus to the Anthropology office. Soon, the secretary was telling her, incredibly, that Iris, Jane, and the ten students affiliated with this project had not been heard from for over thirty hours. Their rooms had been left empty. The desk at the motel had no clues to offer.

Tarkio pulled up out of breath to join the melee.

Secora slapped the letter with the back of her hand, and the secretary cringed. "What the heck is this load of bull?"

The Anthropology Department Chair, Dr. Edward Savage, stepped smartly from behind the secretary's desk and approached the irate woman. "What's up, Ms. James? Can I help?"

Her eyes glittered with anger. "I certainly hope so! Who does this De La Mar fool think he is? Iris, Jane, and the kids are missing!"

"Please, Secora," he calmed. "The American Embassy in..."

"You know he's stonewalling! He has no intention of helping them. What..." her voice softened as she became more vulnerable. "What are we going to do? Cripes! My sister's missing and from all appearances—has been for nearly three days!" She felt her heart sink. What should I do first? Who can I contact? How fast can I fly down there?

Savage tried a different approach. "Am I correct in assuming you will be traveling to Peru?"

"Do you have to ask?"

He reached for the inside pocket of his tweed jacket and pulled out a packet which he slapped into her palm.

"Here are tickets. Return is in one week." He stretched an arm to the dot matrix printer and retrieved two inches of printed pages. "These are copies of all the progress reports Jane and Iris sent me before the disappearance. There might be information there you can use to pick up their trail."

Secora's shocked stare turned into a grin as she received them. She put the wad of reports under her arm—she could read them on the plane and opened the ticket envelope.

"Great! Wh..." Her eyes questioned him. "Who are those extra tickets for?"

"Inside, you will find tickets for five people. Two of your choosing and two have been selected by the Dean of Social Sciences here at the university. One is Azalea Petersen, a former policewoman, who teaches forensics and pathology classes; and Bob Greenwood is a specialist in Peruvian biology. His hobby is tracking."

"Okay. Before we do anything, I need confirmation that this man..." She placed a hand on Tarkio's shoulder. "Tarkio Cyr is to be contracted as my official teaching assistant, so I can be free to go." She pinned Mr. Savage with her stare until he dialed a number. "I'll check."

"I wanna go with you," pleaded Tarkio.

"You're the only one who can't go. Tarkio, I need you to be here." Her eyes demanded as much. "I'll make a point to take you on field trips during semester breaks or during the summer. Besides, what would Anida and Frederick do if something happened to you? Remember your list of mishaps? I'm beginning to agree, hanging around me may not be the best idea."

Tarkio went from crestfallen, to looking a little chastened.

Ed briefly spoke to a voice on the line, and then turned to the young man. "We've worked it out. If your department won't cover the contract, Dean Prufrock will manage the cost from the general fund."

"Isn't either of you going to ask me how I feel about this?" whined Tarkio.

Both Secora and Mr. Savage said, "Do you want this?"

Tarkio grinned. "Sure, I want it. It's the next best thing to going."

"Okay." Secora turned to Mr. Savage and asked, "When do we leave?"

"Azalea and Bob are already packing." Savage continued, "You and your two companions will leave with them from Missoula on the 6:40 p.m. Frontier flight."

Secora pivoted, sending the fringe of her elk skin jacket flying, "Oh, about the computer reports, I guess I'll need..."

"Got you covered." Dr. Savage swung a laptop out toward her.

Tarkio reached for it since Secora already had an armload of paper. Her bad arm was in a

sling these days rather than a brace, she still struggled to carry it all.

"Thanks, Dr. Savage. Really, that ought to do it. And thanks, Tarkio."

Ed added, "I'll need reports from you daily at the very least! Do you have a Satfon?"

"Uh, yes, I guess I do." She nodded, and then gave him the number for the new satellite phone she'd received from Gideon.

Secora was eager to find her sister's last known location before the trail grew too cold or too overgrown to follow. She'd flipped through the email reports sent by Iris and Jane, hoping to glean clues which might be helpful, finally laying the pages on Tarkio's desk to see what part of the mystery he could solve.

She needed to talk to Gideon about Jane but decided that was out of the question. Even though he was feeling better, it would be awkward, possibly traumatic for him. So, she called Jimmy instead, tapping a pencil on the desk while her mind raced. The phone rang a fourth time, and she thought about leaving a message when Jimmy quietly answered. He was still in town watching over his truest friend, but he agreed to help find Jane and support Secora.

She tried to call her father, but the message machine still repeated they were out of town. She left an explanatory message, sighed, and hung up. There was no one else to call. She set out teaching plans for the week.

Tarkio stared at her. Inhaling, he asked, "How about the baby? I don't think we could care for a seven-month-old and Frederick for a whole week."

"No, of course not. She and I belong together, risky as it may be. We are family."

"Hope you don't mind if I say that's insane." His thoughts escalated. "Are you nuts? Taking a child into a dangerous and practically uncharted area of Peru?"

Secora started to respond, but he cut her off.

"Not to mention the cultural terrorists, separatist guerillas, and the bugs!" He hesitated for that to sink in. "Oh, and snakes, maned wolves, and jaguars."

Secora again opened her mouth as if to speak, but Tarkio continued, "Let's not forget the

treacherous jungle and mountain terrain, and the fact housing and amenities are spotty at best. Do you even speak the language? What if you are hurt? What will happen to Monta?"

Secora set her jaw. "You're right. All those dangers are real, yet hopefully avoidable. I will go to the Isla del Sol and ask Monta's Godmother, Alai, to watch over her."

"I can't imagine you fitting a side visit into the week's schedule, at least not right away."

Secora looked down, then away. "Do you have any helpful solutions?"

Tarkio was for once wordless.

"Me neither and I need to leave now. Anida will be waiting."

On the way down the corridor, Secora planned what she would need to pack for she and the baby.

19

TREKKING SOUTH

With her daughter strapped to her chest, Secora slung her hefty leather backpack over her good shoulder, and added the handles of the baby bag to the handle on a piece of rolling luggage. She struggled slightly, as she sauntered from the parking lot toward the entrance of the miniscule Missoula International Airport. When she was nearly there, she was met by a man with black and silver braids wrapped at the bottom in red and blue felt. This was, of course, Jimmy Lizardeye, the half-Lakota, half-Tewa Wichasha Wakan, who was wearing jeans and a soft blue shirt. He carried a large duffel, a backpack, and his ubiquitous beaded pipe bag.

"Hau, Kola!" Jimmy offered his hand, but Secora went in for a hug. He was more like her uncle than merely a friend.

"Any place on earth would benefit from your presence, Jimmy, but nowhere would you be more welcome."

As he stepped back from the embrace, he said, "I thought having a crazy Heyoka along might be of some use." He looked over Secora's head and used his chin to indicate the parking lot.

She turned and spotted Gideon Yellow Thunder looking bleary-eyed as he locked his lapis blue BMW - uncharacteristically covered with more dust and bugs than paint. She watched him stretch painfully before removing two bags from the trunk, the slammed it shut with uncomfortable exertion.

He ambled toward them with long, slow strides. She felt several emotions overcome her as he approached, concern and delight chief among them. Monta spotted him and made an excited squeal.

"You're kidding, the baby is coming?" His monotone words struck her hard.

Secora nodded. "No family or friends here to leave her with.

Jimmy chuckled and said, "Kinda like Sacagawea."

Secora countered, "Besides, you also have a child in this mess, Kyah, right?"

Jimmy soothed, "We'll make the best of it. Always do."

Secora's tone sobered, "Sorry that we must to meet under the condition of our sisters' disappearance, Gideon. Who knew Jane Iris and Kyah would get hijacked in Peru? Yet, beneath all our troubles, I am relieved you are coming on this uncertain voyage."

No answer, but there was a sparkle in his eyes.

She felt the grin on her face broaden. "Adversity has a way of bringing us together."

"Happy to see you too, Secora, I think." He smiled and looked away.

"How have you been, Heyoka?" she asked.

He winced. "You know."

She smiled. "Hey, Jimmy thanks. But I hope you can manage to keep Gideon out of trouble this time. I don't seem to have too much luck with that."

Jimmy drew a long breath. "We'll see if either of you can keep out of trouble for more than a few minutes." The smile slid from his eyes and he asked, "So, who are these people from the university you told me about? Are we going to have to wait for them?"

Gideon nodded. "Doesn't it feel a bit weird for the university to butt in?"

Secora agreed, "It really does. Maybe they feel like they are covering their backsides. One of them is a retired policewoman who teaches forensics. The other guy is supposedly a tracker who specializes in Peruvian biology."

"Still, feels strange." Gideon rubbed his jaw.

She nodded. "We'll want to keep our eyes on them, but the university will pay our way if we tolerate their babysitters."

The three moved into the building to start the process of boarding. As they took seats in the waiting area Jimmy pulled out a book and a pair of reading glasses.

Gideon asked, "So, what's the plan with Monta? I'm sure you had no alternative but to take a baby on a desperate journey."

"As it happens, no." Secora was fatigued and not in the mood to discuss the issue. "I hope to connect with Alai and leave Monta with her. I tried to call her today, but no answer. It was very short notice, and she might have been asleep. It would be nice if she could meet us in La Paz or Puno, on our way out."

"And what if..."

Secora cut Gideon off, "Worst case, she'll be with me whatever happens. I'm her mom..."

"And what—you'll protect her?"

Jimmy took off his glasses and leaned forward, effectively ending Gideon's query.

Secora hesitated, then looked down as she said, "Gideon, you and I know God is the only protector. We are as nothing by comparison. I know I have no special power to keep her safe—no matter where we are. I will do the best I can. That's all."

The strained silence eventually eased, and Jimmy leaned back and reopened his book.

As their flight was called, two strangers came up to them. "Darn it," whispered Secora, "thought we got lucky."

The new arrivals were still breathing hard during the introductions, "Hello, I'm Azalea Petersen." An angular gray-haired woman, possibly in her mid-fifties, offered her hand all around.

The man appeared to be sixtyish, wearing wrap-around sunglasses, a cowboy hat, and boots. He nodded and said with a Texas drawl, "I'm Bob Greenwood. Excuse me, is that baby traveling with us on this trip? I... I don't think..." He looked to Azalea for support.

Azalea looked strained. She pursed her lips, and said, "There is no way the university will cover an infant, in case of death or injury, nor can..."

Secora stared hard at the woman immediately cutting her off, "Thank you for sharing your opinions. Monta and I are here to find our family. I'm not exactly sure what you're doing here."

It looked as if Azalea may have shrunk a few inches as she stepped back.

"So, are we ready?" asked Jimmy.

"Uh, not quite yet," Secora responded absently. "There's one last person I hoped we'd see." *Dad, are you going to make it?*

Jimmy watched her as the second call was made for their flight. "No time for that now, Secora. Trust that person will make it to Peru if it is meant to happen."

She looked into Jimmy's kind eyes. "Of course you're right, Jimmy." But her features sagged as her ticket was processed.

The others were ahead of her, already boarding. Secora noticed Gideon's eyes never left the two interlopers. She began to wonder what secrets Azalea and Bob weren't sharing with them.

Jimmy took a seat between Petersen and Greenwood—none to their liking. They weren't going to do much visiting over or around him. Bless him thought Secora.

Gideon took the seat next to Secora and Monta. He mumbled, "Still aching from West Glacier and not looking forward to spending thirty hours tied up in small spaces."

"Yeah. This is not likely to be one of the more pleasant trips we've taken."

A sparkle touched Gideon's eyes. "Wait, have we had any pleasant trips?"

A smile broke over Secora's face. "No, I guess we haven't."

"Can't wait for the honeymoon," he joked.

Secora looked at him sharply trying to hide a smile then looked away.

After a moment, she said, "We did have a couple of bright moments."

"I suppose, like breakfasts at vendor stalls in Bolivia. But mostly, traveling with you is a recipe for pain and disaster."

Secora rubbed her left arm. "Aww," she groaned. "I wish you weren't so right about that. We'll have to make a point of enjoying as much of this trip as possible."

"If that doesn't work, may I suggest we stay home next time?" Gideon smiled and Secora's eyes lingered on that smile.

Little Monta was not enjoying her flight at all, and she was good at sharing her misery. It seemed like the flight would never end. It was dark when they landed at El Alta airport in La Paz and the adults collected their luggage. Monta had finally given into the Sandman.

Once in the city, Azalea and Bob took the lead. They located the rooms the University had procured, but it was too late to do much but eat snacks and rest. They would pick up the trail in the morning before dawn. Secora took time to leave a voice message on the Anthropology Department's phone, to see if the crew had been found while they were in transit. She tried Guillermo's phone again, still nothing.

They shared a quick breakfast where not much was exchanged, and afterward they squished aboard the bus to the Yungas of the Northern Cordillera Real of Peru. The five travelers had to find places to squeeze in where there were none. They were all separated and uncomfortable.

Unfortunately, the bus broke down after it painstaking attempted to traverse a rockslide. The driver mumbled unhappy words and dismounted the stairs with a handful of tools. He was followed by a woman who had been sitting in one of the middle seats. She was leading a brown colored ewe with a white nose and a monstrously large belly.

As the poor ewe waddled for the door, she stopped midway to bear down for birthing, leaking a trickle of amniotic fluid which increased into a spill. The rivulet began to flow downhill toward the exit. The woman muttered while she tugged at the sheep, who was intently focused on her personal needs. The animal tried to comply in mid-contraction even though the floor mat was now slippery. Boom, down she went in a tangle of legs and udder.

"Ayudame por favor, alguien? Please, help me... anyone?"

Secora was third in line behind the ewe. No one else offered to help the straining animal. She sighed and gave the baby, along with an extra diaper, to Gideon, who looked a bit nervous.

Azalea peeked out from a row about three quarters back, and said, "Not a good idea to get involved in local business."

Secora glared back. "What are you going to do—jump over them to get outside?"

She'd had quite a bit of experience with sheep and goats years ago, but she thought that part of her life was long over. Rolling up her sleeves, she reached into her leather backpack to grab a pack of moist towelettes for cleaning her hands and her right arm before applying a pair of disposable gloves. She excused herself while squeezing between passengers and made her way up to the laboring ewe.

By now, the poor sheep had been stuck on the floor for several minutes, yet there was no sign of feet coming out of the birth canal. Secora reached in with her fingers to do an exploratory sweep. The contractions were lessening as the ewe began to tire, but she pushed against Secora's hand. As she'd expected, the first lamb was a breech. Secora twisted her head to the side as she tried to find the feet. As she did this, she noticed that Gideon was holding Monta up high so she could see her mother. *Bless you, Gideon.* She pushed inward on the backside of the lamb until she was able to grab the ankles of the back legs and slide them carefully up over the pubic bone. She used two fingers of her other hand to try to protect the pubic bone and the lamb's umbilical cord. If it pinched against the bone or entangled in the baby's legs, the lamb would try to breathe while still inside the mother—a dangerous situation—and the lamb would immediately need resuscitation.

She asked Jimmy, who was seated nearby for his soft blue shirt. He recoiled. She looked at him again with a hard stare, and he pulled it right off, surrendering without a further fight. Secora, gently, but firmly, pulled the big brown ram lamb out with no further delay. She wiped and massaged his head, especially around the nose, while holding him in a head-down position. The baby finally sneezed and flapped its wet ears. She handed him to Jimmy, wrapped up in the shirt. The Wichasha Wakan hadn't a clue what to do.

Secora nodded. "Thanks." Then she fished out a second lamb, a little black ewe with a white topknot. This time, someone handed her another shirt without her even asking, and she accepted it gratefully. She checked the mamma ewe one more time, and sure enough, pulled out a third black ram lamb.

The owner communicated her gratitude to all of them for the help. In response, a couple more shirts were thrown to clean up the mess so people wouldn't slip on the way out.

Three people were now reluctantly holding slimy lambs. Secora asked them to carefully step over the sheep and take them out the door, where they could dry in the sun. The ewe lay panting, stuck in the aisle, and the lambs began to 'maa' for their mom.

After a few moments of hearing her lambs outside calling for her, the ewe bleated and struggled to stand up on her wobbly legs. With help from her owner and Secora, she clambered down the stairs, bleating maternally in answer to the 'maa-ing' of the newborns who were soon searching for a meal.

By the time the driver finished his repairs, the mamma had cleaned out her placenta, and her new offspring were still struggling to suckle. Monta was following the action and occasionally looked back at Gideon's face as if to ask a question. Gideon just shrugged. The baby acted very interested in the sounds made by the lambs and the ewe.

Secora used her nightgown to finish wiping the floor of the bus dry then she placed the slimy garment in a plastic bag. When she was done, she sat in the nearest seat and drank a bottle of water. Everyone re-boarded the bus, and the sheep's proud owner was returning the yucky shirts to Jimmy and the others.

"I'm not wearing this," said Jimmy. The other passengers agreed and chose to remain topless.

As they returned to their seats, Bob said to Secora, "How could you do that?"

Secora shook her head, shrugged, and looked away. He added in a harsh whisper, "That was disgusting."

As she turned her gloves inside out, Secora retorted, "You're a biologist, right?"

Gideon interjected, "Want your baby back?" Secora grabbed Monta, kissed her, and replaced her in the protective front-facing pack. They were several miles down the road before the travelers began talking and laughing again.

"I'm a little worried because I haven't heard anything from Alai," Secora said softly.

Gideon sounded reassuring. "It was pretty short notice. From what I remember, she and Guillermo don't sit around the house waiting for the phone to ring."

"I know." She looked into his eyes. "But I have a feeling this is different."

20

OJO REDONDO

Mist gathered in the mountains before Secora and the others reached their destination—a tiny nameless settlement hidden in the clouds. It was perched in the Peruvian Yungas on the edge of a warm, verdant canyon. She noticed tiny plots of bananas and other tropical crops that the locals coaxed from the surrounding jungle.

As the bus eased to a stop, it was easy to make out the small inn-like structure where the team would rest for the night. When they were told this was the place to exit by the driver, the five dismounted with a few other riders who immediately vanished into the forest.

Gideon panned the area, stretched, and sidled up to Secora, and Monta who was gumming a cracker. "That guy, Bob, never looks me in the eyes. He always wears those sunglasses. What's up with that?"

Secora regarded Gideon seriously. "We are going to have to be extra careful. I'm not letting you out of my sight."

Before they moved into the building, Azalea offered bottles of water all around. They were gratefully accepted.

They asked at the desk if there was any news about the students. The two people in the lobby shook their heads in silence. Secora took the biggest room available for Gideon, Jimmy, Monta, and herself. She thought good thing I can change clothes surreptitiously, until she remembered the state of her nighty and cringed. "Looks like we have some laundry to do, Jimmy why don't you give me your shirt?"

He looked up in surprise and said, "No, you two stay here with the baby, I'll do the laundry. Better toss me your scuzzy nightgown."

"Thanks Jimmy. I think I saw a washtub by the wall in the lobby," said Gideon, who was looking pretty beat.

Secora brought the nightgown out from the plastic bag, and noticed it was beginning to smell interesting. "Here are little plastic bottles of soap and vinegar, hope this cuts the slime. Could you wash the big plastic bag too?"

"Guess we'll see," said Jimmy eyeing the gown and his mashed-up shirt questioningly. "Either way, I think you ought to plan on wearing something else to bed tonight, Sloth Girl."

They put their other belongings away, and the laundry was drying before they found an Eatery and had a nice meal of local empanadas. Secora was correcting Bob's pronunciation, "The name of the place is O-HO Ray-don-do, long 'o' on 'don.'"

"Piss off," Bob replied and looked away, unimpressed. She wondered about his aloof attitude; it seemed as if his persona was becoming quieter, maybe even dangerous. They wandered back to the motel past a guinea pig vendor. Secora swallowed hard at the thought of them being a food source.

There was a single shower head outside the rooms with a curtain around it. The water wasn't warm, but Secora needed a rinse. Afterward, she hauled herself into the room and collapsed on the floor with the others for a few hours' rest.

It was still dark when Secora's satellite phone buzzed, scaring her.

She jumped up and pulled it from her backpack, answering in a whisper that she hoped wouldn't wake everyone.

"What?"

"Oh, it's Tarkio with an update, Secora. What time is it there?"

"Way too dark to tell. How are Fredrick and Anida? What's up?"

"Well, my beautiful family is fine, but your friend Alai called your office phone, and I was here, so I answered."

"Yes, what did she say?"

"Things aren't good there, and she doesn't want you to go there with Monta."

"Why?"

"Didn't say, exactly, just that you should keep her with you and watch for trouble."

"That's it? Trouble from where? Is Alai, okay?"

"She sounded like she was crying. By the way, classes are going well; the students told me to tell you 'hi.'"

"Thanks, Tarkio, but Alai and Guillermo mean the world to me. Please keep me posted. I'm glad you and the students are getting along. We hope to return in a few days."

When Secora signed off, she became aware eyes were watching her. She turned sharply; it was Gideon, he asked, "Is everything okay?"

"Not really." She explained what she'd heard from Tarkio through sudden tears she couldn't staunch. "I'm worried."

He sighed. "It'll work out. Better rest before Monta gets cranky."

"Thanks. If she does, I'll give her to you."

She renewed her smile as he rolled as far away as possible.

They rose at dawn to the smell of breakfast being prepared and they ate gratefully even though Azalea complained that they paid too much for the meal.

Secora said, "Sounds like a phrase you use often and indiscriminately. I doubt thirty-five cents will noticeably diminish your account," adding several extra coins onto her own bill.

As the smirk fell from Azalea's lip, she mumbled, "I don't like you very much."

"Well," said Secora. "The important thing is finding those kids and getting them safely home, right?"

"Maybe we should start out now?" offered Jimmy.

Azalea paid her tab and they hefted their gear. After about five minutes of walking along a road, they started down the old Jeep trail to the research area.

Within moments Secora couldn't tell there had ever been humans in the vicinity. The path closed almost immediately. It was barely discernible through undergrowth and shrubbery. It was as if the Yungas had completely enfolded Jane Roanhorse, Iris Snowden, and their eleven archaeology students including Kyah, in a quiet cloud.

She checked a notch cut into one of the trees, placing her fingers lightly inside to test the dryness of the sap. If the crew had been abducted by guerrillas, she wondered, are we ready to take on a small army? Just what parts are Azalea or Bob willing to play in this mission? They *must* be carrying weapons.

She asked Azalea, "What do you and Bob hope to accomplish down here?"

"We have a job to do. If they're alive, we bring the kids back." Azalea smiled.

Following a GPS marker, Bob finally led them to a place where Secora felt they were following the actual trail the archaeology team had used on their daily trek to the Ojo Redondo Chachapoya site. She prayed silently they would safely find all the team members and would not be forced to leave without a happy conclusion to the disappearances.

Jimmy walked next to her and said softly, "Trouble could come at us from anywhere."

Azalea was behind them, picked up the thread. "They could have been killed by humans, insects, or animals." She put on a burst of speed and pulled alongside. "But I expect there was interference from a disgruntled indigenous group or something more sinister altogether." She scrunched her face at Secora. "I'm paid to be suspicious. It's hard to imagine that poisonous ants or snakes would have killed them all, right?"

Bob pointed out the vegetation was already regrowing where the team had previously carved the path to the site.

"These severed stems are going to make our navigation difficult," grumbled Jimmy as he swung one of the machetes they'd picked up in town at nearly a foot of bristly new growth. The stubble would often slap back at their shins, rather than succumb to the hefty blades.

As they trudged on the light began to fade, and the moist air became rain. The forest turned both stunning and mysterious. Birdsong flitted like shafts of light through the trees once the rain stopped. Secora caught the piercing voice of a lyrebird.

On a much-needed break, Bob came and sat with the women after taking a trip to the trees. "Did you know that the Yungas hold onto vestiges of ancient or as yet unknown biota?" he asked.

Secora wished she could see if his eyes were bright behind those sunglasses... to gauge whether or not he really cared about lifeforms. Then responded, "And traces of silent human nations."

"More importantly," offered Jimmy. "What are we going to do when we find out what troubles our family might be experiencing?"

Nobody had an answer. So, they picked up their gear and took off again. Secora found herself bending over, dodging branches much of the time. Not an easy task while protecting little Monta. She tried to switch the baby pack to her back, but when she did, Monta howled; she was not pleased when she lost sight of Secora's face.

"Here, let me take a turn." Gideon reached for the little one. "She can look back and see you."

At a momentary loss for words, Secora took Monta out of the baby pack and let Gideon strap it to his own back.

He smiled kindly. "There. Enjoy the break, Mom."

"Don't know what to say—besides thank you very much."

Gideon smirked. "Don't worry, when I have babies, I'll bring them over to Auntie Secora's all the time."

Secora glared at him, mulling over all he meant and not much liking the implications of "Auntie Secora."

At the second rest break, Bob pointed to a strikingly beautiful coatimundi with kits as the family passed over their heads. Secora was amazed by their lovely striped fur and dexterity as they calmly walked the branches above. Her Satfon rang again, and she saw it was Tarkio's home number. She stood and stepped over to the tree where Gideon waited with Monta. She answered, "Hey, Tarkio, what's up?"

"Hey, boss, thought you'd be interested to know I found out who the owner of the mammoth site is—or should I say was, because it is in the process of changing hands."

"Do I want to know?" She became distracted as Gideon took the baby out of the pack and set her on the ground. Monta stood clinging to his fingers.

Jimmy looked over and said, "Would you look at that?"

Secora closed her eyes to concentrate on what Tarkio was saying.

"Maybe not, but here goes. It *was* owned by Professor Donald Chastain, but he is selling it to some cowboy from Texas who wanted to frack the place for oil. The dig was done in preparation for the sale to go through... to a buyer named Robert Greenwood."

At first she couldn't speak.

"Secora, are you still there?"

After a long breath she said, "You don't say. You're amazing, Tarkio. We're almost to the Ojo Redondo site now, with Azalea Petersen and Bob Greenwood."

After a silence from his end, she heard. "Get the hell away from them, Secora!

I'm serious."

"Thanks, would you please look underneath the mammoth molar? I left a slip of paper there with two phone numbers..."

She could hear him shuffling things on the other end. "Okay, I have it, now what?"

"Could you give each of them a call and fill them in on what you've discovered? I have to go now."

"I'm on it."

"Talk to you soon, I hope."

After she hung up, Gideon asked, "What?" Secora quickly told him in hushed tones about Tarkio's discovery.

Gideon said, "Guess that explains the hidden eye thing—they are the dead green eyes of the bastard who attacked us and murdered Kamal. He must have shaved his beard and added the drawl, hat, and boots."

Monta turned to Secora as she squatted to see the baby eye-to-eye. The little one tried to take a few steps toward her but fell on the leaf litter. "Come here to Uncle Gideon. I will protect you from..." Out of nowhere, Secora leaned across and kissed him on the lips. "What's that for?" Gideon looked puzzled.

Secora also kissed little Monta who was watching with somber eyes. "To snap your mind out of what it was thinking so we can act normal. Unclench your jaw." After a few moments, they walked back toward the others.

Bob was looking at Jimmy and clearing his throat. "The fear Azalea and I have is terrorists are the cause of the archaeological team's disappearance."

Azalea took up the topic. "As you said, the rumor is the site may have been overtaken by these so-called culture terrorists. People who take a dislike to the suggestion there were pre-Incan Caucasoid settlements which inspired and influenced pieces of early South American civilization. In their minds, it would degrade the accomplishments of the current local communities."

Gideon stopped near Azalea with Monta. "It could just as easily have been a band of local separatists, looking to benefit from loot, and hostage money."

Bob purposefully turned to Secora. "How do you propose we pry them safely away from their captors?"

"Best not to ask too many questions," Azalea warned him. "Too many eyes and ears."

Secora rolled her eyes and shook her head. Oddly enough, frogs and toads took over the entire conversation.

Jimmy glanced at Gideon and began to move forward. "Almost there," he encouraged.

Forty-five minutes later, they reached an overgrown glade which the GPS confirmed to be the base camp of the Ojo Redondo work site. They stood at the edge of the jungle and looked at a small, cleared area. A tiny meadow on a saddle ridge between two rises. It was such a pretty little place, maybe about fifty yards in diameter. On one side, a miniature cliff rose about thirty feet crowned with trees and brush. On the other, the jungle came up to the edge of the meadow where they had entered.

Without GPS, Secora believed this place would be nearly impossible to find. The five of them fanned out looking for bodies or signs of looting.

They were rewarded with broken equipment in a fire pit and disturbed soil near the cliff.

Bob suggested, "People were lying down here, maybe overpowered by the aggressors."

Secora suppressed saying, ya think? Luckily they didn't find blood or bodies. As the others turned away, she casually uncovered the stone with the apparent altar disc, and then quickly concealed it again. When she finished, she noticed clods of dirt, which had recently rolled down the little cliff.

Bob offered, "I'd say there were at least twenty people in this mix.

Twelve in the university crew and..."

Secora corrected, "Thirteen in the university crew. There was a high school student with them."

Gideon was on the edge of the meadow with Monta. They were walking next to Jimmy who was looking intently into Gideon's eyes as he filled him in on the call from Tarkio.

Azalea spied some camp remnants, including the empty beer cans and the broken plane table, along with a couple of coolers the contents of which had been spread around and picked through.

Bob lifted the splinters of the university's satellite phone. He ran a finger beneath his glasses, wiping sweat from under his eyes. "This doesn't look good."

Secora's inner voice was shouting, *duh*. She prayed, Iris, please keep Jane and the students safe.

21

OUT OF THE WOODS

T he soldiers treated Jane and her crew cruelly as they hurried past Condor Lake, batting at merciless waves of bugs. Jane thought those blasted soldiers are too hard on the kids.

They had been bushwhacking downhill toward the Northeast for nearly two hours. There was little occasion to slap at bugs because the trailside brush was tangling with their hair and burdened arms and scratching at their legs. Eventually, the weary mob stumbled onto a track that quickly opened onto a broad path. The trail descended steeply toward a thunderous river which they heard but had not yet seen. Frequent rivulets crossed the trail creating spectacular cascades which disappeared over the edge to feed the large waterway.

Without so much brush in this area, the captives moved ahead more freely, but not swiftly, because the trail sloped so sharply and was slick with water for as far as anyone could see.

Iris told Jane she could feel shin splints nagging her, and several crew members were already whimpering in agony.

Jane looked questioningly at Kyah. He nodded, so Jane said, loudly,

"We need to rest," whereupon, she sat down unceremoniously. The others gathered and sat which bought them only a moment's rest.

One of the captors fired a bullet that cracked a nearby piece of basalt. "Guess the break's over." Jane arose. In the end all Jane and Iris could do for the teenagers, was to add a couple of heavy items to their own burdens, and hope the students could make it to whatever destination awaited them. The laptop dropped to the ground and was blasted to bits by one of the soldiers, as people scampered away. Jane understood, falling behind was not tolerated.

Down they trotted; Jane thought that the trail was never going to end. Then the dreaded event occurred.

"Ow!" Amy twisted an ankle and fell to the side. Jane heard it pop. The girl was in obvious pain and couldn't stand after several attempts. She was too lame to move and remained seated on the mossy, muddy path enveloping herself in great sobs of pain and fury. She snarled belligerently at a guerilla who prodded her roughly. He smiled and raised his rifle toward her. The rude man clicked the safety off his weapon.

Jane and Iris supportively backtracked and flopped down beside Amy. Jane said, "Mira! No vamos de aqui sin comida y algo de beber."

Aparu and Gilgamesh whispered together.

Iris translated for the students. "We won't leave until we are allowed to have something to eat and drink," The others gratefully fell nearby. They weren't budging either.

"Callate! Vamos o morir!" The leader, Juan Quintos, ran up and sneered in Iris's face while he repeated, "Callate! o morir!"

"Then go ahead and kill us," Iris answered with fire in her eyes. "You can haul this junk yourselves!"

"There are no artifacts here interesting enough to sell," he sneered as he called her bluff and signaled a man with a machete.

In English, he said, "Kill her first as an example." He pointed to Iris, who seemed unfazed.

One of the robed men pleaded, "Esperate por favor. Wait, please! You have made your point. We Gueros are capable of preparing a meal for everyone in only a few minutes, and then we can move again."

Quintos growled, "You skirt-wearers naturally would want to do the cooking. Go ahead. You have five minutes."

From vast satchels slung across their shoulders, the gracefully robed men and women withdrew beverages, grains, and various herbs, which they blended to the right consistency and served out of their own bowls to the guerrillas first, and then the crew.

A tall slender man with hazel eyes, blond-streaked hair, and a red mustache approached Iris with one of the bowls. She looked at the food, which smelled quite appealing, but the

man looked into her eyes dead-on, and subliminally moved his head side-to-side. Iris understood.

As if offering a prayer of thanks, she looked upwards and said rather loudly "Ix-nay on the Ood-fay!" While she burned her eyes into each one of the crew, she added, "I-ay eanit may."

The students played with the porridge, stirring it excessively, or throwing a spoonful out as if it had a bug in it.

Then Jane and Iris returned their eyes to the man, seeking further instructions. He sipped first from the cup, which he then placed in Iris's free hand and nodded. She bowed slightly and affirmed, "Gracias, Senor." Then, turning to her colleagues added, "This is to our health. Salud!" Then she gulped some of the fragrant liquid and passed it on to the others. With her eyes, she continued to fend off any would-be eaters among her crew, who were still stirring their bowls and playing convincingly with the food. More elixir was given to Iris and the others, who began to feel much better.

The guerillas all ate hungrily and surprisingly became violently ill, and after that, comatose. All their gagging and retching made everyone, even those who weren't sick, vomit. The stench was awful.

Next, the Gueros moved the fitfully sleeping soldiers into the trees for shelter where they tried to make them comfortable. They, matter-of-factly, removed all their weapons, calmly tossing them over the cliff into the torrent. Last, they removed the right boot from each of the soldiers to disable them, without crippling them too badly.

A woman explained with minimal English the soldiers might not be as evil as their leader. The crew members nodded.

The team swiftly retrieved essential equipment and several artifacts for the local museum, while Guero men lashed three branches together and laid the crippled girl down on them. They shouldered the conveyance and bore her along an intricate route continuing downward to the shore.

Iris attempted to stop them. She was determined to return to the Ojo Redondo site where anyone sent to search for them could find them. Her request was answered with an emphatic, "No."

Jane quipped, "I guess we're not really out of the woods yet!"

Soon, everyone was again moving swiftly through the brush, down a narrow path following the ridge on the canyon wall toward the smooth beach of the expansive river. When they finally arrived, Gueros emerged from unseen grottos onto the beach. The students were awed by their able companions.

Iris said to Jane, "Does it feel like we've wandered back in time to an ancient civilization akin to that of the Chachapoyas we've been researching?"

Jane stared incredulously. "Yeah... it certainly does"

Kyah looked amazed. His eyes were glistening when he told his mom, "These people are cool, like the Duendes. Could we move here permanently, Mom?"

Jane smiled, so proud of a son who could appreciate people everywhere he went. Her thoughts were interrupted by popping sounds coming from the hill above them. Incredibly, a gunman was shooting at them again. They could make out through the brushy thickets that he was one of the soldiers, who had managed to follow them down the trail to the shore. Additional shots were fired in the direction of the escaping students. Most of the bullets were wild, but two found marks. One hit Sammy's calf, the other hit Amy's forearm.

Several nimble Gueros managed to climb up beside and behind the two shooters, then doused them with what appeared to be a particularly severe pepper mixture. The soldiers were screaming but they were tough, and it required a second dose of the scalding pepper potion to disarm them. A curly-haired soldier pushed into one of the robed men, the gentle man who had asked to provide the food and lashed at him with a hidden knife. The two other Gueros put the fighter down and knocked him unconscious.

"They have hurt Gilgamesh!" yelled Aparu, one of the Guero men to Jane and Iris in broken English.

Jane hollered, "I would have killed them." Then she said to Iris, "Those soldiers may be alive, but they will be unable to move for a long time."

The mysterious guardians kept the knives but tossed the guns as far as possible into the river below before making a break for the beach to join the others in their retreat. On the way down, it became apparent that Gilgamesh had been severely injured. The knife had torn into his abdomen, and he could no longer run. His tunic reddened before the onlooker's eyes. One of the Guero women ran to find some cool moss to cover the wound, but the gentle man insisted on remaining behind.

Iris and Jane went ballistic. They refused to leave anyone behind for any reason, even though the others assured them it was the wise thing to do.

Strong branches bound with grid marking string had been used to create the makeshift travois which Amy previously used. The sister-friends grabbed it and started toward the bleeding man. They were soon joined by others in the hasty rescue.

With difficulty, they managed to carry Gilgamesh right up to one of the boats at the shoreline. He was placed along with Amy and Sammy in a dugout canoe manned by several oarsmen. The craft flew away, surprisingly agile in the water. Three other boats followed suit. Because the Gueros hadn't planned on company, there wasn't enough space in the boats to ferry everyone across in one shot.

Iris, the remaining students, and several of the Gueros crouched under a colorful cliff overhang to wait. The compact cavern had been carved out by a broad roaring waterfall. It was wet but safe.

Jane was whisked away to one of the wooden boats by the man who introduced himself as Aparu. She boarded reluctantly with Kyah and three of the college students. Afraid trouble would again break through the brush. She and her son offered a Lakota prayer of protection for Iris and the others left behind.

Aparu hopped aboard after pushing the large canoe off the sand and took a seat. Jane looked up in amazement at the brilliant rainbow pattern of the cavern rock which had been stained with minerals in stripes of black, reddish-orange, yellow, and gray. She waved goodbye to Iris. It wasn't long before she and the others were dropped off, while the boats returned for the others.

While waiting on the far side of the river, Jane watched in horror as one of the returning boats capsized near the shore, turning its dark brown wooden hulk to the sun, it sank perpendicularly.

Jane squirmed; the water must be very deep. God knows what horrid creatures make the river home. Most of the passengers swam quickly to shore, cheered on by Bruce with his curly red hair and scarf. "Only God knows what's in these waters."

It appeared that one of the robed oarsmen was missing, but after a few breathless moments, he popped up having reclaimed a large bag of herbs and a coil of rope from the flipped dugout. He labored with the sack until several arms grabbed him out of the water.

After they checked his condition, the Gueros tugged on the rope, which had been attached to the submerged craft, drawing it in with their efforts. Once all boats were beached, everyone rested before they moved on. Bird calls were made, presumably to update other Gueros in the area. Oarsmen paddled the dugouts upriver along with the injured.

When the river was behind them, the anthropology crew was dropped at a temporary camp nearly a half-mile away, where a nourishing porridge awaited them.

Jane and two of the Guero women watched as an advance party departed. She suddenly felt confused and dissociated. Her equilibrium was traumatized by the massive quiet of the forest and intermittent mist. "It's claustrophobic. I can't see any distance." She tried to explain her feelings to the women who were becoming nervous.

"Enemies might pop out from anywhere." She looked for a glimmer of understanding in the eyes of her saviors. Seeing none, felt compelled to continue. "I live in open prairie." She tried to explain with her hands. "This forest is scaring me."

One of the women nodded and called out to Aparu. The hazel-eyed healer arrived. Pointing to his chest he repeated in broken English, "Aparu my name."

She thought no way could I forget you, then acknowledged, "I remember."

He attempted to alleviate her rising panic by rubbing her forehead, yet the fear was increasing. So, he reached for her arm, and they left camp, immediately disappearing into the forest on a lowland trail and moving toward a concealed valley in an uncharted region of the massive Yungas.

Tears ran from her eyes when she saw Kyah catching up to them. She felt lonely in this big country, but at least she was not truly alone. On the way, Aparu said in broken English that the others would leave shortly after they caught their breath and loaded their remaining supplies. Jane sniffled, nodded, and wished desperately she had a wad of Kleenex.

22

THE CLIFF CITY

An hour and a half later, Jane wondered why they hadn't caught sight of the others and whether this scenic but crazy trail would ever end. Aparu signaled they would rest in the valley bottom on top of a large boulder, "For safety from animals."

Jane's eyes questioned.

He responded, "Big animals." He stretched his lean, beautiful arms out as far as they would go, then brought them back in, and stretched again.

Jane's eyebrows rose appreciatively.

Kyah said, "Wow, Mom. What could that be? Must be like an elephant."

Jane brushed the hair from her son's eyes. "We'll ask your Aunt Secora when we see her."

Aparu tried to say the animals' names in his language, but she didn't understand the words he used and slowly wagged her head.

Kyah asked, "Do you think Secora will come here, Mom?"

Jane drew in a deep breath and looked at a flock of passing parrots, and said, "It wouldn't surprise me."

"How will she find us?"

"Good question, but I'm pretty sure she will."

It was time to leave again. A light mist began to fall impeding travel, but eventually the canyon split around a tall rocky outcrop which they followed by way of a well-worn path to the right. The trail straightened, and rose steadily as it navigated a rising cliff wall. Jane could see from about halfway up, that part of the cliff had collapsed inward and huge rocks had shifted down the slope. This left a cleft cut back into the mountain. Inside the gap was a spectacular veiled city which no one from the river or the canyon bottom would ever see.

Inside was an ancient ruin, a cliff dwelling that had been cleared of brush and rubble and was currently being used by the Gueros as their sanctuary.

When they finally arrived at the gash in the wall, Jane realized that Gilgamesh, Sammy, and Amy had somehow survived their journey and were resting under a healers' care. However, the man who had been knifed did not look well. He was surrounded by family, friends, and a singer. Glanced at her watch; Jane noticed it had been a good four hours since they had left the camp by the river. Still, she saw no sign of the others behind them.

She and Kyah had time for a cursory exploration. The cave roof rose well over one hundred feet, and the opening was maybe a quarter of a mile across. She was still marveling at the roads and paths among the usable buildings when Iris and the rest of the crew came into view a few minutes later.

Iris ran halfway across the cave to hug her. "Jane, are you okay?" When they were satisfied each was managing to cope, they took stock of the eight students, as well as the artifacts and gear they were able to bring with them.

Several crew members had suffered nasty bug bites which needed attention. Others had scrapes and cuts that might be susceptible to infection. Aparu, a woman called Sarai, and a man introduced as Kantun made sure each was treated for their maladies.

Next, Jane and her team assembled to discuss their new situation. "Obviously, our initial objective has taken an unexpected turn." She sat down cross-legged. "For now, we will record our experiences as a case study... protecting the town's privacy. What shall we call it?"

Bruce blurted out, "Case E101...the "E" stands for enigma."

"That sounds fair," Jane agreed, as she rubbed one of the many itchy bites on her face. "Thank God for our malaria shots. Anyway, the code we must adopt is to keep this group protected from any outside interests."

Sarbjeet affirmed, "At all costs. It is bad enough they have been exposed to whatever diseases we are carrying."

Iris agreed, "True, we must also protect these kind and spiritual souls from the vicious material interests of our world beyond the river."

"We need to practice super hygiene—keeping our distance as much as possible," continued Sarbjeet.

Thanh said, "Sanitize our hands!" Everyone nodded.

They drafted an impromptu non-disclosure document and affirmed they would later figure out what, if anything would be mentioned to the university in the future. Following the meeting, everybody stretched out for a much-needed rest.

Kyah had already disappeared, while Jane rested near Iris who sounded wistful, "Wish we were on our way home"

"Me too, girl, me too, but aside from the bugs and bullets, there are so many positive aspects to this adventure."

"Excuse me?" Iris sounded shocked.

"Well, look at the fact that we've found a remnant of a culture, people who live as if they were descendants of a Chachapoya tribe."

"I guess there is that..."

"And, Iris, I don't know if you've noticed, but these people are awesome. I am fascinated by the men, especially the one named Aparu. He has the kindest gray-brown eyes."

"Is he the guy who brought you here?"

"Yes." Jane nodded sheepishly.

"Yeah, well, don't get your hopes up, girly girl, these fellas seem kind of monastic to me."

"So, you haven't noticed the guy who's been hovering around you?"

"Oh, you mean, Kantun?" They heard footsteps approach. When the two women looked up, both smiled, noticing he was right there beside them.

He smiled back—at Iris. She shut up and lowered her eyes shyly. Jane smiled.

"'Nuff said. Iris, I think you're blushing."

"You're probably right, but even if they aren't monastic there are enough women and children to account for every male here."

"Thanks, Iris, for throwing snow on my daydreams!"

Later that day, Jane and her new friend, Aparu came to visit Iris, but she appeared to be sleeping while Kantun rested nearby, so they walked quietly away. Instead, they found a rock to perch on, and worked on strengthening their communication skills using words, sign language gestures, and laughter. Aparu seemed shy and blushed more than once.

Jane showed him some of the notes and Polaroids from the Ojo Redondo dig. Aparu disappeared for a few moments and returned with a cloth bundle. Inside the cloth, there were written documents stored in a woven box. Aparu pulled out the writings and Jane cocked her head to try to make sense of the symbols.

Iris awoke and joined them saying, "I don't need an interpreter to see the mutual admiration in your eyes." She winked at Jane, and then she approached and touched the attractive weave of the cloth and the decorations on the box. "That almost looks like Ancient Greek, or a Cretan script."

"Right, because you know what Cretan looks like?" Jane challenged.

"One of Dad's friends, Gavin Andrews, was a linguist." She rolled her eyes. "He was so cute. Anyway, he gave a guest lecture on Cretan writing in one of my classes and happened to mention there were rumors of Old Cretan script on signposts in South America." She shook her head. "Not the oldest version, because that was completely pictorial, and not the set of more simplified symbols from around 1,650 years ago, but the one from around 1,900 years ago."

"Get to the point, Iris."

"Well, it would look like this."

Jane asked, "Wasn't that the same vague time as the visit from the mysterious Messenger you were talking about? The Weeping God or Viracocha, who wandered this area while trying to find His believers for the new revelation?"

Iris yawned and nodded. "I guess so, but His journey would have been later than the invention of the language, right? Sorry, need more rest." She curled up on the ground near the rock they were sitting on.

Jane also chose to rest again. She woke at dusk when a slight drizzle began to bead up and trickle down her chiseled features. She looked over at Iris, who was also stirring. Both had been covered in several layers of brightly colored cloth. A woman was sitting a few yards away. Jane blinked and recognized she was the one who had helped them avoid the danger of poisoning from the food in the large nutshell bowls that morning, and, of course, Kantun had his watchful eye on Iris.

She couldn't see anyone else in the courtyard, although there was movement around the stone-walled dwellings. They reminded her of the cliff dwellings in the southwestern states. She sat up wrapping the blankets around her. Then she inhaled aromas of food preparation. The air smelled of a warm and fragrant meal and flatbread. Suddenly she realize how famished she was. A bite of savory food would be wonderful.

Kantun came over, half bowed and said things in a language which was lost on her. Seeing her perplexity, he pointed to himself and repeated the word "Kantun."

She acknowledged, adding that she was "Jane."

He repeated her name a couple of times to get the right sound, then offered his hand to help her rise. She timidly followed him into a stone building where two oil lamps were lit. It might have been some sort of dining area where several people savored the contents of generous bowls. With a smile, he motioned her over to a kettle and gave her a bowl of her own. He then took a seat and ate beside her. A moment later, Iris joined them. Smiling but groggy, she sat on the other side of Kantun. He immediately rose to fill a bowl for her.

"Thanks, Kantun, and good evening to you both." She tasted the food and closed her eyes. When she finished, she said. "I enjoy listening to the musical flow of this mysterious language. Its etiology escapes me, but Mom and Dad would be so amazed by it if they could break away from wherever they are teaching this month."

Jane ignored Iris and relished the simple grain, vegetable, and egg dish which was so tasty she was afraid that one bowl might not be enough to fill the vacancy in her stomach. Luckily, it was all she needed. She began to wonder where the students were, as none were in sight. It must have been a premonition, because Kyah soon found her and reported the crew had already eaten and had hiked into the valley bottom where they had been shown the tracks of a *very* large animal.

"Did you snap any pictures?"

Kyah was excited. "We sure did."

"Be sure to show them to Secora. What are you guys doing now?"

"We're going over the top to see what's in the next valley."

"Of course, you are. No more than an hour, okay?"

"Two, please?"

Jane smiled wryly. She trusted her son, but she was not comfortable with the massive forests around them. "One hour, and be careful."

Kyah kissed her cheek and ran off.

Jane felt awed but relaxed in the company of the easy-going, graceful people of Cliff City. Perhaps it was similar to the way Frodo felt in the company of elves. *What a contrast to my own daily routine.*

The girls wandered over to check on Sammy and Amy who both said they felt awful, but they had been receiving food and medicine, and were made as comfortable as the situation allowed.

Jane had a difficult time looking at the damaged limbs, but she noticed the herbal infusions had kept infection out of the gunshot wounds. She thought, *these poor children, torn by violence.*

Iris was kneeling beside them, quietly offering Baha'i healing prayers.

Jane closed her eyes and added a wish from her heart for their speedy recovery. She said, "Guess you two will have stories to tell the grandkids." They laughed half-heartedly. It was time to let the two of them rest.

As the evening progressed a handful of crew members returned with Kyah, and a handful of Guero youngsters. They all sat together peacefully as lamp shadows began to dance and blink. Jane asked Aparu how Gilgamesh was faring. He said that their leader was stable, but far from well.

Weariness had once again befriended Iris even though it was still early. Kantun noticed and escorted her to one of the mats in a neighboring sleeping room which had a single oil lamp burning.

Jane smiled as the two left, then winced, not quite knowing how to ask where the little girl's room was. Aparu must have expected something like that, and came over to help her up, and pointed to an enclosed area.

Really, they have plumbing? Guess that's not so far-fetched; they had a similar system back in the days of Tiahuanaco. She said, "Thank you Aparu, and sleep well. I'll see you in the morning." He smiled as he nodded, then left.

As Jane lay down, she wondered if they would find a way out of this situation, although the last few days had been wonderful. She drifted off to sleep thinking, *Secora I don't know if you can find us, or how you could even cross that huge river. Please keep my brother safe.*

23

TRACES

During a rest break, Secora pulled her full-length alpaca Ruana serape from her backpack. She slid it around her shoulders while considering the next step, in light of Tarkio's revelation about Bob Greenwood. She could feel Jimmy and Gideon's questioning gazes and looked at them both but said nothing. Before long, it was time to move on. The team moved back and forth across the valley and down the slope searching for clues.

"I think I see tracks leading this way," Azalea said as she moved down the narrow valley that descended along the little cliff.

A thousand yards further down, Gideon, Jimmy, and Secora found a limestone overhang at the edge of Condor Lake. They followed a path around the formation, until the rock curved inward becoming a small cave where they were staggered by the sight of two raw human skeletons.

Azalea strutted over and said, "Those bones are pinkish-white, and there is a bit of splintering and cracking. So, they're too old to be from our archaeology crew." The retired policewoman pulled out a couple of bags from her pack and automatically prepared to collect samples for DNA testing.

Before going into the woods for a personal break, Secora said offhandedly, "Don't forget the gloves."

After Azalea finished and left the cave, Secora also collected a bit of the bone and labeled it in case it could be useful for later research. "These two may have been victims surprised by the same group that found Jane and Iris. At any rate, the police in La Paz should know about them." Jimmy and Gideon heartily agreed. She took out her camera and snapped a couple of photos. "I have a funny feeling that these two haven't moved on."

"They do need help," Jimmy agreed.

Bob kicked at the dirt and prodded, "Let *us* move on." Then he took off.

Secora called out, "We're going to say prayers for these people."

"You don't even have a clue who they were," Bob hollered back.

"Think of it this way," Gideon's voice boomed from the overhang. "If you and Azalea died out here alone, wouldn't it be nice if whoever discovered your bones paid a little respect to you and your lives?" His voice took on an edge. "No matter who you were or what kind of person you turned out to be."

Bob looked shocked, and turned away scowling, and muttering an unintelligible response as he sat on a nearby stone to wait.

Secora shot a wry smile at Gideon.

Jimmy took the sacred pipe from its beaded bag and respectfully polished the bowl against his shirt. He offered the pipe to the Creator and the earth as began to raise a voice.

"O Grandfather, you who designed all created things;
every rock, sea, river, and plant.
You who brought into being the two-leggeds,
four-legged, and the wings of the air - hear us.

These souls must return to you in peace.
We ask assistance from the spirits of the Four Directions
to guide them safely on their journey.
Hetchetu Aloh."

Secora said a prayer for the departed from memory.

"O my God! O Thou forgiver of sins,
bestower of gifts, dispeller of afflictions!
Verily, I beseech Thee to forgive the sins of
such as have abandoned the physical garment
and ascended to the spiritual world.
O my Lord!
Purify them from trespasses, dispel their
sorrows, and change their darkness into light.
Cause them to enter the garden of happiness, cleanse
them with the most pure water, and grant them
to behold Thy splendors on the loftiest mount."

As soon as she finished, Azalea bustled in again. "What's the holdup?"

Gideon reminded her, "You were a forensic detective, right?"

She looked at the skeletons with renewed interest, kneeling beside them looking for evidence. She was able to locate a few tatters of cloth and metal, which she collected, along with an assortment of photos she snapped. She said she would mail everything to the university at the first opportunity, along with her report.

Gideon picked a flower from an overhanging vine and knelt on one knee, placing it near the remains. "Go in beauty."

When they finally stepped back out into the sunshine, they were in for another shock. As they looked uphill toward the cliff they had recently left, they noticed the form of a man hunched over inspecting the ground around the carving and altar.

Azalea said, "This is a clear case of vandalism—or worse." She pulled her pistol and shouted at him, "Stop immediately! Or I'll shoot."

He did stop and turned as he stood up smiling like a silver-haired, blue-eyed Cheshire cat.

Secora said, "Hold your fire, Azalea—that's my dad, Dr. Sage Dalton, and the woman beyond him is my mother, Dr. L.W. Dalton."

With the gun now pointed at the ground, Azalea said, "Oh, I had no idea ... Donald never mentioned..."

Secora caught the slip. "Donald? Thought it was Ed Savage, Chair of the Anthropology Department who employed you?"

"What are they doing here of all places?" Gideon changed the subject, astonished.

L.W. smiled as she came over and embraced her daughter. "I heard something that inspired me to return to Peru."

Her dark hair and skin tone complemented Sage's paleness perfectly. She does look like an Olmec princess ran through Secora's mind. That's how her dad had often referred to her.

Jimmy winked at Secora and said, "Guess things had a way of working out after all."

Secora sent him a knowing smile and nodded.

L.W. took Monta in her arms and kissed her, then handed the baby to Sage. "Ed Savage at the Anthro office filled us in with what was going on with Iris and Jane."

Secora looked anxious. "I tried to call you! I left you a message but never heard back."

"Sorry, we didn't receive your message till we'd already arrived in Peru," L.W. responded as she again put her arm around her daughter.

Sage was holding the baby over his head and saying, "So you must be my sweet little granddaughter, Monta?"

Was that a panic-stricken glance Azalea gave Bob? Secora wondered.

"Uh, Mom, Dad, I'd like to introduce you to Gideon Yellow Thunder—Heyoka. And this

is Jimmy Lizardeye, mentor and Wichasha Wakan. They are my indispensable warrior buddies and close companions.

Sage and L. W. nodded grinned with their handshakes.

I'd also like to introduce you to..."

L.W. took a few steps over to Azalea and Bob and offered her hand. "Ed told us about Azalea and Bob, so nice to meet you both."

The tracker quickly stepped away looking at the ground. He drew everyone's attention away when he called, "Hey guys, you should see this—looks like there was some sort of skirmish up here. That rock over there appears to have been splintered when it was hit by a metal object."

"Like a bullet?" asked Jimmy flatly.

Bob glared at Jimmy. "Yeah, maybe like that."

They spread out, looking for more information, and converged on a path beaten into the foliage leading northeastward. The bushes were scratchy against their arms and legs, and bugs swarmed as they neared the water.

"Here's a computer destroyed by gunfire," Sage panted as they continued.

Secora heard the thunder of a forceful river in the distance as she hurried to catch up.

Forty-five minutes later, they came to a spot where a group of people had sat. There were masses of flies on a smelly acrid residue.

"Vomit?" suggested L.W.

"Ugh, I think so. Lots of it! Disgusting!" replied Azalea.

"Think I'm gonna puke," said Bob...and he did. Afterward, he said, "I need a break."

"Okay, but let's clear out of this dreadful place first," said Sage.

When they descended another half mile, Secora heard her father say,

"Oh my God, there's dried blood over here—and old drag marks." She turned around to join him in scrutinizing the leaves and the ground cover.

Jimmy, who was farther down the hill said, "Drops of dried blood and drag marks over here too. Kinda looks like someone dragged a travois down toward the water – maybe more than once."

Secora noticed that Azalea and Bob were searching the surrounding brush thoroughly, apparently looking for clues or bodies. Azalea said, "Looks like a couple of bodies were dragged over behind this bush, but they got up and left."

"What does that mean?" asked Bob.

L.W. moved some bushes aside. "Don't know, but we found some resting places here, also."

Gideon sounded surprised when he said, "Wait; there are a couple of boots left here. Both are for the right foot. Now there's a mystery."

With all senses alert, the travelers wandered down the rest of the trail, until it splayed out toward a sandy beach that ran about a mile along the expansive river. They found no people, no bodies, and nothing else of interest. Tensions began to ease, but Secora felt perplexed about what to do next.

She'd noticed three caimans on the beach when they arrived. Bob's gun killed two, and the third left without further encouragement. Monta burst into tears at the sound of the gun, and a bevy of comforters quickly surrounded her, much to the infant's surprise.

Azalea warned, "Stay off the sand. There are disease-causing, blood-sucking, flesh-munching chigger fleas. They'll consume your feet, hands, and anything else they can reach."

Secora sighed. "Thank you, Azalea, and thank God we have shoes, clothing."

Spreading out, they decided to take a break on various pieces of driftwood. Most took the opportunity to eat a sandwich or other snack, while they pondered options. Bob was not so inclined. He walked down the shore until he looked like a speck.

While finishing a peanut butter sandwich Secora noticed L.W. was visiting with Azalea. She unsealed a fresh bottle, added water to fruit juice powder, and shook. Now, who has Monta?

"We need to feed the baby." She smiled and gave the bottle to Sage. Monta was definitely interested. Grabbing the offering, she began sucking hungrily. Next, Secora dug around the baby bag for a container of graham crackers, which she laid on the log for when it was needed.

She spied Gideon away from the group and decided to join him, leaving Monta to play, standing on the log near Sage, who grasped her around the waist while she held her hands out like a tightrope walker.

Gideon must have noticed, because he rose and walked toward Secora. "Wait, I'm coming over there." The Heyoka sat down beside the aged professor.

Monta was determined to walk by herself now, but when she tried to step and move, she clung to Sage's fingers like a tiny gibbon. Moments later he placed Monta on Gideon's leg. In turn, Gideon casually told Sage, "Bob Greenwood is a dead-eyed killer who doesn't deserve to live. I think he is here specifically for Secora and me. Others would be collateral damage. He is merciless." He shook his head and repeated, "He showed us no mercy in West Glacier."

Sage, unfazed, continued to look at the river, pointing to an oncoming caiman as cover for their conversation. "And Azalea?" he quietly inquired.

Gideon answered, "We're not sure how she fits in but she was sent by the same people."

Sage asked Gideon, "I assume my daughter's not making a move until the research crew is rescued, right?"

Both Gideon and Secora nodded. "It figures, we might need the manpower."

"Bob is almost here." Secora grabbed the baby who needed to burp.

"We'll go so they won't expect trouble," she said as she walked back toward the others patting Monta's back. She overheard Sage's parting shot, "You two get into so much trouble—you ought to be married."

Gideon laughed as he said, "My thoughts, exactly."

She grinned to herself. At least he wasn't still talking about "Auntie Secora". When she sat back on the log near her backpack, she said to Jimmy, "Jane and Iris would likely have crossed the river. But how, and in which direction?"

Jimmy was squinting across the broad watercourse. "Do those people across the way appear to be climbing into canoes?"

When Secora followed the direction of his eyes, she noticed humans the size of ants in the distance. "Perhaps an outpost of watchers has spotted us."

Jimmy stood and shaded his eyes. "Looks like they've pushed two dugouts off the far shore."

Moments later, oarsmen paddled past mid-river in super-sized dugouts, and Jimmy yelled, "Incoming."

"I hope it's good news," said L.W. nervously as she trotted over. She whispered in Secora's ear. "Sage and I suspect that someone has been following us. Maybe more than one person." Secora's eyes grew large, and she leaned closer in response to the question in her daughter's eyes. "It's merely a hunch. We haven't seen them, but I don't think we're wrong." She tickled Monta and smiled.

Secora nodded, whispering loud enough for Jimmy to also hear, "Tell Dad if you have a moment alone; this could be a good thing." Now it was L.W.'s turn to wonder.

As the boats neared, Bob pulled his pistol and stood at the ready.

"Stow the weapon," ordered Jimmy. "What's the point, Bob?"

The biologist looked rattled but put the pistol back in a side holster. Secora immediately noticed the boatmen had light skin and blue, green, or hazel-colored eyes. Their fine-textured hair shone in shades of blond or light brown which amazed her—*similar to Alai.*

Sage was already at the water's edge, babbling excitedly. "Remember what I told you, honey." Her father gave her a side hug. He'd taught his girls there had been many cultures and a number of great civilizations which dominated the jungles and cloud forests of Andean valleys for thousands of years, prior to the Incas whose empire lasted a mere hundred years before they were taken down by murderous Conquistadores.

The prow of the first dugout pushed up onto the sand. "Ur Mazd," hailed one of the boatmen. Then he continued in English, then Spanish, "We, are Gueros. Somos los Gueros."

Sage's family bowed; Jimmy nodded solemnly.

The boatman must have noticed more of a reaction to the English, so he said, "We were watching the river for anyone who might be seeking our other guests."

"Guests?" asked Sage in English. "We are looking for two women with many children." As he removed his fedora, he half bowed again. Secora followed suit, as did the others who weren't quite sure what was happening. At this point, they didn't need a special reason to honor their potential rescuers.

"Come with us, they are safe."

Sage grinned at his wife. "I find it fascinating they hailed us with 'Ur Mazd.'"

Bob asked, "What's that, a shortened version of Ahura Mazda?"

Sage turned to "Dead Eyes" with surprise. "Yes, Bob, It's the name of God rendered in the ancient tongue Zoroaster used." The few Gueros who understood Sage's words in English were suitably confused.

The Gueros could not have found a more appreciative group of humans anywhere on the planet. The astonished travelers picked up their gear and loaded it into the dugouts. The seven and a half team members fit in easily and the masterful oarsmen shoved off for the return trip across the river.

Sage softly mused, "Wonder if the Gueros still remember Viracocha?"

Though nobody asked him, Sage began to hold forth. "The Chachapoyas were known as 'Warriors of the Clouds.' This is like going back in time over 2,000 years, to the early days of their activity."

"Uh, Dad, maybe people aren't interested in an impromptu archaeology lecture."

"Can't help it, dear, this is phenomenal!" "Go ahead," urged Jimmy.

"The rise of farming, and the subsequent appearance of permanent human settlements, eventually allowed for overlapping civilizations to develop in South America. For example, the Paracas, Diaguitas, and the Calchaqui, who survived because the Utcubamba River Valley was isolated from the coast and other areas of Peru by large rivers and difficult terrain. They found exceptional ways to farm, and were also skilled artists, excelling in colorful clothing and painted pottery. Among them were architectural masters who took their trade with them wherever they traveled."

He stopped to look at his wife. "Honey, this is really where you shine."

L.W. was visibly awed and added, "Like Alai's people, those tribes were reflections of an earlier culture. Many had lighter skin and hair colors. They wore ear spools and created exquisite textiles. It was not unusual to see tiered red hats worn as status symbols. They originally had a charismatic, perhaps even a messianic religion. This has been my life's study, but I wouldn't have dreamed in a million years I would meet a descendant of these lineages. I mean, meeting Alai, Secora's intended mother-in-law, was amazing enough."

L.W.'s words jabbed at Secora's heart. She was assailed by thoughts of losing Diego until she almost felt nauseous. Now there was no one to carry on the line of Alai's people. She *wondered what is going on with Alai.*

24

UNITY

W hile crossing the massive river, the canoes dodged several caimans which Secora didn't want to see, so she closed her eyes. After a moment, she felt relaxed for the first time since she'd received the news of the girls' disappearance several days ago. In her head, she repeated thank you, God, thank you, God, thank you, God, then inhaled deeply, wondering how their story had led the archaeology team to these Gueros. Without warning, her focus was broken by loud chatter as a cluster of black monkeys whooped and screeched from trees on the nearing bank.

Moments later, Secora squinted at the people on the shore. One of them was smaller than the rest.

Gideon's voice was filled with emotion, "Oh my God! It's Kyah— he's safe." After they pulled the long canoes up on the sand, the whole family hugged the boy and wandered into the lowland bush led by Gueros, who were exchanging information in their own language. Secora thought she could make out a couple of words, but not enough to make any sense of what they were discussing.

Bob, A.K.A. Dead Eyes, was in his natural glory. He was snapping photos and recording sounds, almost gleeful now his search and rescue skills were no longer needed. Secora thought,

Huh, maybe he really does have a flair for biology. She returned her attention to Gideon and Kyah, reunited and inseparable now. The boy turned and looked at Secora, or rather, Monta. He loped back with his arms stretched out to grab the infant. "I can't believe you have this beautiful baby. Can I hold her, please?"

She felt a grin spread from ear to ear. "And I can't believe you're so tall."

"Five-foot-six-and a half," he bragged.

She handed Monta over. "And you still look like you weigh about a hundred pounds."

He laughed and told her he wanted the baby snuggly to carry Monta up the trail. A couple of hours later, they began to climb toward a high cliff wall. Secora wasn't the only one fatigued. It took the old-timers quite a while to ascend the path to the top. L.W. might even have fallen off a boulder in the trail, if it weren't for the quick reflexes of Gideon and Jimmy. As they climbed the last rise, spectacular housing structures came into view, reminding Secora of the largest cliff dwellings she remembered from the Southwest, but much more expansive.

Not only did the vastness of the stone city blow the travelers away, but Secora also marveled at its lovely people with their unusually colored eyes. The decorative hairstyles and long earlobes—a few of which displayed colorful earspools, also enchanted Secora. She watched as most of the travelers greeted the Gueros warmly.

With arms extended, their hosts yelled, "Ur Mazd! Ur Mazd!"

"Ur Mazd." Sage Dalton raised his hands in homage as did Secora and L.W.

"It's like visiting Zoroastrian heaven!" he added.

As they rounded the turn into the plaza, he gleefully declared, "No. You know what this is? It's like visiting Tiahuanaco during its heyday."

L.W. suggested, "It also looks like the towers of the people of Ad who rejected their great prophet, Hud, in early Arabia; before every living thing was buried by God's great storm, under thirty feet of sand."

Secora replied, "Yeah, okay Mom, nice comparison but kind of morbid."

L.W. continued, "That's fair. How about the Chachapoya towers at Kuelap and Gran Pajaten instead?"

Secora laughed. "Now you're talking." I've read that the Chachapoya encircled their major urban centers with massive stone walls which would span up to sixty feet. In a few cases, the walls protected more than four hundred interior buildings."

"This place has its own natural wall." Sage rubbed a hand through his silvery hair as he walked beside L.W. "Dear, wasn't Kuelap known as the 'Machu Picchu' of the north?"

"I think it might have been, my love, but I can't remember. I'm sure Jane and Iris can give us specifics from their research."

Secora eyed her mom and then looked up to the towers in the cliff, searching for connections. "They say it was as powerful as Machu Picchu—for those who saw it, but too remote for most visitors to see. Shouldn't we concentrate on *this* moment, and *this* magnificent refuge?"

"Yes, you're right," laughed Sage. As he pointed out to L.W. and anyone who would listen, the various architectural patterns structures in the Guero village. There were circular stone rooms, and towers with conical roofs, as well as rectangular rooms. The walls were often decorated with symbolic images or dancing figures.

"The Chachapoyas also cut raised funerary platforms into spectacular mountain slopes. Usually, the tombs faced outward and could be seen from several canyons at once. The mummies seemed to have traits of European tribes. Most might had had, red, light brown, or blondish hair. Maybe later, a few black-haired Incan magistrates were included.

Many of the corpses were eviscerated like the Egyptians and..." A hand covered his mouth.

"Whoa. Get a grip, Dad," laughed Iris as she and Jane trotted over to welcome Secora and her parents with tears in their eyes.

"It's so very good to see you all again!" Iris seemed giddy.

"Even me?" asked Secora.

Iris took the bait. "Well, maybe, this once..." Then she buried Secora in a hug.

Monta cried out, apparently jealous. Kyah tried to calm her, but L.W. reached her arms toward the pouty baby asking if she might hold her.

Secora was more than happy to continue the mommy break while L.W. took Monta to sit with the other women and their little ones. She didn't want to be that mom who said, "Children have germs," or "Don't spread diseases." Yet, a voice was screaming inside her head, telling her diseases could literally be spread between continents here. She must trust God and the abilities of the healers—and hand sanitizer. She smiled and handed a bottle to her mother.

Iris walked beside Secora. "Sis, I was so mad at you... but now, I couldn't be happier to see you." She swung her arms around Secora and started to weep. "I've missed you so very much."

Secora found a place for them both to sit so she could console her kid sister, who at twenty-six was thirteen years younger.

During a brief silence, they heard Sage's voice bleed through. He was still regaling listeners with stories about excavations of spectacular ruins, exquisite pottery, impressive tombs, hand-made ceramics, and also cloth that was frequently colored red.

"Their painted walls depicted stages of ritual dances, and couples holding hands."

Secora looked past Iris to see who was listening to this lecture. She burst out laughing with the image. Among the audience members, she noted Azalea was seated next to the Daltons looking bleary-eyed. She heard footsteps approaching from behind and repositioned herself on the stone to watch Jane approach with a shy-looking Aparu in a flowing robe. His eyes were a striking gray, brown. Gideon also came up from the opposite direction and stood beside Iris and Secora.

Jane began by introducing her brother to Aparu. Gideon, who was now holding Monta nodded respectfully, then sat beside Secora and asked, "Are the two of you getting married?"

"That's the plan," Jane chuckled.

"What does Kyah say?" Gideon stood up again as he watched his thirteen-year-old nephew trot over.

"Kyah says, right on, Mom!" He shoved his fist into the air in a sign of solidarity. He hugged his uncle with tears building. "Love you."

"Me too, Kyah." Gideon choked, "Almost thought I wouldn't see you again."

Kyah stepped back so he could look into his uncle's eyes. "What does that mean?"

"I don't want to talk much about it, but I almost froze solid in a cave."

"Like a Popsicle?" Kyah's eyes were huge.

"Yeah, but more like an uncle-sicle." Gideon laughed trying to make light of the situation, then added, "It really wasn't very funny."

Kyah buried his head in Gideon's chest and hugged him for several moments.

Secora's attention was drawn back to Iris who was explaining she'd learned a lot in the last few days.

"About...?"

"I have also met a beautiful man named Kantun."

"Are you serious?"

"We'll talk about it later."

Secora set her jaw and said firmly, "Spill."

Iris admitted she could now comprehend the vagaries of love which Secora had experienced with Diego.

Secora took Monta back from Gideon—then handed her to Iris.

"You ready for a precious one like this in your life?"

Iris gazed into sweet Monta's face. "Well, I'm not sure about adopting a child, but, yes... love allows me to think of more sweeping visions, like being a parent."

"I'm very happy for you, Iris, and I want to meet Kantun." At this invitation, Iris stood and left with a smile.

Jane, Aparu, Kyah, Secora, and Gideon trailed behind Iris, to meet a young man who was waiting alone.

Iris's joy and expectation were genuine and Secora was thrilled for her baby sister. For once, Azalea and Bob weren't foremost in Secora's mind.

After introductions were completed, every one of Secora's party met with and checked in on the eight relatively healthy university students. Next, they all moved over to the quarantine area near the rear entrance of the village.

The man, oddly enough, named Gilgamesh after a Sumerian Noah-type Prophet who lived thousands of years ago, was struggling to recover. Sammy was suffering from his swollen leg wound, but Amy's arm didn't seem to slow her down. Still, it would be nice to send them off to a Missoula hospital as soon as possible.

At this point, exhaustion had taken a toll on Secora and her extended family members so they wandered off alone or in pairs to find private spots to rest.

After restful meditation on their situation, Secora went to look for Jimmy. He was across the plaza nearly a quarter-mile away. As she walked, she took in the sweeping view of the canyon and the cliff beyond, and froze in consternation. *Oh boy, when Dad sees this, he'll never stop talking.*

There indeed, were wooden faces staring at her from across the canyon. A tomb containing dozens of sarcophagi arranged side by side in vertical rows, sat like dolls on ledges which had been carved out of the rocky cliff. They rested at the same approximate elevation as the stone city. Secora was stunned to see such a sight. The gray weathered sarcophagi stared back as if in awe of seeing her.

Conical or bullet-shaped wooden husks wore partially painted masks—faces you might recognize from Europe, complete with large eyes, hats, beards, and friendly gazes. Secora assumed they contained cross-legged corpses who sat with arms crossed in front of their faces. And from what Dad told her, the burial relics included metal goods, pottery, and beautifully woven cloths. She observed that a number of the burials had deteriorated, and a few mummies had straggly reddish hair peeking out. Her breath was taken away when she noticed several of the caskets depicted painted extensions like the outstretched Wings of Isis, Horus the Falcon, or the Zoroastrian Farvahar. A pattern found throughout the Middle East— and according to Jane and Iris, also on the altar at Ojo Redondo.

She couldn't help but turn toward each of the figures in astonishment, taking in a vision from a past which she'd only heard of. A few of the faces exhibited black-ringed eyes as large as dinner plates, which could easily be seen across the distance.

A prayer of gratitude and thanksgiving escaped Secora's lips. "Awesome, in the deepest sense of the word," she expressed to no one.

Her dad stepped beside her and touched her shoulder as he whispered, "I literally fell into one of those beautiful Sarcophagi when a pair of machine-gunning German thieves strafed an associate and me. Because of that incident, I recognized that L.W. was a living, breathing replica of the holy woman entombed in that sarcophagus."

"I've got to admit, Dad, not too many guys tell a love story like that."

"That part especially fascinates me," said Iris as she came up and hugged both of them.

Sage nodded with an impish grin, and said, "You know, Pedro Cieza de Leon described those people as unusually fair-skinned like the Inner-Asian tribes, and quite beautiful. He also described their wives as being beautiful for their gentleness. Of course, he also thought many deserved to be Incan wives and to be taken to the Temple of the Sun."

Kyah walked up with L.W., Aparu, and Jane, and made a face saying, "That's so sick, Grandfather."

L.W. agreed, "Enough talk about that."

Sage was dutifully humbled. "Yeah, please forget I ever repeated that part."

When they finally arrived at the place where Jimmy sat cross legged, Secora sat on the hard-packed earth next to him. He turned to her and said casually, "I'm learning about spiritual beliefs from this gentleman, Gilgamesh Spitama." She nodded solemnly to the man who was bandaged around his mid-section, thinking he must be masking the pain.

Jimmy continued, "L.W. stitched up his injured duodenum, and I think he'll heal pretty quickly now."

Gilgamesh nodded.

"He agrees," acknowledged Jimmy.

"I surely hope so." Secora was puzzled. "How did he know your thoughts? You two have a telepathy thing going on here?" Both men nodded.

"Whoa." She bowed her head to each of them.

That afternoon, Secora let the university know what was going on from her perspective, and that the whole crew was alive and basically okay. Apparently, Azalea had given her report a few hours earlier.

Jane and Iris grabbed the phone from Secora and gave the details of their capture and escape, in their own words to the Anthro Department. They also requested to remain another week after the students left. At this time, they shared nothing about the enormous ethnographic study they were living and how it might tie into the original Chachapoya project.

Secora moved on to look for her child. She was taken by surprise to find L.W. and Sage had her along with the baby bag, sitting on a wall opposite the sarcophagi. Two friendly women were feeding Monta a type of mash. The baby made one of those head shakes associated with a "yuk, it tastes horrible" experience. But then she opened her mouth and ate it anyway. Everyone was laughing and sympathizing until she opened her mouth for another bite.

Surprised, Secora asked, "What is it?"

"That's a fair question. Not really sure, dear," L.W. replied. "We think it is a variety of squash." She held up a button-sized gourd. "Good for babies, they say. We've got this, honey. Take some more time for yourself. Your Dad is leaving shortly to visit the girls and their, um, uh... their fiancés. I think the men will be asking permission from him and Gideon. But dear, I'm not sure Iris is ready for such a huge change. Jane and Kyah certainly are. They seem very committed."

Secora agreed and then taking her mom's advice she slept for hours. According to Iris and Jane, the students and the rest of the family spent a peaceful afternoon, and early evening in the heavenly city. Many spent their free time recording aspects of culture, history, prehistory, or the biota.

Later in the evening, there was a circle of people enjoying music and dancing that was different from anything Secora had ever experienced. Graceful at every step, in toward the center, and back again, twirling, dipping, and gliding—intoxicating. Secora recalled the frescoed dancers painted on the walls. The fibers of their costumes and the weave and color of their hats and shawls were strongly influenced by the charismatic Chachapoya culture.

Though the entertainment was magical, she became awkwardly

aware she was sitting with Azalea and Bob. She couldn't ignore them, so she randomly asked, "What's it like to be at someone else's family reunion?" She could see that Bob was non-committal, so she fished. "I hope you're not too bored now the mission is nearly accomplished."

In the silence which elapsed before Azalea answered, Secora heard her father talking and smiled.

"It is documented that the peaceful Chachapoyas eventually killed a few of the merciless Incan governors, captains, and soldiers. This sadly resulted in their continued slavery, imprisonment, or death."

Secora craned her neck around and spotted her father. Most of the university kids were hastily scribbling notes as Dr. Dalton spoke.

"Many of those who weren't killed were forced to resettle in the remotest locations of the empire, and due to their harsh treatment and pitiful subjugation, many of the Chachapoyas chose to join the encroaching Spaniards rather than fight them."

Her attention was pulled back to Azalea, who was now drawing lines with a little stick on the dust which covered the hardpan. "We *are* eager to return home now that the crew has been safely located," said Azalea with a stern look.

Secora wondered how they were going to stop Bob or Azalea from talking to people at the university about the Gueros. Then it came to her that neither of them appeared either to understand or speak Spanish or Guero. That could be a blessing. Their information should be extremely limited, and they did not know the city's exact location.

When the dancers and musicians signaled the end of their perfor-mance, the visitors extended an impromptu offering of gifts. It evolved into an exchange. The students placed into a pile items like key chains, pens, paper, cheese and cracker snacks, and candy bars. Amy helped Sammy, who was hobbling with a crutch, to deliver one of his comic tee-shirts.

The Gueros ran home and returned with beautiful cloths, bowls, and crystals. The evening closed as the students and other guests thanked their saviors and hosts. Eventually, people began to separate and disperse. Jane, and Iris, and their fiancés sat with Sage and L.W. Azalea and Bob sat near Jimmy, who had once again boldly inserted himself between them and Gideon. Secora grinned. *Forever bless his courageous heart and soul.*

It was dark now, and everyone finally appeared to feel safe and secure. Secora said, "Good night; Monta and I are turning in." They found a little place where they could nestle with a quarter-inch of sand to soften the hardpan. She spread out her leather jacket for Monta to lie on; and then covered both of them with the Ruana shawl. The little girl began to breathe steadily almost immediately.

Secora wanted to fall asleep, but worrisome thoughts flickered in and out of her mind. She prayed illness wouldn't befall either the Gueros or the North Americans and wondered about what would happen tomorrow. Best case scenario, the boatmen would take all of us downriver to the town of Arequipa so we can catch flights back to Montana - *But what about Azalea and Bob?* When will they make their moves? It was hard to think of that dark possibility at this serene moment and it gave Secora a chill. At that psychological instant, she felt a body drop down behind her.

"Hello?" Secora asked warily.

"It's me," Gideon's voice answered, "Might as well make it easy for the bad guys to find us."

"That's not funny—at all. I'm a black widow and you shouldn't be here."

"Whoa? What are you talking about?"

"Rick... and Diego, and don't pretend you can't see what's happened to you since you met me."

"The icy mine had nothing to do with you."

"Except for Billy and whatever he discovered - and told me about. Things didn't work out so well for him either, now you mention it. In fact, I wonder if he is still in the burn recovery unit, or if the poor man is even alive."

"He's probably fine... all right, so you are a black widow."

"Again, not funny," she barely whispered. "But honestly, I'm so glad you're here." Monta adjusted herself, cuddling closer to her mom. With a smile, Secora fell asleep in relative peace.

25

VILLAGE LIFE

"Wake up, sleepy head."

Secora acknowledged Iris's charming voice by groaning with her eyes still closed.

"The dawn is disappearing, and so is your daughter."

Secora popped opened her squinting eyes long enough to confirm Monta was indeed crawling away. She sat up, yawned, and reached out to grab the little leg she could still reach. Automatically, she took a diaper from the baby bag and began the process of freshening Monta.

Secora startled when she heard a groan from behind her. At that point, she smelled his Old Spice cologne. *Oh, it's Gideon.* She smiled remembering he'd spent the night next to them.

She wiggled a pair of heavy-duty jeans onto Monta and let her crawl around while she changed her clothes modestly beneath the shawl. When she was done, Secora turned partway around and put an arm on Gideon's sleeve.

"Hey, Gideon, we're still alive."

Another groan was his only response, so she shook out the shawl and covered him head to toe.

Jane had taken Monta in tow. The baby wanted to run but wasn't quite skilled enough with her coordination. She had to settle for toddling with her arms out to the side for balance. When Jane was tired of bending down, the baby fussed at being picked up and held. Jane cooed, "I know you were on a roll, little one, but disaster was only a step or two away."

Secora heard Iris suggest to Jane, "Let's go see what Mom and Dad are up to."

Kyah ran up to Jane and grabbed the baby. "I need to borrow her for a moment, okay Secora?"

Jane looked to Secora.

"Sure, I guess... but no cliff climbing," Secora called after him as she joined her sisters.

"I promise," floated back.

The girls heard Sage and L.W. laughing from a place deeper among the ruins, toward the back of the cave. They went in to explore. On the way, Secora noticed Bob, secreted in a corner, speaking into his phone. When he noticed her, he turned away as if guarding his conversation.

Sage was regaling Gilgamesh and a few other Gueros. Secora noticed that kindly, Aparu was translating.

"Your amazing ancestors strongly resisted the Incas, but they were overwhelmed in 1475 even though they had prepared for the invasion for nearly two years. In the end, the Incas climbed 28,000 feet to conquer a major Chachapoya town, intending to destroy everyone inside—but get this," Aparu abruptly stopped translating and whirled around with puzzlement on his face.

Sage waved the phrase away. "Never mind, please tell them the Incas were met by several women. Their leader was a former mistress of Tupac Inca Yupanqui. They asked for mercy and forgiveness which the Incas granted. The place where the negotiation was held was declared Cajamarquilla, a sacred place closed off, so no man, animal, or bird would ever again put feet inside the area. The surrounding town became a sophisticated cultural center, and they say the ruins are even now, fairly well preserved."

Secora sensed a short break and said, "Good morning, Mom and Dad, we should start breaking camp this morning." Sage nodded.

Iris offered. "We can help you."

Any further thoughts on the subject were interrupted by sounds of excitement as a hunting party came through the plaza carrying the body of a large young tapir which would provide food for all. Its fur was a lovely brown with a pattern of white spots and stripes. Secora was in awe of the creature. She hadn't even thought about one, since the time a group of them had run her over last summer and knocked her unconscious. She shook away the unpleasant thought. So much had happened since then.

Gideon strode up combing his shiny black hair. Secora felt her smile grow into a ray of sunshine.

"Hey, good to see you." Gideon joined them with a half-smile and a blanket wrinkle on the side of his face.

Sage noticed the unusual dent on the young man's cheek. "You okay, buddy?"

"Yeah, I guess so. Just woke up."

"Oh, that explains it."

Secora watched them leave. The girls and L.W. sat down for a visit. But Secora suddenly felt a shiver and left to find a warm spot by the morning fire. Bob sidled up to her, saying nothing.

She wanted to run away, but instead, she asked, "Hey, Bob, are you tired of this place?"

Pretending to warm his hands, he leaned over and said, "Yeah, it's cool in the morning, but too hot for me day in and day out."

"For me, too, I should probably live in Alaska." Secora's laugh felt a little forced. Making small talk with a murderer wasn't so easy. "Have you been able to find any interesting plants or animals since we arrived?"

"Oh yeah, I found dozens of things worth studying. I was having great success this morning, until I ran across a Fer de Lance in the valley. In a heartbeat, running around finding stuff... lost its allure."

"Oh, man. There are lots of scary venomous creatures here. I'm realizing how nice it will be to return home to Montana."

The man with the dead green eyes said, "I think a massive animal is hanging out in the canyon below this cliff."

Her eyes questioned his. He continued, "Yeah, the kid showed me a photo of tracks which kind of look like they belong to a hippo, but bigger. Can you believe it? A hippo. Want to check it out?"

She wondered if he was trying to isolate her to fill a contract. After a moment, she said, "There's plenty of suitable vegetation to support a small population of large creatures." She could see a sparkle glittering in his eye underneath the shades as she looked at him from the side. "I also thought I saw peculiar tracks cross our path as we came up here yesterday."

He stood back from the fire. "I've decided to do a little more poking around this morning before we go. You interested?"

"Not really, but you shouldn't go alone. Most of the large creatures in South America are nothing to mess with. They've had to survive a mean variety of predators for thousands of years—those tracks might even belong to one of those mean predators."

"Predators with hippo tracks?"

"Yeah, probably not, but they might still be dangerous." She sucked her teeth. "How big?"

"Can't really tell."

"Last year I'd have loved nothing more, but I am a mother now and I've sobered up about messing with big critters. It's not as tempting. Remember how the Fer de Lance made you feel?"

"Your loss." He wandered away and was replaced at the fire by Azalea.

Secora started the conversation. "So, Azalea, what do you get out of this trip besides a free lecture series by the famous Dr. Sage Dalton? Were you bored in Montana, or was it the lure of the wild? Did you want to step out and see the world?"

"Well, I'm retired, and the extra cash was appealing."

"What's it like to be retired? I think my parents are going a bit bonkers with their retirement."

"I keep busy."

Secora turned to the older woman looking her in the eyes. "How did you hear about this job? Seems like an odd place for you to be. I don't imagine there was an ad in the paper for this kind of thing." She felt like adding, it would be such a perfect place to get rid of someone, away from prying eyes.

"No, I heard about it from an employee who works there—at the university. He mentioned it in passing. How about you?"

Secora looked up and sighed. "Well, it would have been hard to keep me away from my family members and the students under these circumstances. How about Bob? Did you know him before we left Montana?"

"Hmm? No, why should I? Biology isn't my thing."

Secora turned when she heard the commotion. Students were grabbing their gear and preparing to leave the area. Kyah rushed up with the other children, and he lifted Monta into Secora's arms. "Thanks," he said and took off. "Need to help my mom get ready."

Secora suggested, "She might still be in the back of the cave. Let's go check there."

Azalea walked beside her. "Again, I have to ask, why would you bring such a tiny baby with you to the jungle, Secora? This is a really dangerous place."

"An excellent question, Azalea, there are tough choices to make when half of your family has disappeared. If Iris and Jane were back home, I would have tried to leave her with them. Before you ask, my parents were obviously out of town, and I was trying to get them to join us here, and thank God, they did. There was no one else, and the babysitter couldn't handle two tiny children for an extended period of time. Monta is far too precious to leave with a stranger. Did you hear how I came to be her mom?"

"Huh-uh. I assume it was the usual way." Azalea's voice sounded a little scratchy.

Secora cleared her own throat in response. "Not to get maudlin, but my fiancé died weeks before we were married. So, we were never together, and I couldn't have his child."

"Oh."

"This little girl baby was found on a mountain next to her dead mother. She was brought to my fiancé's parents with the hope they could find her a home. They decided she should be mine since their son could no longer give me a child of my own. It was a real surprise. I knew nothing about babies"

"Donald Chastain told us it was an illegitimate child... you don't really want to know what else he said about you."

"So, you know Donald? No kidding, small world. Anyway, little Monta and I have been learning together how to make this work. Would you care to hold her?"

"Oh, uh, no thanks."

I didn't think so. You wouldn't want to become attached to the enemy. But then, she continued, "When I return home, I hope to be able to leave her with my sister or Jane instead of taking her with me to work. When she grows a little older maybe I can find daycare, or maybe my parents will help."

"I guess it would be pretty hard to dig up mammoths and the like, with an infant."

Secora's eyes shone a bit fiercely. "Mammoths, huh? That's kind of specific. It might not be as bad as one would think. Anyway, winter quarter is dedicated to classes. Fieldwork isn't scheduled until late spring."

Azalea looked at the ground as she walked. "You know, I wouldn't mind going on a dig."

"Really? What kind of dig would you be interested in?"

"I don't know, maybe a mammoth. It all sounds so exciting."

"Azalea, dear, I think the intrigue is a myth. Mostly, the work is as boring and repetitive as knitting."

"Oh?"

"You are basically deconstructing a piece of ground one centimeter at a time. If you find a root or rock in the way, you make a note, remove it, and continue down. It is like precision nonsense. Most of the time, you find nothing to reward your efforts."

"But what happens when you do find something? Is it amazing?"

"Guess I'll have to let you know, if I ever do."

They were interrupted by popping sounds like gunfire, echoing from the canyon below.

"Where's Gideon?" exploded from Secora's lips, as she looked around wide-eyed and tense. People started to yell over the canyon edge in Guero and Lakota. At first, there was nothing but silence. Then she heard groans, huffing sounds, and the crashing of trees as large animals stampeded below.

L.W. raced over to Secora. "Have you seen your father lately?"

"Yeah, he was walking with Gideon about twenty minutes ago. I don't know where either of them is now."

Azalea said, "I think Bob was going down there to look for a mysterious animal. That kid, Kyah, had a photo of tracks he wanted to check out." Another, louder sound boomed up from the canyon.

Azalea asked if the noise might have been gunfire. "Sounds like he might have found his large animal."

"Mom, please hold the baby, I'll find out."

L.W. didn't look like she wanted to stay.

Secora said soberly, "Mom, please."

"Okay, go. Go."

26

TOXODON

Secora's feet were flying, and her heart began to thud inside her chest as raced down the trail to the creek bottom. Probably a dozen others—students, family members, and Gueros were all flying down the trail with her. Her adrenaline screamed, and her breath roared in and out. She hollered, "Dad, Gideon. Where are you?"

They ran to where they thought the sounds came from and saw broken trees and torn earth. Secora saw Sage, then Gideon who was holding onto his bleeding arm, both were on the ground. Gideon's sleeve was turning a telltale red, and he looked like he was in shock.

Sage stood up and turned toward the crowd, mumbling, "It happened so fast, couldn't stop it, just happened." He shook his head. "Secora, they looked like giant hippo-sized guinea pigs. Didn't see if they had horns on their faces... weirdest..." His voice trailed off as Secora put her arm around him.

"I swear Dad, everything down here except a caiman, looks like a giant guinea pig to you."

Recovering a little, Sage said, "Yeah, that's probably why you like it here so much." Kyah and Jane helped Gideon up. Secora hugged both men gingerly before leaving to read the scene.

The body of Robert Greenwood lay six feet away in a contorted mishmash of mud and blood. His head had been kicked clean away from the body. Secora saw his glazed, green eyes seemed to be wide open with surprise—or fear, perhaps both. She stared, incredulous. Finally, she returned to Gideon and Sage. "Thank God you two are okay."

"I am," said Sage as he tipped his head toward Gideon. "He's not."

Secora hugged and kissed her dad and checked Gideon's arm. "Is it broken?"

"Don't know. It hurts too much to try to move it. I'm pretty sure Dead Eyes was trying to kill me. If it weren't for Sage..."

Alarmed, Secora nodded. "Very likely, the gunfire probably stampeded the animals. Kyah and Jane will take you to the village where Mom or Jimmy can clean the wound and brace your arm. I have to figure out what happened, okay?" She kissed his cheek then left.

On the side of the valley, she spotted several clear tracks. "What the heck is this?" Way too big to be a tapir.

Some tracks had three toes, and oddly, some appeared to be made by combat boots. Secora tried to remember what kind of boots Bob had been wearing, when Azalea arrived and began screaming. Secora ran back, to comfort her and move her back to the city.

The trip downriver was canceled for the day. There would be a burial for Bob, and the university was notified of his loss. Ed Savage at the university couldn't understand why Greenwood hadn't followed Sage and Gideon to safety. "Why did he wait too long?"

"I'm sorry, Ed. He was already shooting, perhaps at Gideon, which caused the animals to run, so he made his stand. I'm sure the charging beasts were on him instantaneously."

Azalea was now in shock, she wailed as the call ended. Even though Secora was shaking from the disaster, she went to the retired police-woman—the only one who tried to comfort her.

In the end, Azalea chose to believe Bob had died protecting the others.

Sage and Gideon's version began when they went on the excursion at Bob's request. They rambled through the lush vegetation for a few minutes, before they noticed large, chewing-gum-colored bodies in the brush. The men tried to leave quietly, until Bob, who was in the lead pulled his pistol and fired. He hit Gideon who was already trying to jump out of the way of the large oncoming beasts. Sage saw the danger and gave the injured Lakota an extra push, and they both fell into the thicket.

Ed Savage called back within the hour and told Secora the university was trying to figure out how to retrieve the body since they'd officially acknowledged the news of the untimely death.

Secora was thinking, yeah, he should have been killed weeks ago. But she said, "The corpse should be handled with an immediate burial because of the heat and predators. "If you want to dig it up later, at least you'll know where it is."

Sage grabbed the phone from his daughter and heartily supported her idea, while Secora began planning. There weren't any real shovels, so burying him wouldn't be an easy task.

"Don't think they agreed with us, honey. I think they'll be sending a courier for the body. We should let people know in case soldiers find their way in here or a helicopter shows up."

They took a break to organize and eat lunch. Two hours later the mystery about what they would do with the body was resolved. A black helicopter flew in—terrifying the Gueros. Many cried out or fell to the ground in fear. It hovered at eye level with the city courtyard. A line was dropped, and three plain-clothed individuals slid down. They proceeded to load the remains, such as they were, into a bag. Then the corpse and its impassive pallbearers were immediately lifted into the sky.

The chopper veered away from the village, turning 180 degrees. For a moment, it hesitated, then the nose started into a dive. The pilot corrected quickly, and the vehicle returned to his control.

"Must have caught an eyeful of the sarcophagi," chuckled Sage. "It was probably the wooden faces with the flowing beards like 'ZZ Top.'"

Secora chuckled as she shook herself to the present. "That was awfully quick don't you think?"

"What?"

"For a chopper to pick up the body."

"I prefer not to think of it, dear." He looked down and walked away.

Secora watched as his zeal from thinking of the sarcophagi dissipated. When he was tired, she realized that her father looked much older than she thought of him being.

She skipped a few steps to catch up. "Did you notice anything unusual down in the valley before the stampede?"

"Yeah, everything down there was unusual. Plants were huge, the beasts were huge."

"How many of the animals were there? Did you get a look at them?"

"I guess there were more than six—less than ten. Oh, and they had rhinoceros-like faces."

"One last question, did you notice any other men or machines while you were there?"

Sage looked like she had asked him if he thought Martians could really be pink. He shook his head and said, "I need a rest. Your questions are making my head hurt. Love you, dear. I'll circle back to you a little later."

Secora felt like she was in a daze as question after question assailed her mind. What does Dad really know about what happened? Did Bob lead her father into the valley as bait to single out Gideon? Do the

Gueros know more than we do about this? What do *they* think happened? While Secora was seated, meditating on these questions, and playing with Monta, Gideon walked down from one of the towers and joined them. His arm had been bandaged, but there was still shrubbery peeking from his hair.

"So, we're leaving tomorrow morning. All packed and everything ready?" he asked.

She removed a twig from his head. "More than ready, I really can't wait to be home."

"Crazy about what happened to Bob."

"Yeah, crazy." She replied distantly. She looked up at him. "Sorry, Gideon, do you mean his death or the recovery of his remains?"

Gideon leaned against her shoulder. "Both, I guess. I'm tired and the arm hurts."

"You do look exhausted."

"I am, but I feel so relieved to be free of... you know."

She put her arm around his back. "Me too."

After a thoughtful silence, he commented, "In some ways, what the mapinguari did to the government men last summer was very similar to Bob's demise."

"Oh, the smashing, I'm not entirely sure there wasn't another dynamic involved here." She looked at his arm. "It stopped bleeding, how's the pain?"

"Since you asked, it hurts like..."

"Uh-uh." She put her hand over his mouth. "Children are nearby. I get it. Sorry."

"The healers gave me a concoction made with green and purple leaves. Maybe it hasn't taken effect."

"Perhaps you'd be more comfortable lying down. Also, I have Ibuprofen and Tylenol."

Gideon curled up in a nest she made. He mumbled, "Looks like Jane and Iris are doing better than okay."

"Yeah, I wonder how it will work for them. I hope it turns out better than with me and Diego."

"Different time, different place, different people. They will find their own ways." Gideon said as he lay on the shawl, which Secora had taken from her backpack. A little nest of diapers cradled his head. She found a beanie in the pack and put it on her own head, while she settled down cross-legged beside him like a guard dog, in case Azalea was around.

"So, how is the new office in South Dakota working for you?"

"At first it was kind of slow, not many big investors. But the business in Montana is doing quite well, and lately, there have been a few decent nibbles from Rapid City. I think we should be up and running soon."

"That's good to hear. Maybe I'll come out to see it sometime."

"Maybe." Gideon's breathing became steady.

"Guess the medicine is taking effect."

L.W. stopped by to pick up Monta. "Thanks, Mom, I do need another break. I don't know how you did this—day in and day out." Secora handed her the carrier pack, helping L.W. to strap it on.

"Thank you," L.W. said as she glanced at the sleeping man. "Poor Gideon, he has the worst luck."

"You mean ever since he met me. Go ahead and say it, Mom. I'm a black widow, first Rick, then Diego, and now Gideon."

"I wasn't even thinking that," L.W. said with a sadness in her voice. "But now that you mention it..." She laughed out loud.

"What's so funny?"

"You are. Thinking these unrelated events have anything to do with you. Get over yourself, dear."

Behind her mother, Secora could see Kyah trotting by. "Hold up there a moment, Kyah. I need to see the picture you were showing to Bob."

"Oh yeah, Iris and Jane said I should show it to you right away."

"And when was that?"

"Only a couple of days ago."

"Go find it, please." Kyah ran back in the opposite direction.

L.W. said, "I need to find Sage. That will be harder than usual, because I can't hear him. He isn't talking so much today." She giggled. "I'll actually have to hunt him down." She gestured to the sleeping form with her chin. "You two take care of each other, while I catch up on overdue grand-daughter time."

Kyah returned slightly winded. Secora was surprised to see he had a video camera with him. He flipped the viewer open and showed her a clip of clear but very curious-looking tracks, was she looking at three-toed imprints or four? Kyah was staring as keenly as Secora. She viewed the video again. Kyah had placed a cheese and cracker snack pack inside the back print for scale. He said, "The snack pack was four inches across, and I could have put four of them inside it."

"Interesting, thank God it's an herbivore."

"What is it?"

"Well, weird as it may be, it appears you've found the tracks of a kind of Toxodon."

"Cool! What's that?"

Secora drew a picture in the sand of a hippo-like guinea pig beast with an elongated face.

"Don't they have horns like a rhino?"

"Probably not, if they do, they would be more like a buck deer in velvet, not completely formed."

"Wait a minute, Aunty; I'm going to bring someone over who for sure knows what they look like, okay?"

"Okay, but if you see Jimmy along the way would you ask him to come by when he can?"

"You've got it." The boy was gone in a flash.

While Kyah was away, L.W. returned with Monta who looked drowsy. Secora placed the child between herself and Gideon.

"Think I'll take a nap, too." L.W. waved and wandered off. "Thanks, Mom." Monta snuggled in and fell asleep within moments. Secora removed her hat and used it to cover the baby's head.

"Hau, Sloth Woman."

Secora squinted upward and shaded her eyes as Jimmy walked up. "Good to see you too. I wanted to ask if anything about today's events felt off to you?"

He puffed out a laugh. "So many ways to answer." Then his sneer quickly dissipated. "Unfortunately, I know what you mean - unseen assistance."

Secora nodded. "Exactly."

He continued, "Quite possibly. Guess we won't know for sure." He looked away and nodded. "It was what it was. Glad it's done."

Secora picked up a pebble, examined it, and tossed it aside. She didn't have anything more to say.

Jimmy bent down to look at Gideon's arm. "Poor kid can't catch a break. He's dodged death more than three times in less than a year."

"He's alive. I'd say he caught a few breaks," Secora replied wistfully.

"It needs to stop."

She hung her head and said, "Yes, it does." She tossed another pebble. "At least now, he can go home without looking over his shoulder all the time."

"How about Azalea, when's she going to make her move?"

Secora scratched her head and drew in a deep breath. "Good question. She is worried about there being a baby involved."

"Too bad our invisible friends didn't know about her."

Kyah joined them, walking for once. "My friend can't come but says he thinks they don't have horns. But he also said they are usually very peaceful and have never stampeded before today. Something must have spooked them."

Jimmy and Secora looked at each other and said, "Interesting."

Secora added, "Maybe from more than one direction. Thanks Kyah that is important information. You'd make a good detective."

He snorted, "I already am a good detective." Neither of the adults laughed. They smiled in agreement.

Despite the insanity of the day, there was a nice memorial for Bob. Sage and his whole family said prayers for the departed and the Gueros offered a solemn dance of farewell.

"I wonder if they're cousins to the Kallawayas or Alai's people," asked Jane as she and Aparu came to stand near Secora and Iris. Kantun stood only a short distance away.

Jimmy offered a prayer to the Creator and each of the four directions for Dead Eyes's safe passage and much-needed spiritual improvement in the next realm.

Azalea was nowhere to be found that evening, leaving Secora to wonder what change, if any, this would make in her plans.

Jimmy swung by Secora's spot on his way to visit Gilgamesh. "I'll keep a sharp eye on Azalea tonight."

"Thanks Jimmy. Much appreciated."

27

AREQUIPA

Secora and her friends were gathering firewood for the Guero fires, determined to be useful as a thank you to their hosts for taking care of them during their stay. She, Jimmy, and Gideon to a lesser extent, had been gleaning branches and some driftwood, from which they made a huge stack. Kyah and some of the students kept whittling it down as they hauled armloads back to the cliff city.

"Well, at least we can breathe easier now the big danger has passed," Gideon said.

Secora stopped and leaned on a branch like a cane. "Guys, I need to talk to you."

They glanced at her without registering her point.

Secora looked all around the area then said nervously, "The danger may not be over."

"You mean Azalea?" sneered Gideon. "She doesn't seem nearly as bad as Bob. Old, and pedantic, but not horrible,"

"No one is as bad as Bob," mumbled Jimmy. "But your worst danger is bringing Monta here."

Secora felt shocked he would say such a thing.

Gideon sighed and agreed, "Bringing a little girl into this jungle, has already been dangerous, on several occasions?"

They both knew her reasons, Secora was speechless.

He added, "I guess the good news is neither the Rio Branco Police Station, nor the hospital, is far from here."

Secora's eyes were dripping tears by this point.

Gideon noticed. "Hey, sorry, that sounded mean." He put his good arm around her.

"No, it's worse than you know, Gideon." She was careful to account for Azalea's whereabouts and spotted the woman up on the ridge. Satisfied, Secora sat down on a rock before continuing. She whispered. "Sorry to bring this up now, but I need to share it with someone. Gideon, you once said I could cut the small talk and trust you, so here goes... that is, if you are still willing to listen?"

"I think it's already too late for me to reconsider."

"After you left my apartment in a huff, I went to find Billy, and he was, of course, gone."

"I suppose you took the little baby with you," said Jimmy.

"You know I did. What neither of you knows, is Billy had left me clues and artifacts, and even photos in an email. More importantly, there were lab tests which completely supported his data. He needed me to for validation, because I would understand the value of his find, not very many students of prehistory would."

The guys listened intently.

"As I said at the hospital this was a taboo site—the dates are far too early for big-name archaeologists to accept. They'd happily disregard the dates or tear his work apart, but Billy had irrefutable proof. So, he conveniently disappeared before he could get the word out to anyone but me. Now I have even more information than Billy unearthed, and I'm also a target. I've felt that from the very first day in Bellingham where I was spied on and chased. We all found it strange and worrisome when the university sent two babysitters with us."

"Hmmm," grunted Jimmy.

Secora responded, "If real babysitters were necessary, why weren't they sent with the original crew?"

Gideon thought about it. "You've got a point. So, who's in charge of this cabal?"

Secora wasn't finished. "Azalea mentioned to me that she knows Donald Chastain, who has a lot of respect for the founding fathers of anthropology. They didn't believe humans were in America before 13,000 years ago. He might want to destroy the skeleton and any other evidence Billy or I found at the site. And Tarkio told us Bob was buying the mammoth dig property from Donald. Yesterday, Azalea expressed interest in my work at the mammoth dig. She brought the subject up— even asking to join me on such an outing. If she still wants the information, she will come after me, and try to make sure the discovery dies with me. I'm a loose end."

Gideon placed his hand around his jaw.

All were silent until Jimmy said, "She'll need to make her move before you return to Montana."

Secora instinctively looked for Monta, who was nearby, touching stones and drooling.

She picked the little one up and held her close.

Jimmy rubbed his hands together, and then picked at a splinter in one of them. "What if you leave the baby with Iris or your parents?"

"I'm worried that if I take off by myself, she might hold whoever takes her, hostage until she's certain I won't disseminate Billy's information to the public."

Too late for that," Jimmy reflected.

Gideon summed up, "Secora can't take the baby, nor can she leave her with anyone else. All of us need to stick together like a herd protecting a calf."

"What if we become unavoidably separated?" asked Jimmy.

"We won't," Gideon answered.

"But if we did..."

Secora said thoughtfully, "That would be a problem. Maybe I could survive a trip through the countryside, maybe not. Would Azalea kill Monta too? Or just take her. What?"

"You could beat feet to Bolivia and Alai. I have a map. Let's make a plan," Gideon stated with conviction. He swung his head, slinging the hair out of his face as he pulled a small folded map from his back pocket and flattened it.

"Get this. It looks like the Gueros live near the Malinowski branch of the Tambopata tributary of the Madre de Dios headwaters." He was quiet for a moment.

"You could strike out from here for Juliaca, then over to Puno, and from there find passage to the island."

Secora said. "Maybe if I left now, it would force her hand, and you guys could help me out?" Realizing she'd lost track of Azalea, Secora craned around and found the woman was quietly standing behind them, effectively ending the conversation.

Gideon folded the map and tucked it into Secora's pocket.

She said, "Grab a load of wood, Azalea. We're ready to leave."

Everyone left with an armload of firewood, assuming Secora would either go back with the crew or in case of dire trouble go to Isla del Sol.

While Secora, Gideon, Jimmy, and Azalea prepared to leave South America along with the students, Iris surprised no one by saying she would remain another week with Jane.

Sage and L.W. couldn't have been happier. They would also stay, and return to Montana after devoting time to the girls and their fiancées. Sage admitted he was also excited about recording more of the Guero history and beliefs.

The route the rest of the crew took to the river's edge was a shortcut down the backside of the cliff, to a secluded cove where the huge river curved inland.

Secora as she kept an eye on Azalea, that this shortcut must be how they got the injured people to the cave so quickly. Aparu had said as much. "We had to follow the more distracting route for "guests."

Kyah and the rest of the archaeology crew were bored, and a few of them were milling around the shoreline. Secora mused. Maybe they're looking for frogs or crawfish. As it turned out, the travelers wound up waiting forty-five minutes for the injured students to arrive. It was early afternoon before three of the Guero dugouts were loaded and began to move downriver.

The first canoe left with many of the students. Gideon and Jimmy stuck like glue to Secora while they boarded the second dugout. Predictably, Azalea made a point of boarding the same craft. After they were settled in, Secora became aware of a rising commotion in the first boat where Kyah and Aparu were ensconced.

It was unmistakable. Someone yelled, "Oh my God, it's Kyah. He was bitten by a snake." From the moment Kyah's name reached his ears, Gideon was a flash of motion—bounding out of the canoe and racing down to the dugout which had returned to shore. Once he boarded, he disappeared from Secora's sight altogether.

Things were too silent. If it was a viper, the amazing child probably wouldn't make it. Secora began saying the "Remover of Difficulties" prayer repeatedly until its rhythm became one with her breath, one with her blood. She watched, as if in a dream, as the first dugout lazily drifted back into the current and a familiar voice yelled back in Lakota. Secora recognized the language but not the words. She looked fearfully at Jimmy, who translated.

"They are trying to discern what kind of snake it was. Gideon won't leave his side either way." Secora held her breath.

Another message came in Lakota, "Aparu gave him a powerful

remedy for viper poison, just in case. He is still alive. Sorry, my friends, I'm staying here for the journey."

Secora was in a bind. Gideon was gone and could not help. She wondered if she would be a match for the ex-policewoman. No doubt about it, with her bad arm she'd be at a physical disadvantage both on the boat and in the wilderness. At least out there, an animal might attack Azalea. After all, she didn't know much about the dangerous things.

When Secora looked at her back at her nemesis, there was the glint of a Beretta sliding out of Azalea's pack. She wasn't shy about it either. There was no one close enough to stop her. She raised the gun toward Secora who realized in that moment the bullet which would kill her— would probably pass through her daughter who was strapped across her chest.

Jimmy tried to get up, but Secora held him down. "No, you're too far away. She'll shoot you, and then come after me."

Azalea had been waiting for just the right moment—the right distraction—when nobody was looking or close enough to affect the outcome. Secora saw the silencer and knew she would be gone before anyone realized it. Gripping both her backpack and the baby bag, she flipped backwards over the side of the dugout yelling, "Jimmy, be careful. Love you, Need you."

Slogging for shore, Secora panicked. Should she stay with her sister and parents? Would Azalea move on with the others, or pursue her? She waded the final steps into the undergrowth at the shore hoping Jimmy would somehow be able to safely disarm the aggressive woman while she ran into the dense undergrowth dodging and weaving, hoping not to be bitten, and trying to decide what to do next.

To her dismay, she saw Azalea was already in the water, and would soon be in the brush. If Secora ran back to the village, she could give the baby to her sister or one of the Guero mothers, and then make a run for it. In a flash, she decided against that option. How would I even make it from the river to the city before Azalea shoots me? That stretch would be the ultimate place for an attack, I'd be isolated. Everybody in the city would think I was okay. No one would even know about the change in plans. Okay, plan B, she decided as she raced back to the shoreline.

Flailing her arms and hollering, she waded out to the third boat where half a dozen arms pulled her in. Once aboard, she flattened herself to the floor with Monta. She realized she was still praying for Kyah, Aparu, and everyone else on their boat. She added prayers for Jimmy, and everyone on this trip; especially for Azalea, whose capacity to think for herself, rather than just follow orders was sadly limited.

There was no other choice in Secora's mind; she must find help and asylum at Isla del Sol. She dared only to raise her head high enough to look back at the shoreline as the canoe passed around a huge bend in the river. The tiny figure of Azalea was reacting to her situation in an out-of-control dither. Secora could see her taking aim at her when a caiman surfaced a few feet from her legs. She immediately retargeted the weapon on the imminent threat.

Secora thought she could see Jimmy sitting in the boat ahead. She sighed, deeply relieved. Monta began to cry, and she held the baby close, knowing it was only a matter of time before Azalea forced someone to take her downriver.

When she composed herself, Secora asked a boatman if she could go ashore on the other side of the river. The man looked frightened for her but agreed to the request.

Once she landed, Secora waited, hiding in the bushes to see if another boat would come along with the assassin. She felt paranoid, but no other boats were visible, and she wandered up a little pathway that led through a small village.

Secora and Monta were now officially on their own. She had no idea how to travel through the bush with a child, how long it would take, or even if she had enough food for this journey. She slapped at enormous insects. "If we don't make it out of this bug-ridden jungle soon, Monta, we'll come home unrecognizable as humans, looking more like gigantic welts."

She remembered that when she and the guys had been looking at the map, it would take almost fifty-four hours to walk from Arequipa to Juliaca. It should be considerably less from wherever she was now unless she became lost. Putting fear aside, she took strength from the fact she was on the shore which would eventually lead her to Lake Titicaca. There, she and her daughter should be able to find solace and safety. First, she would travel overland to Juliaca. From there she would traverse to the beach at Puno then take a ferry across to Isla del Sol.

She also remembered that the map showed a smaller lake on the way to Juliaca, which might be a good place to rest for the night. But, not for too long, in case the ex-policewoman was following. If for some reason Azalea couldn't follow, this would only be a miserable two-day inconvenience.

28

THE CHASE IS ON

G ideon anxiously waved gnats from his face. The trip downriver was taking forever. He dearly wished he was sitting beside Secora, making sure she was safe. Yet, there was gratitude in his heart. Kyah was conscious and holding his own. Aparu had said it probably wasn't a viper, but the bite was a shock to the boy's system nonetheless. The worried Lakota was told it would still be hours before they arrived at the drop-off near Arequipa.

The Gueros had not been pleased with the idea of paddling so close to a city for any reason. They diligently guarded their anonymity. But Aparu had consented to go in the lead boat, and he would even step onto the dock with his acknowledged brother since he had some knowledge of English.

When the dreary journey finally came to an end Gideon carried Kyah to the dock, even though his bandaged arm throbbed with the effort. Then, both sat down to rest. The boy smiled and was notably in good spirits. Gideon rose again to make sure the remainder of the group had arrived in good shape.

He ran to the next dugout to check for Secora, and discovered she'd jumped off the second canoe because the older woman had pulled a gun. The students and Jimmy related that Secora didn't want anyone to be caught in the crossfire. Gideon ran a shaky hand through his hair. He didn't want to believe what he was hearing, and his heart began to sink into his gut.

When the third boat arrived in Arequipa with the last of students and without Secora, Monta, or Azalea, Gideon became frantic.

Gideon saw that Jimmy's eyes were downcast, and he grabbed his temples with both hands now, thinking, either Secora is already dead, or she's being stalked. When he'd half composed himself, he approached the students from the last boat to ask what happened. Amy told him she saw Secora swing off into the water, slog ashore, and run into the jungle with the baby. When they last saw her, she and the baby appeared to be fine, and the old woman with a gun was nowhere in sight—she'd been left behind on the opposite bank.

"Well, at least she's alive and unhindered, for the moment." Gideon then asked Aparu, if there was any chance the older woman could catch another boat?"

The gray-eyed Guero shook his head. "Probably not—at least not from us. We have all of the men and women who were willing to travel this far toward danger, on these three boats." Aparu added pensively, "Don't you guys have phones?"

Gideon looked stunned. "Okay, yes. Yes, we do. But... if I call her, the noise might get her killed."

He paced the boards of the dock, knowing that besides Secora's predicament, he had a great deal to accomplish in the next few hours, and he still ached from the calamity in the Toxodon Valley.

He and Jimmy would have to make sure the students made it to their flight, and he'd promised to trade provisions for the transportation offered by the Gueros. Yet he couldn't push Secora's fate from his mind.

Things around him began to change. He collapsed in agony. Jimmy was at his side putting one hand on Gideon's good elbow and the other around his back—bracing his friend, shouting, "Heyoka."

Gideon felt like he was in a warm daze. He could hear the searing shriek of a large raptor, and Wakinyan's keen eyes were staring directly at him.

The Thunder Beings hear your anguish. We will help. We can show you things.

Gideon began to receive images in his mind. Secora and Monta were picking their way through river brush. A small boat was dropping Azalea off at the shore, and her pistol was drawn. It looked as if there might be only a few miles separating them.

The vision was gone in a snap and Gideon found himself panting on the boards of the dock near Kyah. When he looked up, there was Jimmy— and Aparu, Amy, and the other students. Jimmy explained, "This happens when the Great Thunderbird gives him a vision. It will take a while for him to get back to his feet. In the meantime, I'll need three volunteers to come with me to buy supplies and bring them back to Aparu so the Gueros may return home. Most of you should stay right here with the heyoka." Jimmy leaned close to Gideon's ear and whispered, "Call Secora now, while they are still separated."

Jimmy then turned to Kyah. "Can you help the students find food? I see a row of vendors across the docks." Kyah's eyes glazed, but Jimmy continued, "I know, I know—it's scary, but you can handle it, my brother." Jimmy reached for his wallet and pulled out the local equivalent of a hundred dollars. "If there is money left when all of our friends have eaten, give it to Aparu to use for needs that may arise in the village." He asked Amy, who was feeling visibly uncomfortable; to keep her eagle eyes on the river for stragglers, and to see that the provisions for the

Gueros were delivered to the dock in good condition. "Don't accept delivery if things don't look right."

Amy nodded, and Kyah acknowledged, "You got it, Uncle Jimmy."

He snatched the list of provisions from Gideon's chest pocket and ordered, "You, stay here. Make the call." Gideon answered with a slight smile.

When Jimmy was gone, Gideon dug out his Satfon. After staring at it for a few moments, he dialed Secora's number. When she answered, he could barely hear her because she was whispering. He said, "Thank God—you're alive!"

"For now, I don't think Azalea knows where I am."

"She does, but you have a good head start. I'll find you tomorrow." He choked with tears. When he could speak again, he said, "You just have to make it through the night. Remember you have a map, she doesn't."

"Okay, love. I'd better get off."

"Love you." He shoved the antenna down and sat in silence while students ebbed and flowed with different tasks.

About an hour later, Jimmy and the volunteers returned, and doctor Lizardeye handed Gideon a paper cup.

"It's lemonade. Drink it."

"Is it safe?"

"Yeah, I bought the lemons and bottled water, but don't expect it to taste sweet."

The food and other supplies were carefully loaded onto the dugouts. Aparu came to say goodbye to his new friends and wish them well on their journey.

For his part, Gideon stood, looked him straight in the eyes, and said, "Be a good husband to my sister, my brother, and thank you for all that you and the village have done to save us and heal our wounds." They grabbed each other's forearms as was the custom, though Aparu was gentle with the injured arm.

The oarsmen paddled out and found a gentle current for the return trip. The research crew waved goodbye, as an unnoticed piece of history disappeared into the distance.

It wasn't easy to shuttle the passengers to the airport, because it took half a dozen taxis and over an hour before they were all together again. At last, the students were checking in at the desk, while Jimmy and Gideon were attempting to change Jane and Iris's reservations. It was then a speaker announced the flight had been delayed by a storm, so they rested in seats in the terminal. Gideon's gangly limbs were aching, and he felt a huge cramp coming on. He got up to stretch his legs and limp around.

Finally, the boarding call was announced. The sleepy students tumbled out of the chairs and headed down the ramp to board the flight. Kyah hugged Jimmy who said, "Stay strong, young man." The boy smiled.

Then he hugged his uncle so hard that it hurt. Gideon was at a loss for words, and tears stung his eyes. "See you soon." Gideon managed to call after him. Then Kyah followed the others. Gideon sighed once the students were all on the plane. Now, he could plan Secora and Monta's rescue.

The streets were mostly vacant and dark when he and Jimmy left the airport. It wasn't easy to hail a cab or find a hotel vacancy at that hour. When they finally checked in, Gideon flopped on the bed for a few minutes before he could say or do anything more. He heard Jimmy groan from the other bed. Later, Gideon checked his watch. He'd better make a call before he blacked out.

Jeannie and Mitch were beyond thrilled to hear from him, and he briefly caught them up on the situation. They were, of course, appalled, and worried for little Monta and her mom. He told them that, God willing, it would all be finished tomorrow when he caught up with Secora and brought her home.

Next, he asked them to confirm who owned the dig site property over by Birch Bay, Washington. He said he figured the name would be Robert Greenwood. Would they please attempt to purchase the property from his estate, since Robert had recently passed on.

Mitch asked, "I suppose you were able to verify this firsthand?"

"Oh yeah, pretty gory. It also turns out he was the assassin with the dead green eyes who killed Kamal Hasan."

"So, Hasan's men helped you out?"

"No. Well, I don't know how the stampede started... I'm not sure. But I think Secora may have suspected something. I was literally too close to the forest and the Toxodons."

"Toxodons?"

"Yeah, first I was shot, and Sage, Secora's father, knocked me into the brush out of the path of those gigantic hippo-type creatures."

"Wait, wait, wait, you were shot?"

"Yes, Jeannie, but I'm okay, thanks to Sage and the healing powers of the Gueros."

Gideon also asked his friends to contact Clive Bull Bear for help with some detective work. "I would like to see if Clive can locate Billy Riggins, AKA Jake Landsing if he's still alive. If he is, could he take him into protective custody and back to South Dakota? The guy could stay at my place if necessary." He thanked them and said he'd be in touch soon.

One way or another, Gideon had to deal with Azalea and a rescue tomorrow. He needed sleep.

The morning came too early, but he and Jimmy made it across to La Paz, Bolivia, where they were able to rent a beat-up truck and an upbeat ultralight. After grabbing a morning meal, they were off to Juliaca.

29

SEEKING REFUGE

When Secora first disembarked she'd had many questions. How was Azalea still following them? Could she have gotten another ride? Assuming she had, how would Azalea know I wasn't headed on a different path toward Arequipa to join my friends? Azalea simply couldn't have seen where Secora landed. There was nothing but caimans and birds around when she was helped off the boat.

Her departure trail wouldn't have been obvious to any non-local passing down the broad expanse of the river. Perhaps the ex-policewoman could have somehow found out from the returning Gueros. Even so, Secora should logically have a good head start. Still, she felt extremely uneasy, driven to keep moving even though Monta was beginning to feel like a fifty-pound sack of corn. She forced her mind to turn to other pressing issues. There wouldn't be enough food for two days' travel. She had survived without provisions before, but she couldn't let Monta suffer.

She would find a freshened goat either on the road or in the next village she came to, and find out if they might part with her, or at least sell some milk. A doe might be too valuable for people to part with.

Well into the afternoon, Secora heard chickens clucking and rustling around the grassy edges of the path. Then she heard the welcome sound of goats bleating. She picked up her pace and entered a tiny settlement that looked like it might only support a few families.

Fishnets were drying on boxes, porches, and on top of anything else that was up off the ground. There were no cars or trucks visible, just a few boats on a small lake behind the houses. Several children stopped playing and some put their hands up to their mouths as she passed, leaving their wide eyes free to stare at the stranger, a gesture also shared by the adults who began to gather.

"Hola, amigos. Hablas ustedes Español?" She needed to get fresh goat's milk, whether or not she could purchase the goat. "Necesito leche de una cabra, por favor." There was no response, so after a moment Secora sat down in the street and took Monta out of the pack.

The little girl sighed as if saying, "Finally, free." She began to toddle around, but never straying far from her mother. Secora reached into the large baby bag and pulled out a bottle, holding it in her lap. She was careful not to look directly at anyone and kept her eyes on Monta, so as not to be rude.

After a few minutes, she could hear folks speaking to each other and several left the street to get back to work. Nearby, a man turned over a bucket and sat down. From what Secora could see, he might be preparing to darn a hole in one of the nets. A second man and a woman approached, leading a goat with a tight bag. Secora dared to look up and the man made the doe stand next to her. She then grabbed a box of baby wipes from her bag and wiped the teat. She striped a little of the milk to check if there was mastitis. Things looked good, so she applied a disposable plastic bottle liner and filled the bottle. She held up two fingers with a questioning look. The man looked at the woman, and she nodded. Then, he nodded his assent as well, and Secora quickly filled and capped a second bottle. She looked up with a smile of gratitude. The couple gestured that she could take more, but she shook her head and thanked them. She offered the equivalent of a few dollars for the milk, and then she gathered her courage and asked if they had a doe they could sell to her. The man wagged his head, and the couple took the goat back to wherever it had been before.

Secora decided not to push her luck and gave Monta one of the bottles on the spot. Now she would be able to keep the last of the dried formula for an emergency. As she placed the second bottle inside her bag, she took stock of the diaper situation and found there should be enough food and diapers to make it to Puno.

Monta was sleepy when she finished, so Secora packed her up and grabbed their gear. She had just begun to walk out of town when a voice called her back in Spanish. When she turned, there was an older woman with a cranky-looking doe whose knees crackled with every single step she took. The beast came up to Secora and turned her head to the side, looking up boldly with that golden, cat's eye iris. The woman named a price for the creature that was nearly dry but could still give enough milk for a baby.

Though the goat was obviously old and wasn't much to look at, it could provide sustenance for Monta. Secora was thrilled and gratefully paid a little more than the woman was asking because it was her way. In response to the lady's questioning glance, she said it was extra to pay for the rope. The woman nodded, satisfied, then turned away and walked back down the street.

Secora was happy when she left the village, and grateful that some of its people understood and spoke Spanish. She wondered how fluent Azalea might be.

The nanny was none too thrilled about being dragged up the path which Secora hoped was closest to a northwesterly direction. As she passed the net repairman, she asked if there were any jaguars or other threats to goats on the altiplano. He said maybe a jaguar, but no one had seen one for a long time. Then after hesitating a moment, he said there were some large birds that would definitely kill a goat up in the meadows by the high rocks. "They also kill people," he added.

She stared with concentration at his face as he spoke. Some might laugh off what he'd said as superstition, but not Secora. She'd seen far too many strange things to doubt what people said they'd seen. She asked in Spanish if he knew how to fight such birds.

He swung his arm across his chest as if swinging a stick or a bat.

She nodded and thanked him. As she left, her weary body wished she could spend the night in that village, but nagging thoughts of Azalea came to the fore. She drew in a deep breath of fishy-smelling air and hiked on.

"Oooh, can't these horrible insects leave us alone for just a few seconds, Monta? I can't even work a finger loose from all this stuff to scratch."

It was almost evening when her phone rang. It surprised her, and also the goat, and the baby. She stopped to remove the annoyance from her backpack and answered in a whisper. It was Gideon. He shared with her the vision Wakinyan had given him.

Secora smiled as she rubbed on a fresh dose of bug repellant and thought about him saying, "I love you," at the end of the conversation— and she'd let him. It gave her a little lift as she continued her journey toward Isla del Sol and the protective love of her second family.

She looked down at the doe who had a dark red face and front half, and a mostly white back half. "I think I'll call you Tosi. It means goat in Tongan, but why would you care?" She laughed. Tosi walked beside Secora, stomping and switching her tail back and forth as if she was irritated by the name. Secora said dismissively, "On second thought, you remind me of Azalea."

Azalea, how could she be onto us, unless there is another confederate, or did she bug the baby's diapers? What? Then it dawned on her; she carried a phone with GPS. It was hopeless then. Azalea would indeed find her; it was only a matter of when.

The jungle brush became sparse. Here and there, the prairie was interspersed with farms. She passed another small lake. The map had no name for this one. The sun was setting, and she decided to stay at a nearby settlement for safety's sake. She didn't get much sleep that night fidgeting and fretting about the assassin tied to her tail.

At dawn, she was procuring fresh milk for the baby—a real blessing. Before she left the hamlet, she found out there was a truck of produce traveling to Juliaca in a day or two. If she waited, she could catch a ride. The thought was tempting. Maybe the truck could help them bypass the deadly birds. For a while, she weighed the gun against the birds. But in the end, Secora couldn't wait and opted to move on. If the "babysitter" ever saw them, they would be utterly helpless. Perhaps she could find another way to avoid the birds.

Her next stop would be near the town of Santa Lucia, which was surrounded by lush selva, but most of the remaining miles would take her through cold altiplano rock, gravel, and sand. When Santa Lucia came into view with its stone walls, it appeared to be a fairly good-sized town. Secora risked a turn toward several distant buildings where a sign for the El Imperio Restaurant caught her eyes.

"It'll be risky, Monta, but I need to eat something and rest a little." Secora panned the area, including Route 34A, before she entered the building.

Mmm warm food tastes so good! She bought extra to put in the backpack for later, and then mashed a tamale and offered some to Monta, who drew back and shook her head, unimpressed. Secora fed it to the goat, who seemed pleased.

The reward of eating a decent meal at a restaurant was that Secora was strong enough to pick up her pace, as she again headed north toward the town of Imata. While she was still in the forested area, she looked for a stout walking stick that could be used, if necessary, as a bat for defense.

She tried out several which broke under duress. Finally, she found the right one for her needs and moved on with Tosi's twined vine lead in one hand, to keep her close. Now, she felt more like Heidi of the Alps. Burdened with her backpack, baby bag, and Monta's snugly in front. However, it didn't take long for her to feel like Sweaty Secora of the Jungle again. With luck, she would make it to Juliaca tomorrow night or at the latest by the following morning. She cringed at the idea of spending another night in such uncertain circumstances, but if everything went well, she would soon be safely in Isla del Sol.

The land leading into the altiplano was drier, but occasional patches of forest crisscrossed little brooks. In these forested areas, the going was slow. She had to watch that she stayed away from the leaf litter whenever possible, as it might hide deadly snakes. She used the walking stick to poke around if she absolutely had to cross through sketchy underbrush. She was careful to ensure the baby and the goat didn't brush against any nearby branches, since they might harbor venomous insects, frogs, and even vipers.

She had two bottles of clean water left for her and for rehydrating powdered formula if she and Tosi couldn't continue their truce. She took one container from the pack and sipped it whenever she thought about it.

As she drew nearer to Imata, the terrain rose out of the river bottoms and up into the cool altiplano. The altitude was now over nine thousand feet, but Secora was still sweating even though it was nearly winter here. The temperatures ranged in the fifties and sixties, for which she was completely acclimated.

She'd received directions back at Santa Lucia for proceeding to Juliaca without traveling along the highway. Even though the entire trip might have taken less than three hours by car, it would have been far too easy for Azalea to stake out a road or hide under an underpass.

Shaking her head, Secora put aside her doubts that all this secrecy was necessary. It may be slow, but this was the safest path for herself and the child.

Imata was on the Arequipa—Puno Highway. It was a crossroads, and Secora could also see from afar a railroad station, a gas station, and a church. A bus pulled up to stop at one of the other buildings, the purpose of which she could make out. The town featured one street and was otherwise surrounded by extremely flat dry prairie and a few stony hills.

The goat was panting as they passed a sign which boasted the altitude was now 14,603 feet. "That's higher than Pike's Peak. Monta, it's a good thing we were both born in the mountains."

It was late, but Secora and the goat needed rest even though she was terrified Azalea would catch up. They slept a few hours in a shed on the outskirts of town. When Secora awoke, Monta was giggling and cooing to the goat. Secora smiled to see her daughter happy despite the exhaustion and danger. She fed Monta, gathered her into the baby pack, and took off again toward Juliaca.

It wasn't long before the landscape had transitioned from rolling hills and prairie to high rocky desert, where the oxygen level was noticeably reduced as was forage for Tosi. Secora began to worry about her daughter, but hoped that because the little one was born at a high altitude she could breathe the thin air. Unfortunately, the baby couldn't tell her mom how she felt inside.

Vegetation and water became extremely scarce. Secora stopped near a little creek to water the goat and to feed and change the baby. She took the opportunity to drink from the last bottle of precious water. Her eyes wandered to some distant rock formations, where she noticed a sign announcing the STONE FOREST. Her chest tightened.

30

TERROR BIRDS OF THE ALTIPLANO

The air felt cooler, and Secora fussed with an extra blanket for Monta. The aged goat commented "mmmaa" looking up at Secora with those golden eyes. "Not much food for you is there?" Tosi smelled, then tasted the water, and picked at a few weeds around nearby rocks, while Secora opened the map and noticed there were several attractions in the area: notably, the "Waterfalls of the Chili River," and the "Stone Forest," the latter being an eroded outcrop bearing "inspirational shapes."

Secora tried not to panic, but the phrase kept rolling around in her mind. "Deadly birds in a meadow near the rocks".

How will Gideon ever find us? Tears began to overwhelm her eyes, but she shook them off and began to pray, "Is there any Remover of difficulties save God? Say: Praised be God! He is God! All are His servants, and all abide by His bidding!"

Feeling a little better, she folded the map, stuffed it into her backpack, and looked toward the town of Imata. She saw a figure in the distance. Could it be Gideon? Not likely. He wouldn't be hiking if he was trying to catch up. Unless it was a stranger walking the lonely hills with a death wish, it had to be Azalea.

As they climbed steadily upward, Secora noticed the word PELIGRO on the map, which meant danger in Spanish next to a picture of a hiker inside a red circle with a line through it. The word pointed to an area to the left of the Chili River which appeared to be barren rolling hills. That must be where the deadly birds live. *No problem, we won't go there.*

She then noticed grazing cattle in the near distance. There's a heavenly break. We should be safe as long as we are able to see grazing animals. Tosi was still nibbling plants when she could reach them along the way.

Secora sighed as she looked back at the approaching figure. "Between a rock and a hard spot, Monta." The baby looked up, trying to focus on her mom's eyes as if she would find meaning in those words. Secora smiled, then picked up her gear, the stick, and the goat's rope, and began walking toward the cows. When she was closer to the animals, she spotted ponds, grass, and a couple of abandoned ghostly buildings.

After forty minutes, she had passed the herd and looked back. The figure that followed their exact path wasn't much bigger. That must be Azalea, struggling with the altitude. *Not born in the mountains like me and Monta.* That was one thing to be grateful for.

The temperature on high mountain passes could take a sudden drop as a change in the wind might trigger wintery conditions, but so far, the weather was holding at what Secora felt was around fifty-five degrees, a temperature at which she was quite comfortable. Stone pinnacles and a forest of boulders loomed ahead, and she thought she could hear waterfalls. She glanced back over her shoulder; Azalea didn't appear to have gained any ground. But, her head snapped back around when one of her boots struck a stick or root sticking up from the ground. What she'd hit felt off. She returned to look, then kicked at it with the toe of her boot, and eventually pulled it out of the ground. A few rotted feathers stuck out at angles. It was a wing that seemed to be about two and a half feet long, if she could have stretched out the dried elbow. The size wasn't horrible, but the fact there were well-developed talons sticking out of the joint was a huge problem.

Secora was transported back to graduate school exams. "Phorusrhacid," sometimes referred to as "Terror bird." Some of them had been humongous, but this one was the mid-sized Llallawavis Scagliai which stood about three feet tall. Secora shook her head, *should have died off completely by two and a half million years ago.* Come on, what else do I remember? They had solidified cranial bones and could swivel the head and whack their prey. Certainly, they were capable of breaking bones. They were also thought to have had excellent hearing ability, and they lived in open environments near streams, in grassland, or open forest. Adults weighed around forty pounds, about the size of a dodo or a trim Labrador. A few types scavenged, but many ran their prey down, bashed it to the ground, and shredded the bodies with their wicked beaks.

Secora moaned, "Okay, enough of that. I don't want to play anymore." They were in serious trouble. These birds were not only living on the far side of the river, but apparently, they were also nearby. Secora sat on a boulder. Now, more than ever, she felt totally vulnerable and alone.

Azalea caught up with them, panting. The hand holding the pistol was shaking.

"I've wondered whether or not I would have to kill the child at this moment," she gasped.

"Save your bullets, Azalea. We're all as good as dead."

The smile hung on Azalea's face a moment longer, then fell as she asked, "What are you talking about?"

Secora lifted the bones and feathers that comprised the wing.

"What am I looking at?"

"There are birds over the side of this rocky outcrop that are going to bash us down, then tear us to shreds." Secora threw away the wing and calmly said, "We won't stand a chance without a fully loaded machine gun."

Azalea started to smile again.

"You think I'm bluffing? Come, take a look over this rock and keep your head low. More than ten are eating a dead black horse only a hundred and fifty yards away."

Azalea warily obliged, then fell back against the nearest boulder, her chest heaving and her eyes round with fear. Secora noticed the sweat beading on her forehead.

"And those are just the ones we can see," Secora added. Azalea blanched, then leaned over and threw up.

"Why did you take this job, Azalea? What was your motivation?"

"At this point, nothing has meaning. At the time it looked like a way to make easy money. Bob was out to tie up some loose ends. He was going to find a way to kill Gideon—make it look as if it was an accident. I was supposed to force you to give me the Riggins Site information before I killed you. That was our plan. Right off, it went wrong when I saw that baby—I wasn't being paid enough for that. But what was I going to do with her? Should have killed you back at the village, there were mothers there who could have taken care of her."

Suddenly, the goat screamed "Maaaaa!" Secora looked to see Tosi was facing a bird with a jagged beak towering above her on one of the lower pinnacles. Secora whirled around and whacked the bird's neck with the stick. It fell back out of sight. "Aim for the neck or body. The head is pretty solid," yelled Secora. Azalea took the Barretta off safety, and she shot two other birds that showed their heads above the rocks.

"Maybe I could discourage you from returning to Montana," said Azalea. "Don't suppose you'd be willing to take a job elsewhere if I asked you nicely?"

"Interesting thought, but maybe whoever put you in this position needs a reality check."

"I was afraid you'd reject my offer with an answer like that," moaned Azalea.

The women and the goat backed away from the rocks, pressed tightly together.

"I wonder how many more there are," Azalea questioned.

"Hope you have plenty of ammo."

"We'll see."

"Let's try to back our way out of here and head toward the cattle. The birds don't seem to want to bother them," Secora suggested.

She heard a motorcycle racing down the highway, or was it a weed eater? She could use a weed eater right now.

Four of the horrifying birds poured over the rocks. One half-flew, half-ran up to Azalea, and bit her leg open before it dropped from a well-placed bullet. The policewoman cried out. Her thigh was bleeding through her jeans as she dispatched the other three. Secora snatched a diaper from the baby bag and put it over the tear in the flesh, then took off the goat's collar to use as a tourniquet above Azalea's wound while the older woman reloaded.

The goat took advantage of her freedom and waddled off immediately toward the cattle screaming her head off. Two birds ran from between tall pinnacles and raced after her. Secora took the gun and shot one while the other rammed the goat's side. Tosi turned, reared up, and rammed the bird. Azalea grabbed the gun back and shot the second bird before it could regain its balance. Secora gave Azalea the stick to hobble with.

"Run for it!" They followed the goat at their best pace. Monta was frightened by the noises of the gun and the birds. She wailed and tears streamed down her face. Secora thought she heard the motorcycle noise again, or was it a lawnmower? It didn't matter, because now there were five more terrifying birds chasing them.

Secora yelled, "Azalea, we have to turn and make our stand."

"We only have four bullets left."

Secora grabbed the stick like a bat. "Well, make 'em count."

Azalea nailed two of the creatures, then a terrifying image came up over the Stone Forest, and the three remaining birds scattered back into the rocks. A red ultralight buzzed low over the women's heads adding to Monta's woes. Then it went over the rocks and circled back around. It was Gideon, bless him. But Secora thought he couldn't stave off the predators for long.

Then the cattle stampeded.

"Oh my God," panted Azalea who was as pale as cattail down. "They're coming from the other side and killing the cattle now. We're done for."

An old rickety truck burst out of the dust cloud the cattle had kicked up. Secora was breathing heavily, but she became aware that Azalea wasn't making any sound at all. She turned to face her one-time enemy only to see her staring straight ahead. Secora looked in the same direction to see if there was a new savage horror on the horizon, while Gideon continued to fly overhead. Secora couldn't see anything else. Abruptly, the woman next to her dropped to the ground in a silent heap. Secora had Monta in front, so she could not drop down to check on her. She just uttered a prayer, stunned—until the death rattle escaped Azalea's lungs.

After what seemed like half an hour the truck whose engine was running sporadically, possibly due to the lack of oxygen, pulled to a stop next to the women. Gideon landed his craft, drawing it up to the back of the truck. He ran over and kissed Secora and Monta. With gratitude and longing, Secora kissed him back, then turned her eyes to her fallen comrade. Jimmy was already kneeling, and Gideon squatted down.

"She's gone," Jimmy announced.

"Ya 'Baha'u'l-Abha," Secora repeated nine times while the men respectfully lifted the body. Jimmy jumped up into the bed and pulled her forward. Secora got her fringed elk skin jacket out of the baby bag and offered it up to the holy man to cradle her head from banging around as they drove.

Jimmy warned, "You might want to save that for yourself when you see the condition of the passenger seat."

Gideon was already prepping the ultralight for storage at the rear of the truck, and Jimmy helped him lift it and tie it down. Then Gideon hopped in with their dead companion, gritting his teeth. "Hope to survive the bumpy ride in the back of this clunky rig."

Jimmy guided Secora to the truck door. The seat was so old it was filled with horse tail hair. Silver springs with pointed ends where the wires were clipped showed through the tangle. A passenger could easily be skewered by the sharp ends of the coils. Then a thought hit her. *This thing must go back to the 1930s.*

"Guys, wait. Jimmy, can you please get those two birds and toss them in the back? I need them. You know they died out twenty-five million years ago."

There was indistinct mumbling from the men as they wandered out after the creatures. She tried to pick out a place to sit in the cab that wasn't totally devastating for herself or her baby. She wished she had a board to put on top of the seat but ultimately decided to sacrifice the baby bag and its contents. Still uncomfortable, but not deadly.

There was one huge thump, then a second. The added cargo felt like it weighed the vehicle down even more than the ultralight.

"Is that it?" asked Gideon from the window.

"Well, almost. The goat is out there amongst the cattle somewhere."

"The *goat* - way to travel light Secora... and through a flock of deadly birds?" He shook his head, but she could see a hint of a smile as Gideon returned to the truck bed.

There was no sign of Tosi as they passed slowly through the wary cattle.

Jimmy said, "Maybe she just kept on running and went to Imata." Before Secora could say anything, he added, "We, however, are not going back to Imata. We gassed up there on our way out here."

Secora could say nothing and silently hoped the grouchy doe would find a pleasant life. It was all she could do to keep herself and the baby safe inside the vehicle. They met up with wheel tracks that served as a road to the Stone Forest and followed them to the highway. Monta quickly fell asleep with the rocking of the vehicle. Secora swept the little girl's hair back and noticed the red cheeks. "Poor baby, you've been through so much." Darling child, I can't wait to get you somewhere safe, warm... and normal.

She looked up in time to catch a glimpse of the waterfall. A scene which, if you didn't know about the birds, and weren't inside a painful sardine can—was enchanting. When she thought about it, she and Azalea had taken out nearly all of the birds, both a shame and salvation for others.

Along the highway, they passed hills covered with bunch grass, a meandering blue river, and terraced farms. Occasionally, there would be a small lake or pond which seemed incongruously paired with the arid landscape.

31

SAY GOODBYE, SECORA

The four of them, unless you counted Azalea, traveled along Route 34 toward Puno rather than continue the path to Juliaca. They were nearly to the city when Secora could no longer bear the cramps in her legs and arms caused by staying in place and not disturbing the sleeping baby. She tried to look back to see how Gideon was faring, but she could barely make out the ultralight's outline through the dust-crusted window glass. She desperately needed a break and begged Jimmy to stop. They were near the shore of Lake Umayo when she got out and stretched. Next, she untangled poor little Monta from the baby pack, and with the baby safely in a state of wonderment, she went to join Jimmy who was checking on Gideon's condition. He was a rough dusty mess, but he tried to smile and pointed to a tower to divert their attention away from him. They all wandered stiffly while taking in the sight of the large chullpa, pronounced "chuypa" she remembered, which overlooked the lake.

Secora used a baby wipe to remove the dust from Gideon's eyes and eyelashes, then from the rest of his face while she explained this was an above-ground monument, also referred to as a "Tower Sepulcher," because it resembled a very rustic castle turret. These towers were relics of the "Qulla" or "Colla" people. She remembered that many ancient people had used cave tombs, slab-cist tombs, and subterranean cist tombs. But these above-ground Sillustani Towers near Puno represented a burial style which went back, at the very least, to the glory days of Tiahuanaco.

The men were duly impressed, but Monta wanted to hold her mom's fingers so she could explore a little bit. Secora obliged, and added, "The Incas were so astounded that they restored some of the old monuments with stone blocks."

After a few minutes of peace and quiet, they packed themselves back into the old truck and were on the road again. Lake Umayo was only a few miles from Titicaca as the crow flew, but not nearly close enough to fill Secora's urgent need for food, rest, or safety. They followed the road to the right and were soon rewarded by views of the lake in the distance. At last, they arrived in Puno, worse for the wear. First there was business to take care of.

They located the police station and dropped off Azalea and made the necessary report. The dead birds in the back were very convincing for their part of the story. Next, Secora gave them the samples and photos from the little Peruvian cave which sheltered the two unknown skeletons, asking them to be passed along to the appropriate police station.

Afterward, Secora limped painfully to a sporting goods store and bought a couple of large duffels to contain the birds. It was 62 degrees outside, and Secora thought it would be best to pay for a few hours in cold storage to preserve the specimens.

That being done, they dropped off the rental truck and ultralight. They would have to use Gideon's credit card to pay the rental agency the cost of having a driver return vehicles to Arequipa, but no way would he and Jimmy be returning them in person. Gideon made a point of photographing every angle of the equipment in front of the local driver to show its current condition—especially, the seat.

"Drive safely. They will pay you cash on arrival. If for some reason they don't, call me."

Then the exhausted survivors slogged their way to a hotel, dropped off their gear, and rested. Secora fed, washed, and clothed little Monta in clean diapers and duds. Then she took out the Satfon, which was completely dead, and plugged it in to charge. No surprise there. It had been several days since it was properly charged. She and everyone else showered and relaxed while Monta toddled around and in between the beds.

Much of what had been in the baby bag was destroyed, but Secora could easily replace the supplies in town.

Later, they shopped for baby necessities and a few beautiful toys, and then they took in a delicious meal. At first, Secora wasn't hungry. She was well past feeling starved, and her body had given up. But the steamy plates of fish arrived, and after a single bite, her hunger rapidly returned.

When they returned to their rooms, the phone was charged enough for Secora to contact her parents and let them know they'd arrived in Puno. The folks said Jane and Iris's thoughts were mainly on marriage. Then they put the girls on the phone. There was no doubt whatsoever in Jane's mind, but Iris didn't sound as certain. Secora imagined her sister was in a tough spot and tried to draw out her feelings. Although she was still taken with Kantun, everyone around her had expectations. Secora counseled, "Other peoples' expectations are burdens unintentionally placed on you. You have to decide if you want to behave the way someone else expects you to."

Their parents had bought tickets to fly Jane and Aparu to Montana, as well as Iris and Kantun, even Gilgamesh, if he chose to come. They said they would happily make preparations for the weddings up north if that was what the girls wanted.

"How will the guys manage the jump to light speed?" whined Iris.

"Worked in Crocodile Dundee, sort of ... and Bill and Ted's Excellent Adventure," Secora teased. "Don't over-think it, Iris. Stay focused on Kantun and his needs in a crazy new environment. Don't abandon him to go visit friends, shop, or anything else. And realize the adjustments for you both will take most of a lifetime."

"You're right. He's never abandoned me. Not since he first laid eyes on me that day at Ojo Redondo, and believe me this was a crazy new environment."

"My prayers are with you, sis. And with Jane, the guys, and the rest of the Gueros..."

"And the Toxodons, I get it." Iris chuckled.

"I hope there wasn't an outbreak of illness because we were there?" Secora asked.

"No more so than they would have expected under normal conditions. Oh, and Gilgamesh is feeling much better, by the way."

"Thank God." Secora meant it. "He is a special soul and very important to that community."

"Yes, he's the lead healer."

Iris finished by saying she felt better, and that they would see each other soon in Montana.

Secora also touched base with the university and explained all the unforeseen events to Tarkio, and he was "so jealous." She laughed and said she would bring him a big present if the law allowed.

Next, she called Ed Savage at the Anthro Department and filled him in. He sounded a bit confused. Bob Greenwood's body had not yet arrived in Montana. There was some mix-up in the border crossing forms, for reasons he didn't quite understand.

Secora's thoughts flashed immediately to Jamal Hasan. She told him she sympathized and hoped things would work out soon. Luckily,

Donald Chastain was not in his office, and she left a message with the department secretary.

Gideon found out from Mitch and Jeannie that Clive Bull Bear was unable to locate Billy Riggins or Jake Landsing. He looked thoughtful as he hung up and passed the message along to Jimmy and Secora.

"You must be the sole survivor of the mountain tragedy, Heyoka," comforted Jimmy.

The baby was fretful throughout the night. Secora patiently rose and tended to her daughter, walking around with her. Occasionally Monta settled after playing with her colorful new toys. Everyone slept in the next morning. They simply had no energy left.

During breakfast, Gideon said, "Actually, now the bad guys are gone we don't have to take Monta to the Island for protection... maybe we could just go home?"

Secora drew in a breath. "As tempting as that is, Gideon, I feel like there is something wrong with Guillermo and Alai. Tarkio has been unable to get another message to or from Alai, and I definitely feel the need to go there."

"To the Island, it is, then."

Gideon bought each of them tickets at $100 each, and then closed his strained wallet, saying, "You really are an expensive date, Ms. James."

Before long, they caught a catamaran to the town of Cha'lla. They passed several rustic floating villages along the way, complete with the fragrance of methane, and arrived at the island hours later. They were dropped off at the cove, and Gideon carried little Monta while Jimmy walked beside Secora in case emotional or physical support was needed during the climb.

Secora's eyes were dripping with tears as they slowly walked past Diego's empty house and up the path to Alai and Guillermo's cottage.

"Something's wrong," Secora whispered.

"Who's that with Alai?" asked Jimmy.

"Guanaco's wife, maybe?" she said. "Though, I have never met her."

There were eleven or more people up beyond the house, standing around the path, or sitting on stones with serapes and high domed hats to ward off the chill. All of them were looking directly at the travelers. Alai came out of the doorway and greeted Secora with great sorrow in her eyes.

"Welcome home, daughter." She kissed Secora and Monta, then embraced Jimmy and Gideon. "I'm so glad you brought these good friends. This is my good friend Rocio, Guanaco's wife."

"Did something happen to Guillermo?" Secora asked.

Alai dabbed a cloth at her eyes. "Guanaco and Guillermo are being held captive."

"How do we get them back?" Gideon asked nervously.

Secora wondered what was happening here, and how it might affect them.

Alai looked into Gideon's eyes and said, "The family of Monta's dead mother has come." Then she moved her feet around to face Secora. "We must meet with them, Mija."

"Of course." Secora said, with what hopefulness she could muster, "They will want to meet little Monta."

Alai looked to the floor. "They have come to take her home."

In response to the tears gathering in Secora's eyes as the thought sunk in, Gideon wrapped his free arm around her.

"I don't understand." She sniffed. "Why did they wait?" Alai said, "It wasn't the father's fault."

Rocio stepped forward and said, "Monta's father was detained by an American oil-drilling operation. He was treated like a prisoner."

Alai added, "No one was allowed to leave, for any reason. They were essentially slaves until three of the men broke away. Only two survived the effort. Monta's dad was one of those two."

Rocio was emotional. "He has taken the loss of his wife and child very hard. When he heard a rumor that there was a chance the baby had survived and had been adopted out, his emotions overpowered him. The mixture of hope and anger tore him apart."

Alai wiped her own tears. "His search led him eventually to our door. They didn't come alone. About fifteen family members came up to the house while our close friends, Rocio and Guanaco, were visiting. That was two days ago. Some of them have left and have taken Guillermo and Guanaco as hostages. If we do not return the baby the men will be sacrificed." Alai broke down and wept. Rocio tried unsuccessfully to comfort her.

"What? Are you kidding?" cried Secora.

"We have no way to know if they are still alive, and no, Mija, I have 'felt' nothing. I know Guillermo has the power to block my thoughts. Perhaps Guanaco as well," hiccupped Alai.

Gideon guided Secora into the cottage to sit and gave her the baby. Secora was grieving, rocking her daughter in her arms. Then he said, "The story, painful as it is, makes sense. There's no doubt the father has been through hell and did not intentionally abandon his child. He didn't even know she was alive."

Secora nodded, and Gideon continued, "There is a legitimate claim."

Secora couldn't bear to hear the overwhelming words, and she began shaking. Jimmy said, "Gideon, maybe she is going into shock."

Gideon gently stepped closer and took the child, who sensed the sadness and started to cry along with her mom.

Jimmy continued, "After everything you—well, all of us, and sweet little Monta have been through together..." He touched Secora's shoulder, but she turned away.

Gideon put his hand under her chin and turned her face back. "Look at me, Secora. This is really tough—beyond heartbreaking. But you have to follow this path to the end. You have the strength to meet this man, and if he is not totally insane, you must return Monta to him. Waiting won't help. It's time for us to say goodbye."

Secora began to shake harder; she was unable to speak. Gideon and Jimmy helped her stand, and they walked together out the door, followed by the other women.

Secora noticed movement in the crowd on the hill. The people were parting for the passage of a man who might be the father, as well as Guillermo, and a tall, thin man whom she thought must be Guanaco. Secora turned to leave.

Rocio ushered them all back inside and stepped in front of Secora. "No matter how our hearts ache we must think of the father. He was imprisoned, enslaved. When he finally escaped, he had lost everything. He is hurting from the loss of time with his family and his people... the loss of his pregnant wife. He has a spark of hope with Monta. There are so few of her people left; Monta could bring the light of hope to all of them."

Gideon and Jimmy could no longer deny the pain of the situation. All of them were dabbing at their eyes now. Their grief was abruptly curtailed when there was a solid knock at the door—once, then again.

Alai stood slowly. "Un momento," she croaked as she opened the door, her eyes staring at the floor.

A man with a scarred face came forward and looked sternly at Secora. "Yo soy el padre, I am the father." Instinctively, Jimmy and Gideon stood to become a protective barrier for the women and the baby. Secora could tell Gideon was full of emotion, yet tried to seem calm.

The father was also surrounded by grim-faced people, who looked first at Alai and Rocio, then Secora and Monta.

Gideon said, "Perhaps there *is* hope in their eyes."

Monta bawled loudly, and the father's heart seemed to melt. He took a few hesitant steps forward and Secora stepped toward him, looking into his eyes.

"I wasn't the best mom. I know I shouldn't have taken her everywhere I did. I put her in danger several times... Is this penance?" She lifted Monta and kissed her through a river of tears, then her eyes wandered back to the father. "Do we want to give our child to people who would kill another human to get her?"

The father signaled, and the mob brought forth the haggard hostages.

Monta grabbed her mother's hair and tangled her little fingers in the tresses, then screamed. Secora kissed her again and untangled the tiny fingers. She kissed each little hand.

It was then, that a kind, motherly looking woman outstretched her arms to receive the small girl. Her eyes seemed to say, "I'm sorry for your pain, but this must be."

In English, she said, "My name is Teresa. I am the aunt of this child. Her mother was my sister. I promise she will be well cared for and loved, for all of her life."

Secora looked at the floor, and then cautiously handed the child to Teresa. When she looked up again, she tried to smile, for Monta's sake.

"I will see that she is not a stranger to this family. You notice I speak English. That is because Alai raised me as one of her children, and Guillermo is like a father to me. I was the one who brought the little girl here to Alai, so also to you. I'm sorry this has been so hard on everyone." She stepped close and kissed Secora on both cheeks.

"Thank you, Teresa. I'm glad you will be a major part of her life." She hugged the woman and Monta then she turned to the father and dipped her chin, acknowledging her acceptance of the situation. To Monta, she said, "I have to go, baby. You stay with Teresa and let her and your father love you." Gideon handed the man the baby bag and the snuggly. Jimmy gave them the new toys from his pockets.

Guillermo was being jostled toward Alai. He was gaunt but happy to see her. They embraced, and then she led him away. Guanaco's wife cried at the sight of her rail-thin Kallawaya. She put her arms around him and also took him inside. The crowd shuffled away as swiftly as possible. Gideon and Jimmy led Secora back into the house. The rest of the day was spent in tears and in healing love for each of them. Everyone had suffered greatly in his or her own way. Each, in consoling one another, found some comfort for themselves.

32

THE SKELETON RETURNS

G ideon and the entire family took Secora up to the Inca ruins at
dawn the next morning, offering prayers for healing, detachment, protection, and submission to the will of God. She was still traumatized, but the family gave all the comfort they could to help her, and
themselves, recover.

As Gideon watched her torment, he tried to put his own feeling of
loss aside. Secora had not failed to notice and said, "We all love her. I
am the only person in this family who has a hole in her heart. We did
the right thing and now we will move on together." She took a deep
breath and then prayed, "Is there any Remover of Difficulties save
God?" When she had finished the prayer, the family and friends
continued to offer prayers for over an hour before returning to the
cottage and preparing a meal to celebrate family and friends.

When she was seated, Secora watched lifelessly as Gideon took her
hand in his. With his other hand, he withdrew a miniature tape recorder
from his pocket. "We need to move forward. I was hoping I wouldn't
have to pull out the big guns, but here goes. I know how you love
Johnny Rivers' songs."

He snapped on the recorder and turned up the sound so all could hear Johnny croon, "Baby I need your Lovin." Secora felt her heart begin to melt. Gideon got down on one knee and sang along—really hamming it up. Secora raised her eyebrows and began to smile. Her frame of mind went from crippling shock to a cringe, then to outright laughter. She threw her head back and howled. Everyone around them looked at first concerned, and then they also laughed at the ridiculous transition of sentiments.

Water flutes and other musical instruments appeared from nowhere, and a celebratory atmosphere of family took over. More food began to appear and joy spread rapidly. Alai stepped behind Secora and played with her hair. Brushing it back into a ponytail, she said, "Mija, this is your chance. Marry this man, our other son. There is still time for you to give Guillermo and me grandchildren to love and enjoy."

Guillermo offered a hand to pull Gideon back up and clapped him on the shoulder with the other. "Remember, son. No hanky panky until you are married."

Gideon looked chastened, then nodded. "Okay, Dad." Everyone laughed again.

The next day, Gideon woke up with Diego shaking his shoulder.

"This is your time, my brother," he said. "You need to throw away your own sorrow and loss and make her your wife—with my blessings." Gideon rubbed his eyes, and when he looked again, Diego had left.

From the morning sounds, Gideon knew the family was awake so he got up and started his daybreak routine. When he came back to the table, breakfast was set before his place. After he had finished, he thanked Rocio and Alai, and then stood and went to Secora, touching her shoulder. "Come on, it's time for us to leave."

Secora looked at him, then at the others at the table, and the tears began to build. There were nods of agreement all around. She sighed and thanked everyone. "Thank God you are all healers. Life and happiness will go on. I love each of you more than I could tell you."

"Remember what I said, Mija."

"I will," Secora answered.

Within the hour, Gideon, Jimmy, and Secora were on a ferry to La Paz, then on to El Alta airport after lunch. Finally, they were going home. Whenever one of them felt listless, the others reminded them that Monta was very likely a sensitive like Alai and could tell what they were feeling. "So, feel happy."

Waiting for their flight that evening, Gideon wondered if Secora would ever actually agree to marry him. She came over and asked him what other Johnny Rivers songs he could sing.

He answered, "All of them if you want me to. But it might take a life-time. I think he's still writing new ones."

She laughed and said, "I'm sure he is."

"Is there any chance...?"

"Yes, of course there is, at the soonest possible opportunity."

Gideon looked shocked. Then, Secora felt quizzical and said, "I hope the question was about marriage, or did I just blurt that out for nothing?" He stood up and kissed her until Jimmy pulled on his sleeve and announced gruffly, "That's enough, kids."

Kyah, Mitch, and Jeannie were waiting at the airport when they arrived. Tarkio raced up to them saying, "Sorry I'm late. Welcome back."

Jeannie opened a large shopping bag and handed out teddy bears to the travelers. "For whenever you feel sad," she said. They all hugged, and then left in a line, seven abreast, arm in arm, and each with a bear.

Like any other morning, Secora opened her eyes and rubbed them. She yawned, and got up to check on the baby. She was halfway to the crib before she remembered. Sitting down on the couch, she smiled wist-fully. Alai had called yesterday to tell her Monta was settling into her new life. Teresa had brought her by on two occasions for visits. Alai said she looked happy and well.

Okay, then. Wiping the tears that stung her eyes, Secora dressed herself and headed into the department for a few hours of work. It was Friday, and spring vacation would officially begin tomorrow. She would be leaving after her last lab class at noon to drive to West Glacier. Tarkio had not come in today, but she would see him later.

Dr. Donald Chastain would not be in the office today. He was still being investigated for selling questionably obtained artifacts on the black market to collectors with fat wallets. A business he had shared with Robert Greenwood—not to mention his illegal fracking schemes.

If a discovery was out of line with the current theories, like Billy's discovery, he wanted it to not only disappear but at a profit for his retirement fund, kind of like Glen. It was an uncomfortable time for the staff and students around the department. Secora felt bad for the old man. He was so dedicated to his beliefs that he had lost the neutrality of a scientist's eye.

Donald was also charged as an accomplice to murder in the second degree for the death of Kamal Hasan, so he wouldn't be back to the office—ever. Secora was asked if she would like to be the Department Chair, pro-tem, but she refused. Her life was complex enough without that headache.

As she drove her old Dodge across McDonald Creek, Secora remembered Suzie and Ken's offer. They'd said she could find refuge at their Buckeye Dude Ranch and had even hinted that their resort might be a lovely place for a getaway or a honeymoon with Gideon. She had laughed to herself. Getting away from anything or anyone was unlikely.

When she pulled into the parking lot, it was packed with people and cars. Iris came over to greet her, all dolled up in a beautiful burgundy dress featuring embroidered flowers, and her flaxen hair was accented with purple and green ribbons.

Others pressed forward to greet Secora. She couldn't believe her eyes; Jimmy was wearing a tux! She had to snap a picture. Guests and family began to move through the doors as the appointed time drew near. Secora took a place across from the girls and their husbands to be.

Gideon silently came to stand beside her, looking smooth and eye-catching, also in a tux. He pinned an orchid in Secora's tawny tresses. "A suit guy is making money off of you and Jimmy," she whispered.

Jeannie waved from the right side of the circle, catching her eye. And there was Mitch. *Is he actually standing near a girl?*

Sage and L.W. led a party past Secora which included Alai and Guillermo, who had flown into Kalispell. Sage pecked Secora's cheek on the way. Her heart instantly ached to be with the Santiagos. Suddenly she was crippled by thoughts of her baby and wished they had brought Monta. Quickly, she realized the strain would be too much for both her and the child. Maybe later, after they had more time to heal. She wiped her tears.

'Everything became quiet when Tarkio, Anida, and Frederick stepped into the center with a mike.

"Friends, this is a magical day, and if Jimmy would be kind enough to bring forward the brides and their grooms, we will begin with very simple Baha'i ceremonies for each couple, and then our favorite wichasha wakan, our own Lakota holy man, will raise a voice and chant a marriage prayer."

Jimmy ushered Gideon and Jane's mother, grandmother, and Kyah to the center. Jane brought Aparu forward to share their vows in front of her family. Next, Iris brought Kantun and a translator, just in case. The men couldn't take their eyes off their brides; the same was true for the girls.

Gideon offered Secora his arm and said, "Shall we?" They were the last of the three couples to repeat the phrase, "We will all, verily, abide by the Will of God" in their own ceremony.

Kyah started beating a Plains Indian drum, Guillermo played an Andean water flute, and Jimmy began to dance and offer his prayer for the new families. When he finished people began to mingle.

Secora looked up and saw two men standing across from her. Jamal Hasan saluted her, and she winked and dipped her chin in reply. The man next to him seemed oddly familiar. She squinted and thought, he *could* be Billy Riggins—in a former long-haired life. She would have to talk with those two before they disappeared.

Gideon was turning to her so they could finally share a serious kiss which was, of course, the icing on the cake. Then the new couple began to circulate and visit for what seemed like hours and hours. At last, they had a brief, but pleasant visit with Jamal Hasan and his employee who held a pug in his arms and introduced himself as William Landsing and the dog as Cutesie.

"I believe we've met," Gideon smirked.

Mr. Hasan smiled and said, "Hope everything is to your liking?"

Secora answered, "Quite so, thank you."

Gideon said, "Some questions are better not asked. But I feel glad to be alive, and I suspect I owe you thanks for that." He grinned and shook Mr. Hasan's hand.

"You're welcome." The tall man smiled. "Please visit Mr. Landsing or me at the resort any time. You and your expansive family are all welcome guests. In fact, a South American contingent will be staying a night or two with us."

Secora giggled. "We'll be sure to stop by."

Mr. Landsing interjected, "And please, check out the gift table."

Gideon repeated, "Gift table? No gifts were expected." Both men pointed to a table in a back corner. The four of them wandered over and Secora saw copious presents for the Guero couples, but there were also a few for her and Gideon. There was a very long package in black-silver foil wrapping and with red, white, and green bows. The label read "Secora and Gideon Yellow Thunder."

Tarkio and Jimmy had followed them and urged her to open it. So, she did. Inside was a long wood and glass case, complete with a velvet shrouded skeleton in deep repose. He was surrounded, Secora noticed, by Middle Stone Age artifacts.

Secora glanced around. If this had been any other family, there probably would have been screams and people fainting all over the place and for a variety of reasons. But this family was different. Very different, many were healers and sensitives, from the Gueros to Alai, last of her tribe, from Kallawayas to Lakota healers, and precious representatives of the Faiths of Jesus Christ, Mohammad, and Baha'u'llah.

As such, fifty people came by to pay their respects to the departed man lying in state - and offered prayers for this ancient traveler who happened to die while visiting, or moving to, North America.

William Landsing announced, "Arrangements will be made immediately to return this honored one to his tomb with his mammoth companion on property now owned by Gideon and his wife." Landsing grinned under his new cookie-duster mustache. Secora noticed his hands were missing a few fingers, but that didn't seem to slow him down.

Secora whispered, "Thank you, Billy."

"Uh... that would be William. No, Billie or Jake—in case someone still has it in for one of them."

"Right, say, I've been wondering about Carrots, because every time I hear that mule in the Buckeye corral bray, I think of Billy Riggins' mule. Though I never met the critter, I heard him screeching the night someone attacked Billy and broke his arm with a shovel."

"Funny you should mention it... I think that actually is Carrots' voice."

"What do you mean?"

"You know, the way I heard it, Billy visited back in December, just a week or so before you and Jimmy rented the saddle horses. He stopped by there and gave Carrots to Ken and Sue."

"I'm *very* glad they both survived."

"Yep, it appears Billy overcame the man who attacked him, knocking him out with his own shovel by the grace of God. He had already loaded the duffel which held his camera and the notes he'd taken, as well as the gentleman preserved in this case, because this discovery was not meant to be erased from prehistory by Professor Donald Chastain or others like him.

"Although he experienced a great deal of pain with a throbbing, broken arm, Billy undid the tailgate of his pickup, and with the aid of a small hill of dirt as a loading ramp, urged the mule to jump. After closing the tailgate and the stock racks with one arm, he collected his jacket and left for Montana.

By the way, you may wish to check this other package, with the aforementioned photos and notes, when you get home." He pointed to a medium-sized square package wrapped similarly. "The rest of the gift."

"I will. You know nobody seems to have heard from Billy since his hospital stay."

Lansing mused, "I think that's the way he would like it. Especially when the brouhaha about this burial comes to light."

Secora rolled her eyes. "I so understand, my friend."

"I'm sure he remembers your meaningful visit to his hospital room. I think it saved his life—gave him a reason, you know." She smiled brightly. Then the two men gave her hugs and moved on toward the exit.

Secora rejoined Gideon, who had wandered off during the conversation. He was laughing with Aparu and Kantun. Guillermo and Alai were becoming acquainted with these young men, and of course, adding them to their ever-expanding family. Iris and Jane, true to their commitment, never left their husband's sides.

Alai said, "I have something for you from someone very special."

She handed one of the colorful toys Secora had purchased in Puno to the new couple. "Monta wanted to give you a present."

Secora's accepted it with glistening eyes. "Gideon, this is the happiest day ever."

He put his arm around her and kissed the top of her head. "We'll have other happy days, but this one will always be special."

He kissed her cheek just as Kyah flashed a picture. That was a cue. The three brides rushed over to L.W., each grabbing a bouquet, which they hadn't needed for the ceremony—but they needed them now. Giggling, they lined up, side-by-side, and with sweeping gestures, they hurled them backward—at Jimmy. He was startled and caught two of them in self-defense. Cameras flashed again catching the shock on his face, and when he noticed every eye was on him, he flushed, and hurriedly escaped to the men's room with a slight smile on his lips.

The End

ABOUT THE AUTHOR

Diane Olsen is the prolific writer and award-winning author of her debut book titled: Ancient Ways: The Roots of Religion, a Bronze Medal Winner awarded by Christian Illuminations Book Awards.

Diane's debut release of Ancient Ways is thought-provoking and an informative look at the development and evolution of religion throughout time and a well-considered concept—the idea of a connective thread of monotheistic faith throughout history from the birth of human creation. Now comes her new release and book series titled; RISING WIND: The Thunder Beings, Ice and Bone, The Weeping God and the Book of Hope, Like Feathers of a Wing, Rock My Soul and Rays of the light.

Her readers to enjoy as an amazing Multicultural Fiction, Action-Adventure, with Super Natural and Mystery elements.

Born in Colorado Springs, Colorado she now lives in the beautiful Pacific Northwest in Washington State. She was an undergrad at Colorado State University Ft. Collins: Pre-vet med, Anthropology, then attended and received her BA and MA at the University of Montana, Missoula: Anthropology, Archaeology, and Paleontology. She was a Graduate Teaching Assistant for two years.

Diane raised two sons Andrew and Gavin, has four grandsons Dylan, Brayden, AJ, and Asher, and is an animal lover with two doggie girls, "Ladybug and Charlie," along with one or more feral cats. She has raised sheep and goats and about forty other species of critter over the decades.

A few of her favorite books are The Book of Certitude (Kitab-i-Iqan), The Upanishads, and The Great Initiates.

facebook.com/DianeOlsenAuthor
twitter.com/Author_Dolsen

www.ingramcontent.com/pod-product-compliance
Lightning Source LLC
Chambersburg PA
CBHW070859180626
46817CB00003B/827